Marian Calhoun Legare Reeves

Pilot Fortune

Marian Calhoun Legare Reeves

Pilot Fortune

ISBN/EAN: 9783337266868

Printed in Europe, USA, Canada, Australia, Japan

Cover: Foto ©Andreas Hilbeck / pixelio.de

More available books at **www.hansebooks.com**

PILOT FORTUNE

BY

MARIAN C. L. REEVES AND EMILY READ

AUTHORS OF "OLD MARTIN BOSCAWEN'S JEST,"
"AYTOUN," AND "WEARITHORNE"

Fortune brings in some boats that are not steered
SHAKESPEARE

BOSTON
HOUGHTON, MIFFLIN AND COMPANY
New York: 11 East Seventeenth Street
The Riverside Press, Cambridge
1885

The Riverside Press, Cambridge:
Electrotyped and Printed by H. O. Houghton & Co.

PILOT FORTUNE.

I.

"Stephen, why do they ever come back?" says the girl, with a half sigh of longing, clasping her hands on the railing of the sea-wall, as she stands and watches the fishing-boats come in. "They look so free," she says. "See how they sweep in over that blue strip of sea between the islands, —one by one, and now with a flutter of great white wings all together. They are like the sea-gulls: they can fly where they will, away from this island, away to the other side of the world. I wonder why they should come back?"

"The gulls come back, Milly."

"Yes, they *are* gulls," she retorts, a smile at the small witticism chasing the slight cloud from her face, as a sunbeam chases and overtakes and lights up a sweeping shadow on the gusty water she is watching.

It is she whom he is watching: and somehow the cloud has gotten into his eyes, that flitted from her face.

She has forgotten him in the swift scene below
her. Wind and tide are in favor of the fleet
now steadily sailing toward the piers, — one, two,
twenty, thirty, fifty trim small schooners, here
and there a sloop or two, — in through the strait
named by the early French settlers on the opposite shore, the Grand Passage, between this little
Nova Scotian Bryer Island and the deep-coved
shore of Long Island opposite. A hurly-burly of
dark rocks, where the white eddies never rest, juts
out into a point on this side; beyond which, with
the merest belt of blue between, the tiny lighthouse island lifts its rocky pile, its green crest and
white harbor light. The white, trim village, almost
every cottage with its pier and fish-house jutting
from the low cliff out into the water, lines the harbor on this, the whole northeastern side of Bryer
Island; and behind, the hay slopes rise until they
meet the belt of spruce and fir against the sky.
A quiet scene enough upon the six evenings of the
week; but on this seventh, as the fishing-boats are
coming in, every available inhabitant of the village, and that is almost literally to say of the
island, has crowded to the piers.

Many of the women show some token of their
household employment when the good news reached
them, and which in their haste they had forgotten
to drop. One has thrown over her head for covering the towel with which she was wiping her
crockery; while she stands listening to her vol-
uble neighbor, who is gesticulating with a fish-
knife. A few have caught up their knitting, and

are the more loquacious, the more rapidly their unconscious fingers work. As for the children, they are in every one's way, under every one's feet; dancing, screaming, tumbling, not heeding in the smallest degree the cuffs and threats they receive without stint from their elders. For a great joy is often as irritating to the nerves or temper as a sorrow or a pain : and the fishing-boats are coming in, in the wake of stormy weather.

Soon they are near enough for shouted greetings back and forth : and then come personal and family news, jokes and loud laughter; tidings of vessels that are laggards,— all the gay chatter and excitement of return after a most anxious week of absence.

It is somewhat apart from the noisy throng that these two are standing : the man above the medium height, strongly, even powerfully, made ; the girl looking slight and almost childlike, as she leans by the side of her companion, with arms folded on the wooden railing which for a score of feet fences the bit of sea-wall overlooking the piers. The low columnar cliff just here has been helped out by man's hand, building up its fallen stones, quarried by nature ; fragments lie scattered beneath, brown-green with rock-weed and white with barnacles ; and here and there a reach of black basaltic pavement underlies the clear water. The spot is a good post of observation. That the two who are looking down from it, upon the busy scene, are only spectators, is evident; yet there is no doubt of their interest in it.

"Angus has made a good haul," remarks the girl, as an old brown, criss-cross-wrinkled fisherman to whom they have been speaking moves away. "Of course he will not acknowledge as much; but as he has not said one word of grumbling, one can't help suspecting him of good luck. Ah, see there, Stephen: is n't that a strange boat? The one just coming alongside the pier, I mean," she adds, eagerly pointing out the alien craft her quick eye has detected.

"She is a beauty!" exclaims Stephen, in admiration. "She has n't had much of a taste of salt water yet, judging from her paint; and," he adds critically, "she carries too much sail to be altogether safe."

Just then, the little vessel they are commenting on being made fast, a man scrambles from out her, up the side of the pier, — a man in the dress of a sailor, but with very little of the rough appearance of a fisherman after a week's exposure to sun and weather. There is too much dandyism in his costume not to show it is an assumed rather than habitual dress; and though he does not refuse to give a helping hand to the men when necessary, still, landing the fish is by no means a matter of interest to him, and he appears to prefer laughing and joking with the women.

"What a prince he is!" exclaims Milicent, laughing. She has forgotten to look at the fishing-smacks, in the interest or curiosity this stranger awakens. "I wonder where he comes from, and what has brought him here? One would think he intended to stay for the rest of his life, from the way he seems to make himself at home."

"Whom are you talking of?" asks Stephen. He has been watching the handsome little yacht so intently that he has not seen its owner on the wharf. "Where is your prince?"

"Don't you see him? I wonder if he thinks French flannel durable, or only becoming?"

But Stephen, instead of looking in the direction indicated by Milicent, is watching one of the sloops, which, perhaps from carelessness in its skipper, is perilously grazing a ledge of the black pavement here underlying the water. Before he can exclaim, the mischief is done: the fishing-boat has stuck fast. Fortunately, the water beneath the cliff is shallow at this time, and the tide is running out, — a less chance for the little vessel to float off, but not so difficult a performance on the fishermen's part to give a helping hand. In a few minutes the men are splashing waist-deep into the water. There is shouting, swearing, and giving of directions; and then, with a push all together, in unison with a musical cry or chant, which to the uninitiated seems an unnecessary expenditure of breath, the little craft swings slowly round, safely afloat once more.

Stephen was one of the first to go to the assistance of the stranded boat. He took off his coat, and threw it at Milicent's feet; and before she had time to ask even what he would do, he had joined the fishermen.

The stranger is the only idle man ashore. Perhaps he thinks it an uncomfortable position to be working waist-deep in water: or he may have known that his assistance is unnecessary. At any rate, he walks away from the pier, rather than towards the end of it where are the women and children.

Milicent stays where Stephen left her. She is watching the boat with great interest: for even after it is afloat, and the men, dripping wet, have come back to land, she yet stands quite still, shading her eyes with her hands from the glare of the sun on the water.

"She is all right now, and lucky to get off the ledge so easily. Were you anxious about the fish or the fisher?"

The intonation of the voice is so different from that of the fishermen, that Milicent knows, before she turns her head to answer, it is the owner of the yacht who is speaking to her. "Why should I feel any interest in him?" she asks sharply.

"I don't know why, only you seemed to," he answers good-humoredly.

"It was the fish I was thinking of. I was in hopes they would have to lighten the boat by throwing them overboard," Milicent explains.

There is a look of surprise in the stranger's eyes when she turns to answer him. Her blue cotton dress and coarse straw hat, as well as her eager interest in the fate of the boat, misled him into supposing her one of the fishermen's daughters; but a glance at her face gives him a very different impression.

It is a very beautiful face, and the delicately cut features could scarcely have belonged to a class for generations used to hardships and exposure. There is no shyness nor fear in the brown eyes scanning him, though there is much mirth. He thinks it is his unlucky mistake which amuses her; but in reality it is his appearance. She has a great contempt for what she terms dandyism; and for a man to think of the becoming in his dress is sheer silliness, in her opinion.

As it is the blue flannel shirt she is laughing at, it is just as well he misunderstands the cause of her mirth. "I beg your pardon," he says, quite frankly. "I really took you for one of the fisher-folk. I never dreamed you were sympathizing with the fish."

"I ought to have felt an interest in the boat, for it was our winter's supply that came near being lost," answers Milicent. "But I dislike coddies, and would gladly have seen them thrown over-board."

"The fishermen do not share your prejudice against them," he says, laughing. "They were like misers in a gold-mine, and seemed to regret that so many of the fish had to be wasted by be-ing left in the ocean; though to my inexperienced eyes they seemed to have caught enough to supply the world for a year at least. I never expected," he adds, "to find a lady on this rock between three seas."

He uses the word "lady" without hesitation; and yet he is evidently curious as to her position,

—which curiosity Milicent sees and resents. "Will you please tell Stephen I am waiting for him? The gentleman yonder without his coat," she explains, with an imperious gesture, as if she were speaking to one of the fishermen.

He laughs, but does not move. "He is coming," he says. "But he is too wet to walk home with you. Your friend is evidently not afraid of salt water."

He speaks advisedly, thinking she might correct him, and say they are related. But she does not, and only replies, "The tailor does not make the gentleman here, so we don't mind spoiling our clothes:" and then calls to Stephen, who is hastily advancing towards her.

"If I had known you were going to help the men, I would not have come. You can't walk home with me in that plight."

"I did not expect to be of any use," says Stephen good-humoredly. "But of course I could not have stood by, and not have helped Thomas in his extremity. I am sorry, though"—

"Some people could have resisted the temptation," interrupts Milicent, glancing at the stranger, with a laugh in her eyes.

But Stephen does not understand her hint, nor even see there is any one near them.

"If you will tell Miss Ursula that we have saved the fish, she will be glad to hear the good news. And then, if you will say that it was all my fault that you came here, and that"—

But Milicent stops him, with a movement of her hand towards the stranger.

Stephen shakes hands with him, and welcomes him heartily, very much as if he were a guest of his own ; a proceeding which rather amuses the recipient, who has an idea he has as much right to be on the seashore as Stephen himself, but which he takes in good part.

" If I could be of any use to you, and could see the young lady home " — he begins, a little eagerly.

" The young lady knows her way perfectly," she interrupts.

" But you did not intend to go alone ; and I will be too happy if you will let me take the place of your friend."

" Miss Ursula won't be able to find any fault, if there is a stranger with you," suggests Stephen in a whisper, as he stoops to take up his coat.

Still Milicent hesitates. Is her dignity worth preserving, at the sacrifice of so good a chance of escaping from the much-dreaded fault-finding? Scarcely, she thinks, and therefore gives a gracious permission to the stranger to go with her ; leaving Stephen to struggle into his coat as best he may, in his drenched state, and then to take a shorter path across the fields to his own home.

" Are you very much in a hurry? " asks Milicent's new acquaintance. " I have been so little on terra firma of late that a race is beyond my powers, I fear."

" I am not walking at all fast," asserts Milicent, nevertheless slackening her pace.

They have passed, by now, the last of the straggling village houses, its gable to the street, and

double bow-windows, like most of its fellows, filled
with rare geraniums and fuchsias.   There is a
clump of bleeding-heart and white spirea by the
doorsteps; one tall, scant-leaved balm-of-Gilead tree
keeping up a breezy rattle overhead, — at watch, as
it were, upon the cottage, in the midst of its green
hay-field, with the " fish-flakes," or long lattices,
laid horizontally on props, and lining, with their
rows of drying cod, both sides of the garden walk
to the white gate upon the street.   Beyond all
these, and past the point of rocks, and up the
grassy slope behind, climbs Milicent, the stranger
at her side.   " Have you been long with the fishermen ? " she asks him, with a woman's laudable desire to make conversation.

" Nearly a week.   I was at Grand Manan with
my yacht, and fell in with the boats off the banks.
I was anxious to see something of the fishing, and
to know a little of the hardships of the life.   They
are a brave set of fellows," he adds, willing to pro-
pitiate her by a compliment to her fellow-townsmen.

" Do you think so ? " asks Milicent, carelessly.
" They are no novelty to me."

" I acknowledge the fishing is more interesting
than the fishermen," he answers, laughing.

" Even that I do not comprehend.   The fishermen look upon their work as the very hardest, and
complain of the great exposure ; and yet you regard it as mere pleasant pastime," the girl says,
really puzzled by the difference of opinion.

" That is only because the men grow accustomed
to it.   Most things are disagreeable that we are

obliged to do day after day. Still, I have no doubt every fisherman here can remember the delight he felt on his first fishing voyage."

"Perhaps so," she assents, doubtfully. "But I must confess I can't see how work can ever be looked upon with delight: and fishing is decidedly work."

"I can understand how enforced idleness can be an awful bore."

"One need n't be idle because one is doing nothing," asserts Milicent.

"I don't see well how you can help being so. If you are really doing nothing, you are not employed."

"You talk as well on the subject as Aunt Ursula!" The girl shrugs her shoulders skeptically. "I was not idle when I was yonder in Westport watching the boats. Aunt Ursula would have said I had better be darning the house-linen; but I think I was much better occupied."

"The most tyrannical of aunts could scarcely expect you to sit in-doors on such a day as this," he begins sympathetically.

"Oh, I need not sit in-doors. I can take my work where I please. It is the constant stitching, whether I wish to or not, that I detest. And there is no end to it. I suppose most people buy new house-linen every now and then; but we never do. Aunt Ursula says she cannot afford to."

This is said with such a weary, aggrieved tone, that the *ci-devant* fisherman can with difficulty keep from laughing, — which fact Milicent detects at once.   Half angry, half ashamed, she turns sharply round to him : but checks herself in time, wisely thinking it better not to resent his mirth, much as she dislikes it.

"See, there is our house," she says abruptly. "Did you ever see anything so old and hideous?"

A difficult question to answer, unless one could be quite frank, and agree with the questioner.

The house is certainly old, with an uncanny look about its weather-beaten, gray-brown face, which in men and houses hints of haunted rooms and skeletons.   Its builders, unlike the wiser cottagers, were not thrifty of their windows, in this windy climate : there is a great number of them, all stuck into the wrong end of the house : for they stare out from the gable to the open sea, at watch for the prevailing southeast storms.

Not a shrub nor a tree grows near, except that on one side there is a wind-bared skeleton with a few breezy leaves atop; which, however, only seems to make the building more noticeable, as it does not shade it in the least.   The situation is too bleak and exposed for anything but the closest-woven turf pressing to the ground.   A garden might have been made behind; hardy creepers might possibly have been induced to cover up some of the dismal ugliness of the staring walls full of shutterless windows.   But there is evidently no loving hand to do the work.

"It is a large house," Milicent's new acquaintance says at last, not knowing what remark to make but this self-evident one.

"And has a great many windows," adds Milicent. " I never heard any other observation made at the first look at our mansion.' But we have a tree, and that is something that not every house in the village can boast," she asserts, with doubtful pride in it.

"What do you call it?"

"A tree," she says, half suspecting him of laughing at it; "a balm-of-Gilead."

"There does not seem to be much balm in Gilead," he says, looking up into the scant foliage, which makes up in sound what it lacks in shade. "Well, home is home, though ever so homely. It is certainly an old homestead."

"But not ours, for Aunt Ursula rents it. Not that I can remember any other home," she adds quickly, as if she would do away with the impression she might have made that she is new to the place.

She pushes aside, as she speaks, a gate in the gray-brown pitch-pole fence; and for a moment she seems to hesitate whether to dismiss the stranger or ask him in. But he does not or will not notice her indecision. His meeting Milicent is something of an adventure, and he is inclined to make the most of it.

Perhaps the sight of the tall, gaunt figure of a woman standing in the doorway decides Milicent to be hospitable; for she lets him follow her across the yard, as if it were an act on his part that she expects.

"Aunt Ursula, this is" — Milicent breaks down

there, in confusion at not knowing the name of her
companion: but recovers herself in a moment, and
adds — "a gentleman Stephen asked to walk home
with me, as he could not come himself."

"I did not know you were out. I had your promise to do some work which ought to have kept you
occupied all day," Miss Ursula answers shortly.
Neither Stephen's name nor the presence of a
stranger has had the effect Milicent hoped for.

"Stephen came to take me to see the fishing-
boats come in," replies Milicent, carelessly ; and
then, turning to her visitor, she says, "Perhaps if
you would tell me your name, so that I could introduce you properly, my aunt might notice you."

"My name is Urquhart," he answers, not thinking it at all worth while to give any more information about himself.

"You have a Scottish name." says Miss Ursula,
for the first time turning to look at him. "If you
have come here for pleasure you will not tarry very
long. We fisher-folk have nothing about us to interest strangers. And we are far too poor to be
idle ; so you will pardon me if I tell you we do not
receive visitors."

Though it is Miss Ursula's evident intention to
put herself on a footing with the fishing-people in
the village, Urquhart is very sure she has nothing
in common with them save poverty. Her scant,
black dress, almost nun-like in its fashion, seems to
him more a masquerade than her usual attire.
Neither are her hands, roughened by toil, tokens of
a life which is hard and painful — any real evi-

dence that she belongs to the class she has claimed. Rude as her words were, Urquhart does not feel altogether repelled. However, he would not have presumed to cross her threshold after such a dismissal, though Milicent seems rather anxious he should. Her aunt's want of civility has the effect of making the girl much more gracious; and she bids him good-by cordially, as if she were sure they would meet again. When he turns to latch the gate he sees her standing watching him.

"Milicent, are you mad, that you bring a stranger here?" asks Miss Ursula, angrily, as soon as Urquhart is out of hearing. "Cannot your girlish vanity withstand a fool's look of admiration? At least you need not have asked him to the house."

"I told you Stephen sent him," answers Milicent, raising her hand, as she speaks, to shade her eyes, so that she may see Urquhart's retreating figure the better.

"Stephen! What does Stephen care? He would bring the sea into the house if he thought it would give you any pleasure."

"That would be rather an injudicious kindness. But Mr. — Usher, or whatever his name is, will be much more easily gotten rid of. I doubt if he will ever come again, after your reception of him."

"Did you wish me to ask him to dinner? or perhaps you would have preferred my pressing him to stay here? There are rooms enough in the house for guests," returns Miss Ursula, ironically.

"It does not make the slightest difference to me," answers Milicent coolly, "whether he stays here, or I never see him again ; for I don't feel the slightest interest in him.   But he seems to feel a great deal in us.   He is standing at the gate, staring at the house as if it were one of the curiosities of the place."

"It is much more likely that he is looking at you.   Do come in and shut the door, or he will be making an excuse to come back again."

Milicent laughs an odd, mocking laugh, but does as she is bidden.   Nevertheless, she watches Urquhart furtively from the window until he is out of sight.

It may have been that she only wished to be sure he is not lurking near ; for as soon as he is gone, she takes her work-basket, and goes out-of-doors, turning her back on the old house, that truly looks sadly buffeted and ill-used by wind and weather, as it keeps its post, a beacon to the sailors.

On a fogless day like this, the high ground where it stands overlooks well-nigh the whole of the three-mile island ; a rock between three seas, as its visitor has called it. Yonder, Westport Harbor, or Grand Passage, links with silver band the shoreless, boisterous Bay of Fundy — with Grand Manan a mere cloud on its bosom — to calm Bay St. Mary, bordered by the Nova Scotian mainland, the "French Shore," where more than a century ago some stragglers from Evangeline's part of Acadie wandered down to these more hospitable coasts, and have since dwelt there, a people half apart.   Even now, as Milicent looks, she can see where old Denis the pilot's boat comes fluttering into Westport, with the French flag flying from the mast-head.

Far more pleasant than in-doors is it to be out in the soft air, even under the sunny balm-of-Gilead. But Milicent only glances askance at that familiar seat; then, with her work-basket on her arm, she wanders away to where the slope seems to break off with a rolling grassy edge against the sea.

But only seems; for as she nears the edge, with just a fringe of spruce and fir dwarfs bearing off from it, she looks down from the dizzy height upon a strange chaotic world of rock and water. It has been Milicent's dream-world ever since she could remember. Torn out of the side of the island by some convulsive throe of nature, the dark basaltic rocks rise up in pinnacles and broken turrets, as of a huge fortress in ruins, at the girl's feet; and strewn on the wide pavement reaching out beneath into the water lie great octagons, columnar bases, unfinished pillars, — all the scattered fragmentary blocks left over by the Master-Builder. Billows come in raging here at every turn of tide, however calmly they may swell beyond, and spring to climb these battlements, and fall back, broken, on the rocks below. The wild, strong music of their on-rush reaches Milicent; inspiriting as a trumpet blast, but hardly for the sort of work she takes into her hands, as she drops down on a knoll that overhangs the cliffs.

With the low green boughs screening her from

the westering sun, she works on diligently, never raising her eyes from the intricacy of her darning. Nearly an hour passes; but she is still there at her monotonous task. One would suppose she is trying to make up for the time spent in watching the arrival of the fishing-boats, and is determined her aunt shall have no occasion to complain of her broken promise.

On into the late sunset she sits with her work. Even when she sees a shadow drawing near, across the patch from which the firs stand back, and from which she is herself in full view, she does not look up, though no doubt she knows very well it is Stephen's shadow. But she affects to be unconscious of his presence; and he has to approach near enough to speak to her before she even glances at him.

"How did you get home, Milly?" Stephen asks. "Did you like your new acquaintance?"

"He did well enough," she answers, without looking up. "But I can't say the same for Aunt Ursula. I knew she'd be cross; but I did not expect her to be quite as rude as she was. Of course I could only be as polite as possible, to cover Aunt Ursula's brusqueness; and now I have not a doubt he will think I want him to come again. It is too stupid! I wish I had not let him walk home with me; or, better still, I wish I had not gone to the village with you."

"Perhaps he'll take the hint, if Miss Ursula was not cordial, and think it best to stay away. At any rate, the fellow seems daft about fishing, and

I can manage to keep him busy; for of course he will not be here very long," says Stephen, hopefully.

" If he proves troublesome, you can easily drown him," Milicent replies, dropping her work, and looking up at him with a smile.

Stephen laughs; not so much at the prospect of making away with Urquhart as at the smile he has won.

" Let us go up to the High Knoll," he proposes. " The sun has nearly set, and you like to see him die royally."

She has let her work slip out of her fingers; but now she takes it up again, and begins to stitch diligently.

" I have no time for sunsets : Aunt Ursula has brought me up with a round turn. And besides," she says, a sly little dimple lurking about her pretty mouth, — " you would leave me to come home alone, or coolly turn me over to Mr. Urquhart."

" And if I do, you ought not to complain," says Stephen, laughing. " You have completely turned his head. I met him in the village, and he did nothing but talk of you. I found some difficulty in getting him to speak rationally."

" Thanks," says Milicent; and the monosyllable, shorn of all amenities, sounds like a small stone flung at him.

" Is there any harm in my telling you? I am sure I did n't mean any," he says humbly.

" I know you did n't. But if you had asked if

Mr. Urquhart had meant to be impertinent, your question might have a different answer."

"Impertinent?" repeats Stephen, in an uncertain way, as if doubtful whether he has really heard aright.

"Everybody," says Milicent, with a mock air of resignation, "cannot be *exactly* like that famous

' Noll
Who wrote like an angel, and talked like Poor Poll '—

but at least you manage a half resemblance, when you repeat my words like a parrot. Yes, impertinent was what I said. This Mr. Urquhart, after first taking me for a fishwoman, goes to the trouble to rave about me " —

"But he did not say anything that was not perfectly true. It was only that you are pretty" —

"Oh, I have no doubt his speeches were. Only I don't care for them *at second hand.*"

Her face is like an April sky, half cloudy and half laughing, as she flashes up a sidelong glance at him, with those last words.

But the clouds have it. Suddenly, as at some overwhelming thought in the silence, a rush of color floods fair throat and blue-veined temples. She turns sharply aside, plucking with restless fingers at such of the buttercups and the pink sheep's-laurel as grow within her reach. Presently she flings them from her with an impatient gesture, and takes up her sewing again. " Why don't you go and look at the sunset? I can work much faster alone."

Stephen rises at once. There is a look of pain in his face, but not the slightest trace of anger.

"Good-by, Milly," he says. "I did n't mean to be in your way. I am sorry I got you into any trouble. You may be sure I never meant it."

He is looking at her wistfully, but she never raises her eyes from her work.

"There is no quarreling with you comfortably," she says, with a shrug. "One is so apt to get one's ears boxed with a text of Scripture."

"A text of Scripture, Milly?"

"If you did n't quote it, you implied it: 'A soft answer turneth away wrath.' Good-by."

In and out goes her needle, with all the regularity of a neat darn. So low the long brown lashes sweep on the flushed cheek, Stephen marvels how she can be looking at the stitches. Milly's lashes are like no one else's, he is thinking; the silken fringe upon the lower lid is so long and thick and soft, as it curves downward.

He watches her a moment longer; then, as she never moves, but for the small swift hands, he turns away, and walks off slowly.

Still Milicent works on, with praiseworthy steadiness. But when Stephen is too far away to see, she buries her face in the well-worn damask she is mending, — a token of better days, — and cries bitterly.

Are they tears of contrition, or mere silly ones of mortification? It is hard to tell, and no one comes near her to ask.

Perhaps she is not sorry for the neglect. For

after a while she gathers up her work, and goes in-
doors and up to her own room, where she bathes
her eyes, and takes some time and trouble to remove all traces of tears from her face before she
goes down-stairs again.

II.

THAT the seventh day of the week, when the fishing-boats come in, should be followed by the first, when the boats neither come in nor go out (and when, moreover, in this particular case, a furious southeaster was sweeping from the Atlantic to the Bay of Fundy, blotting out this little island in its low-hung clouds and fog), Urquhart regarded as a mistake. But perhaps if this one Saturday could have been followed by a sunshiny Monday, "and fortune's favor filled the swelling sails" of the gay Undine, he would have sped away with just a half-curious memory of the sea-girt islet and its sea-maid, and Milicent would be of those fortunate ones who have no story.

As it was, from lack of other thoughts, he thought of her, and even went as far as the door of the Baptist meeting, the only assemblage of the saints this day upon the island, — the English church having long been closed, and the Methodists suffering from the great Baptist revival of last winter, when a pause in the deep-sea fishing gave space for the fishers of men.

Was her voice in the melancholy hymn he heard from the choir in the gallery, as he held the door in the white tower ajar? It was all of the storms of life, and of the billows going over our head; and through it swelled the undertone breaking on the distant cliffs, — "The floods are risen, O Lord, the floods have lift up their voice; the floods lift up their waves." The young yachtsman, peering in on the weather-beaten, earnest upturned faces of the fishermen, as they sat presently listening to the preacher, telling them of the haven of safety they were steering for, had it borne in upon him that his voyaging through life, in the Undine or otherwise, was a mere summer-sea sail, and that it is these men who occupy their business in great waters who see His wonders in the deep.

But as it was not these men Urquhart had come to look at, he went away rather piqued that among the few women who had ventured to breast the storm, Milicent should not have been there to amuse him.

He might have ventured up the wind-swept slope where the big gray house loomed through the fog, but that neither was Aunt Ursula among the congregation. So there was nothing for it but to struggle back to his lodgings, where he had already mastered the leading facts in the History of Acadie, interviewed the Prince of Wales in the full trappings of Grand Master of the Masons, and made a study of the tomb of the late Captain Featherstone, depicted on the opposite wall under a much-weeping willow, where, behind a handkerchief rather bigger than the tombstone, drooped a willowy figure of quite different proportions from the comfortable Widow Featherstone. There was nothing left for Urquhart to do but to wonder what the pretty girl was doing — what she could do, would do — on this rock between three seas.

Fortunately, Mondays will come in due course; storms will go, suns will burn up fogs, — or so at least, declares Mrs. Featherstone.

But the sails of the Undine are drenched, as if her spiteful uncle Kuhleborn had been aboard; her decks are over-wet; and the sea's broad bosom is still heaving in troubled remembrance of the storm: so that there is nothing to tempt a fair-weather sailor outside the harbor. Urquhart may as well see something of the island, — and, by the way, of a certain islander.

The balm-of-Gilead is lifting its crown of quivering gray-green leaves above her empty seat; even the close-woven, springy turf, that dries so soon, is too wet still for the girl to be sitting out-of-doors. Instead, she has been stitching away at her window all the morning; having evidently set herself a task she is making all speed to get to the end of.

Milicent, as she sits there, is like the day, like the sea, at which now and then she glances as she works on. In truth, the child's face is not unlike the sea in its changes: every cloud reflected there,

as well as every sunbeam; storm and calm; and
again days when it is turbid and dull-looking,
and outer circumstances and surroundings seem to
make no impression. These variations of mood
and expression are Milicent's chief charm. The
other day she was captious and perverse; to-day
she is sunshiny, yet withal, like the sea, a little sad.

It is not until some time after the primitive din-
ner-hour that she has finished the last piece of
work in her basket, — a coarse red fisherman's-shirt
that needed buttons, — and takes all, a great pile
her arms can scarcely carry, down to Miss Ursula.
Then she comes out-of-doors, with her hat on.
She stands on the step where she can see over the
village below, as if she were looking for some one.
But there is nothing to be seen, except a woman
turning the fish on the flakes; a wavering line of
children coming from school, along the winding
street; and one or two laggards of the fishing-fleet
going out even now.

After lingering a while, Milicent crosses the
yard to the gate. Outside of it, she turns her back
upon the sea, and goes up a somewhat steep road,
which stretches before her, towards the middle of
the island, until lost in the belt of low woods.
Presently she comes in sight of a low white cottage, the porch of which is covered in with clem-
atis and green matrimony-vines. There are two
Norwegian firs before the porch, their dark green
branches sweeping the ground. Willow-bushes
and lilacs are planted through the grass, giving the
small lawn such a bowery effect that one scarcely

remembers the absence of trees. There are rustic seats placed where the view of the sea is finest, — a more distant view than Milicent has from her own windows, yet near enough in a storm, or on a calm, still night, for the roll of the waves on the rocks to be loud.

Milicent opens the gate in the white picket fence.

There could not have been a greater contrast than the pretty cottage, perfect in its neatness, and set cosily in the soft, bowery green, and the great staring, many-windowed, unpainted barn which Milicent calls home. No doubt the difference is very plain to her; for she stands at the gate for some time, looking at the cottage. Yet there is no discontent in her face, but a tender, grateful look, as for some kindness shown her.

Milicent does not go towards the cottage, but to a seat half hidden by the lilac-bush. She takes off her hat, and lays it down on the bench beside her, letting the sea-wind blow her hair about at its will. It is evident she is waiting for some one, and is not at all impatient.

If she is waiting, she is not watching; for her back is turned to the house, and before her is a stretch of fields which runs down to the Green Head cliffs, a way it is not likely any one would come.

Though Millicent is sitting with her eyes fixed dreamily upon the sea, and her back to the cottage, she sees it very plainly. When she was a child, and first came to live on the island, this was as unsightly as her own home. The boards were unpainted and weather-stained, not a tree would grow, and the rough salt wind in the winter killed out the grass. It was not until Stephen had come of age, and had taken the property into his own hands, that the metamorphosis began. It took untold trouble, as well as a long time, to discover what would grow in such a sterile and exposed spot; for even the grass had to be coaxed into luxuriance, as if it were an exotic. But it was a labor of love with Stephen, — a tender, generous love, which would fain have even the surroundings of the loved one beautiful,—and this is his success.

Milicent has been sitting there fully half an hour, when Stephen returns from one of his distant fields. His quick eye detects some one under the great lilac before he is near enough to recognize who it is. He goes forward slowly, as if not caring to welcome a visitor, but soon quickens his step. The grass deadens his foot-fall, so that he is at Milicent's side before she knows he is coming.

"See, Stephen, I have come to you to ask you to pardon me. I was horribly cross and unreasonable on Saturday: but if you only knew " —

Milicent does not finish her sentence: indeed, it is a bad habit of hers to break off with a word or two lacking.

But Stephen is not exacting; he does not desire an apology. It is very sweet in Milicent to come to him; and though he had felt hurt, now he is heartily ashamed of himself, and is sure he should have gone over as he usually does to Miss Ursula's every morning. Feeling this, no wonder Stephen

kisses the hand Milicent has stretched out to him,
as a loyal subject might kiss his queen's who has
just pardoned him.

Milicent has taken up her hat, making room for
Stephen on the bench ; and the two sit there side
by side, not caring to talk. The red light in the
west is reflected in the clouds in the east, until they
are rose-colored. Even the water has caught the
tint, and the sail of the little fishing-boat flying before the wind is pink.

One of the strongest links which bind Milicent
to Stephen is his always quick perception of her
moods. As she seems inclined to be silent, he
does not care to talk, but is content to have her by
his side ; doubly content in that she for the first
time in her life has sought him herself.

" It must be very easy for you to be so good
and kind as you are, when everything is beautiful
around you," Milicent says abruptly.

" It is not always as beautiful as it is this evening. In our cold, bleak winter, you know, the
cottage does not look much better than the ugliest
fishing-hut."

But Milicent does not seem to hear him.

" Perhaps I too may feel the influence of this
peace and quiet, in time," she goes on. " When I
leave Aunt Ursula and — and the other trials,
and come here to live, I may grow quite different
from myself now."

" If you would only come at once ! You know,
Milly, it is my great longing and desire to bring
you here," says Stephen, eagerly.

"I can't just now, but soon, perhaps. Ah, Stephen, you do not know how I long to call this my home."

She speaks softly, almost tenderly. There can be no doubt that she means just what she says.

"It won't be long before you will fix a time? If I can look forward to something definite, say next winter, or even the spring, Milly " —

"I can't tell you this evening. I know it seems hard and ungrateful to put you off; but indeed I can't help myself. If you will wait until to-morrow; or next month will be better. It will be just as soon as I can," she adds, laying her hand on his arm. For she has left off looking at the sea: instead, her eyes are on his face, and she sees there a wistful, questioning glance, as if Stephen were not altogether satisfied.

"Tell me when you can," he says, gently. "I am all ready for you, and have been so for a year and more. But, Milly, you speak of trials that I do not know of, and as if you had n't everything in your own guiding."

"You forget Aunt Ursula. Or don't you consider her a trial? You are not a girl, and can't tell how it vexes me to have her carping at everything I say or do. Certainly I consider Aunt Ursula one of my trials."

"Then you admit that you have others " — Stephen asserts, gravely.

"Oh, any number of them," she answers almost gayly. "Is it not a trial to be as poor as we are? Why, I have n't had a new dress for a whole year now! Only think of it, Stephen, not a single dress for a year, and the last one was a cotton one! You 'll do better for me than that, when you marry me? See, I shall make a bargain. You must give me two dresses a year, unless the hay is bad or the fishing fails. Then I 'll be content with one."

She is looking up at him with saucy, laughing eyes; all the soft, tender light has gone out of them.

For the first time, Stephen does not respond to her change of mood. For some reason, he feels baffled rather than amused, and not at all inclined to give up questioning her as to what she means by her trials.

If Milicent does not care to answer, she must be relieved by seeing a man coming slowly up the road to the cottage. She points him out to Stephen, and rises to go. "Some one on business, no doubt. He need not see me if I go at once. I am sorry, for I hoped you would walk home with me. But you will be over soon."

She leaves him abruptly, before he has quite determined whether he will not elude the man, and go home with her. But he has made the appointment himself; so he must let Milicent go without him, though he longs inexpressibly to talk to her.

Milicent does not return by the road, but by the fields to the cliffs. She skirts the big potato-field; the patch of wheat covering a space about as large as a good-sized pocket handkerchief; another, well-nigh as big, of barley; and then she crosses the crumpled swell of the ridge against the sky, to where Green Cove offers its tiny square-cut shingle beach, a doubtful shelter for a hard-pressed boat. Beyond the hill, upon the farther side, stands Milicent's old gray unhome-like home. But the girl chooses rather to reach it by the roundabout way of the sea. So she clambers down as fast as she can, not stopping to take breath until she stands on the lower level of rocks, a Giant's Causeway which the tide, halfway out now, has left bare.

Once on the rocks, Milicent walks more slowly. She is in no haste to reach home. She can think of Stephen, and of the future, where she has no doubt much happiness awaits her. It would be heaven, that future at the cottage, compared to her present. The poor child has not yet learned that at least one half of the misery in our lives is but the crop of our own sowing.

As she goes on, still towards the harbor and the jutting point where it begins, she turns a rocky parapet, and sees, upon a ledge almost at her feet, a man in a red flannel shirt, such as she was mending this morning. His slouched hat with its broad brim shades his face effectually. A basket of fish and his fishing-tackle are on the rocks by his side, the former showing he has had good luck to-day.

The fisherman's back is turned to Milicent, who no sooner recognizes him than she walks softly, as if anxious to pass him without his seeing her,— a feat not difficult for her to have accomplished if fate had not been against her, making him chance to look round just as she comes where he is seated.

His face is bronzed by exposure, the lower part
entirely covered with a heavy black beard. His
eyes are of that peculiar shade of gray which can
look cold as steel, or can flash black with passion.
Certainly his eyes are the most noticeable feature
in the face he turns on her.

"Where have you been?" he asks abruptly, as
Milicent, finding she cannot avoid speaking to him,
walks quietly on.

"To the cottage."

"To the cottage!" he repeats, mimicking her
tone. "One would suppose you were some fisher-
girl looking after her man that is to be. Girls in
your position receive visits instead of making them.
They like to be sought" —

"Girls in my position are seldom sought," replies Milicent, stopping and facing him. "Any
man of common sense would rather marry the
roughest girl in the village than such as I am."

"And I for one would not blame him for his
taste," is the cool answer. "I never saw a more
devilish temper than yours. One cannot even give
you a caution without putting you into a passion.
If you wish Stephen to hold you cheap, go call on
him, by all means."

"He 'll hold me cheap enough some day," she
answers bitterly.

"And if you go courting him and paying him
visits, he 'll bring it up to you. Men are not generous," he goes on, not heeding her last remark.

"Some men seem to have all that other men
lack" —

"Of course Stephen is one who has much more than his share. But take care not to tax him too heavily. After all, Stephen is a man; and when he finds you marry him only to get your own head above water" —

"You know that is false" — interrupts Milicent, her eyes flashing.

"False! Have a care how you select your words. However I may choose not to interfere with your plans, you will scarcely deny my right to do so, I suppose."

Milicent makes no reply. An intolerable blush overspreads her face. "Tell Miss Ursula I will bring some fish for supper," Thomas says, all at once assuming the monotonous drawl of the fisherman.

It is meant for the benefit of Urquhart, who has come upon them suddenly.

Urquhart had seen Milicent standing there; but, like her, he had not seen the fisherman until he had come down the rocks.

The blush has not died out of Milicent's face, nor the angry ring from her voice, when she must answer Mr. Urquhart's good-evening. Thomas takes not the smallest notice of him.

But Urquhart cares very little for the good-will of Thomas, though he evidently intends to join Milicent, who seems uncertain whether to let him or not. She glances down in a puzzled way at Thomas; but he is busy in gathering up his fishing-lines, and does not look at her. So she walks on with Urquhart.

She does not know that when both backs are turned the fisherman has lifted his head, and is following her with his eyes. There is a strange look in them, — a dark look of pain, of anger.

But the first is the stronger: the flash dies out of them; there deepens a yearning in them, as he stands watching the light figure flitting from rock to rock. Her hat sways at her side; the sunset is in her burnished hair.

The fisherman turns sharply away as if there were something in the pretty picture just then defined against the sky which he cannot bear.

It strikes Urquhart in a different light; but Milicent does not give him much time to observe it, for she has sprung down from the rock before he can offer his aid. So he can only ask her, —

"Have you been walking far?" by way of opening the conversation.

"Not very," she answers curtly.

"Are you fond of the exercise?" he goes on questioning.

"I have never tried any other."

"Certainly you have tried driving."

"I certainly never have. You have not made good use of your time on the island if you have not discovered that there are no carriages on it, unless you except the one at the light-house across on the Fundy side. I might go in an ox-cart, as the fishermen's children do sometimes."

"But you might try riding," persists Urquhart.

"We have no horses, except that at the aforesaid light-house. But I am wrong to say I know no other exercise, " she adds, "for I can pull an oar as well as any one."

"I am sorry I have n't my horses here. I am sure there could be nothing finer to drive on than a sandy beach ; and I know you would like it."

" There is not a yard of sand-beach on the island ; and I am glad they are not here. There is no use in learning to enjoy pleasures one will never perhaps have again in one's life," philosophizes the girl. "Besides," she adds, "if the horses were here, perhaps I would not drive with you."

"Why not ?" asks Urquhart, amused by her heat.

"Because I am not at all sure that it is customary in your world " —

" But it is, I assure you. I would ask any lady of my acquaintance to drive with me. Perhaps, however, your customs here are different ? "

He does not know that she has just been rebuked for a lack of coyness, and that she is determined not to offend where a stranger is concerned. Perhaps, if he had known, he would not have stooped for that tuft of bluebells waving from a crevice of the rocks, — which she does not refuse, but draws indifferently through her hands, while she goes on speaking.

" We have no customs at all," she answers him. "It is only when a stranger comes that we bother ourselves about such trifles."

" Don't bother yourself about them on my account," says Urquhart, laughing. "I 'll promise not to presume on your sensible, primitive ways."

"That is wise. You know there are no people so easily aggrieved as those who are not quite sure of their rights." And then she adds, with the evident intention of turning the conversation, "Stephen tells me you have taken lodgings in the village."

"Stephen?"

"Yes, Mr. Ferguson."

"Is it one of your customs to call people by their Christian names?"

"If we have known each other since we were children, and have been constant companions."

"You make me wish I had always lived here," begins Urquhart; but catching a glimpse of an angry flush on her face, he hastens to add, "Your friend has been very kind, and has procured me far more comfortable lodgings than I thought I could possibly get here."

"Where are you lodging?" asks Milicent, with sudden interest, as knowing every one in the village.

"Let me see if you can tell me. A trim little body, rather fat, very fair — in complexion I mean — and rosy, and emphatically jolly, unless her face belies her."

"Which it does not. Altogether a taut-looking craft, as Mrs. Featherstone herself would say."

"I observed she was nautical in her mode of expressing herself. Is it" —

"The island dialect," he was about to say, but fortunately stops, while Milicent goes on with a laugh: —

"Oh, yes! Perhaps she never signed articles, but for all that she is as good a sailor as ever passed a weather earing. She has even been wrecked, and carried off chief honors in the newspaper account of the disaster. Captain Featherstone has been dead only a year or two, and she thought nothing of shipping two or three children and going off with him to the States or to the West Indies, to England or South America, — in whatever trade he happened to be at the time. Captain Richard, she will tell you, though he'd a fine figure-head of his own, was n't altogether to be trusted for straight sailing ; and she liked to take her trick at the helm. But since she will have no particular desire to steer *you*, you are lucky to fall into her hands, if she takes a kindness to you."

"I believe I may flatter myself that she has," says Urquhart, smiling, " since she assures me she does n't care the drawing of a rope-yarn how long I stay on the island, as I 'm not a whitewashed Yankee. I wonder how she knows ? "

"Oh," apologizes Milicent, "she means one of those American traders who sail in here with a cargo of goods, and open shop for the three summer months, with their counters full of what they call ' lawns ' and ' mosquito-nets,' — things that we don't know the use of ! But they rather interfere with Mrs. Featherstone's own shop. They are about the only summer visitors the island has."

"So that explains why I find the neighbors a little suspicious of me. It is difficult to make them believe I am staying for the pleasure of fishing."

" But are you ? " asks Milicent, turning round, and looking at him with evident curiosity.

" Certainly. What else can possibly keep me ? "

" I can't say ; only I think, with the fishermen, you might be better employed."

" But unfortunately I am among the drones in the world's busy hive, so have no employment but that most tiresome one, the search for amusement."

" Don't your friends object to such employment on your part ? "

Urquhart's attention is rather more given to the wondering brown eyes that question, than to the question itself.

" I don't see what business it is of theirs," he says, half absently.

" I should think they might reasonably object, if they have to take care of you."

" Take care of me ! Well, thank Heaven ! I have not got so low in the scale of humanity," says Urquhart, with very evident satisfaction.

" I thought you called yourself a drone, and I 'm sure the drones live on the honey made by the other bees," is Milicent's conclusive argument.

" Then I am not literally a drone, for I assure you I buy my own honey," replies Urquhart, laughing.

This bit of information seems of very little interest to Milicent, for she begins to talk of something less personal. At the gate, she bids him good-evening ; and Urquhart, remembering Miss Ursula's reception on Saturday, supposes Milicent will not care to risk another of the same sort for him. Milicent has frankly said they are tenacious of their rights in all mooted points of etiquette; so the safest way would be to ask Stephen to introduce him. If he were once received at the house, he could depend upon himself for all further steps toward an intimacy.

Milicent disappears round the side of the house, ignoring the front door, and going by the kitchen. There she finds Miss Ursula preparing a kind of nondescript tea.

She looks red and warm from the heat of the stove; but Milicent knows better than to offer to help her.

"I should think you would find it fatiguing to walk so much. Such a fine lady as you should set up her carriage," Miss Ursula says sharply, when Milicent appears at the door.

"Perhaps I shall some day," answers the girl, lightly.

"Pray, will it be soon?"

"I can't tell; but the future is so uncertain, one can't help thinking there must be some luck ahead."

"Bad luck, then. The future will be no kinder than the past, unless you do something yourself to mend it. That is the way with young people. They sit still, their hands in their laps, expecting the good things of life to fall into them. Where one is fortunate enough to catch anything, a dozen miss."

"Did you ever catch anything that was pleasant, Aunt Ursula?" the girl asks, wistfully.

" If I did, I have shaken my skirts free of them. What is the matter with Stephen, that he has not been near the house for two days ? "

" There is nothing the matter with him. Only I have been to see him instead."

" And picked up another man on your way home. I suppose you think it a fine thing to be noticed by a stranger no one knows anything about."

" I am sure I don't care whether he notices me or not. The road is open to more than me, and I can't help who walks over it. We are to have fish for tea," Milicent adds, as she turns to leave the kitchen.

" Are we ? " asks Miss Ursula, ironically. " I should like to know what else there is to eat in this God-forsaken place."

" The place is good enough. There was n't a blot upon the earth until man was made, and even he can't spoil the sea. But it was n't the herrings I meant. I knew they were for tea when I reached the gate."

" So you were ashamed of the herrings," says Miss Ursula, as if she rather enjoys any feeling of annoyance Milicent might have at the fumes of the fish.

" If you mean that was the reason I did n't ask Mr. Urquhart to the house, you are mistaken. There are other things I am much more ashamed of, than the herrings. Aunt Ursula," cries Milicent, passionately, " I won't be stopped and found fault with, as I have been this afternoon. And I 'll not marry Stephen unless I tell him everything about myself.　I know you want me to marry him; but I'll not do it with an untruth upon my conscience."

She does not give Miss Ursula time to answer her, but goes swiftly up-stairs to her own room; so she has not the mortification of seeing that this outbreak of hers has not discomposed Miss Ursula in the least.

"She is her mother's own child in more than appearance," Miss Ursula thinks, as she returns to her labors, for an instant suspended. "She is proud and passionate, and such girls never make smooth paths for themselves through life. A little stumbling may be good for her, and make her more humble and gentle. Stephen will be better without her than with her; yet I'll do nothing to help nor to hinder him."

This compromise seems to satisfy Miss Ursula. Milicent should manage her own affairs, — she would wash her hands of them. Alas for Miss Ursula! She had formed plans of her own in life, and had longed for them as eagerly as Milicent is longing, and with far greater chances of success: and they had all failed. That spare, gaunt figure in black, bending over the fire, half stifled with the fumes of the herring, is a far more eloquent sermon on the vanity of human hopes and desires than any ever preached by a golden-mouthed Saint Chrysostom.

Yet it is being preached in vain to Milicent, who is impatiently trying to get rid of evils which Miss Ursula has learned to bear without a murmur.

III.

" Who is the fisherman with such a splendid growth of beard?" Urquhart asks Stephen, the next morning, in the village.

" I suppose you mean Thomas. He certainly has an uncommonly handsome one."

" This Thomas seems to be an insolent fellow "—begins Urquhart.

" He is a dangerous one, so you had better not call him insolent to his face. Those cold eyes of his can show the devil in them if he is roused; though usually he is good-natured enough."

" I never was much afraid of the devil," Urquhart says, quietly. " It was your pretty little friend, Miss Milicent, I was anxious about. I saw her on the rocks to-day, talking to this Thomas, and I am very sure he was impertinent, for she stamped her little foot as if in a rage. I thought the best thing I could do was to hasten to her rescue. But when I got up to them, I found he was only telling her about some fish I think he wanted her aunt to take; and the young lady walked home with me as if she had not been scolding this same Thomas."

" Well, the whole of that story is easily explained," says Stephen, laughing. "Thomas lives at Miss Ursula's, and is her fisherman."

"Her fisherman? What an odd servitude."

"It is a very necessary service, where fish is so important an item in housekeeping as it is here."

"Yet I should think Miss Ursula might buy all the fish her household needs from the fishermen in the village, and not take into her family so dangerous a man as you represent this Thomas to be."

"But the fishermen will not always sell; and besides, money is not so very abundant with us. It is surely convenient, as there is no man in the family, to keep a fisherman, who for his board and lodging catches fish for them. I suppose every community has its peculiar customs or ways of management. Certainly this has been Miss Ursula's for a very long time," Stephen adds, a little coldly, as one is apt to do when what one has always been accustomed to is criticised by a stranger.

"Then I am afraid Miss Milicent is a little termagant, if she can fly into such a rage with her aunt's fisherman. I don't mean anything derogatory by the word," Urquhart hastens to explain, as he sees Stephen begin to look grave. "There could be nothing handsomer than her eyes, when the devil peeped out of them. I admire a woman under a flash of temper; for the truth is, I have seen more of their smiles than of their frowns, and a perpetual smile is apt to be a little insipid."

The perfect egotism of this speech does not seem to strike Stephen. No doubt he is thinking of Milicent rather than of what Urquhart is saying, for he returns, "She can be very meek and gentle, if she is a little fiery on occasion."

"Can she?" asks Urquhart, laughing. "The change must be delicious, though I confess it is past my belief. By the way, I want you to take me to the house. I have met the young lady twice now, and it is but civil in me to call on her."

"I don't know,"— begins Stephen, with evident hesitation.

"Of course you must ask her permission; if she refuses, I shall be obliged to acquiesce. But if you choose to manage it for me, I am sure she will let me call."

But the better acquaintance Urquhart desires comes about easily and naturally this same morning; though he could not have expected it, in turning off from Stephen to find his way to Greenhead cliffs.

It is not hard to find, as Stephen has directed him. The springy turf makes the curvings of the upland seem short enough; and Urquhart is soon clambering down from the green headland, by what is most like a flight of huge stone stairs flung out of place by some upheaval of nature.

At the bottom of this flight, one stands fronting the first of the five strange little beaches, with the cliffs towering up a hundred feet above them. These cliffs are every one a massy pinnacled tower, jutting out to meet the sea-lashed ledges, and every two with a tiny cove between, — a court paved with oval gray stones as big as a man's hand, yet smooth and flat as wave-washed pebbles.

The high tide covers them, and lashes against these inaccessible fortress towers of the island, submerging the stairs that lead away from them. But as yet, one may pass round their foot from court to court; and even, in one place, behind the buttresses, which leave a passage-way from chamber into chamber.

Urquhart has paused upon a ledge which juts out, facing them, a barrier between them and the sea. The barnacled rocks show the reach of every tide. The same white fret-work is on the base of the columns, and covers one broken, jagged shaft; which was once perhaps the portal of the widest chamber of the five. They are all unroofed now; the splintered summits tipped with a fir or a wild rose, a scant handful of grass, or some close-clinging, crimson-leafed weed that reappears like a vine here and there along the joints of the masonry.

The tide is still withdrawing reluctantly, and with now and then a backward rush of some loitering wave. So Urquhart knows that he has time to loiter, too, and he stands looking up at the massive pile and listening to the gurgle.

But is that the gurgle of the waves? True, they might very well be chanting, in that long-drawn rhythm, —

> " We are passing away,
> Like a long summer day."

But when it breaks off suddenly into a lively Scotch reel, —

> " Sailing awa' to Germany,
> Laddie, laddie,

> What is it ye 'll bring back to me,
>   Bonny, bonny laddie?
> I 'll bring back a broom to ye,
>   Bonny lassie, bonny lassie," —

Urquhart is seized with a sudden desire to explore these cliffs. Is it possible that there may be a cave among them, with some canny housewife of a Nova Scotian mermaid?

He says as much to Milicent, when he comes upon her, seated on the shelving shingle, in the inmost curve of one of the beaches, just out of sight from where he was standing on the ledge. She has a little heap, not of white sea-foam, round her, but of coarse white towels held together by their fringed borders; and with her red and white Indian basket by her side, she is busily hemming and humming away. The near grating of the shingle under Urquhart's tread makes her look up with startled eyes across that pile of white.

Then Urquhart makes his little speech anent the housewifely mermaid.

"If it were in auld Scotland, now," he says, "it would be quite in rule to look for one. But in this New Scotland of yours" —

She lets her hand fall, with the needle in it.

"You do not know, then, that we too have them? — that the Indians believe in mermaids? At least our Micmacs do. There used to be an old Indian on the other side of the island, a *very* old Indian, Piel Jack by name, who I suppose was baptized Pierre, as the Micmacs don't pronounce the letter *r*. The cove where he lived and died is named for him, though you *will* hear people call it *Pea*

Jack. He used to tell Stephen and me about the mermaid he saw, and the migumoowesoo that haunt the woods and shores, and sing a man's heart out of his breast with their sweet voices."

"I can well believe it."

The girl is glancing up quite earnestly at the young man, who leans on a ledge of the dark buttress before her, looking down at the wonderfully pretty, speaking face, and the idle little hands clasped over her forgotten work. Perhaps it is some prick of the needle lying there which presently pricks her conscience ; for she starts up, gathering the crumpled white folds together.

" Ah, how lazy I am ! Aunt Ursula is not so far wrong when she says one hour at work with one's back to the sunshine accomplishes more than a whole out-of-doors morning. But then, could one turn one's back on such sunshine as this ? The Fundy does not give it to us every day. And when the fog rolls in — not one of our warm fogs, with the sun making a pretense of being a moon, and peering down at us out of a drifting veil — but a gray, close, damp, dismal blotting-out of the whole world " —

" That is the sort of day to gather round the fireside," says Urquhart. " You with your workbasket " — picking it up from the shingle for her as he speaks — " ensconced at one angle of the blazing hearth ; and at the other " —

He sees her give a shiver, as she averts her eyes. Then she turns to him, saying lightly, —

" All very pretty, if, instead of a blazing hearth,

we did not, as the Irishman says, in this country keep our fire in a big iron pot. But listen! there is something which the Fundy gives us, besides fog. The tide is coming up; and though I might 'suffer a sea-change' into a mermaid, yet you "—

> " 'I would be merman bold;
> I would sit and sing the whole of the day,
> I would fill the sea-halls with a voice of power:
> But at night I would roam abroad and play
> With the mermaids in and out of the rocks,
> Dressing their hair with the white sea-flower,' "

quotes Urquhart, a little afraid of his own audacity as he remembers the lines following, of how,

> — "holding them back by their flowing locks,
> I would kiss them often under the sea,
> And kiss them again till they kissed me: "

but reassured when he meets Milicent's unconscious eyes.

"Who wrote that, Mr. Urquhart? I don't like it in the least. It would n't do at all. It is all very well for mermaids to be sitting on rocks, combing their sea-green locks; but a merman, — what could he do? "

"Might n't it be rather lonely for the mermaid?" suggests Urquhart, carefully abstaining from quotation to this girl, who apparently knows more of Shakespeare than of Tennyson.

She shakes her head; her pretty, smiling lips are moving, but what they say is drowned in the heavy thud of an advancing wave on the low-lying wall of rocks, — the outpost, as it were, of this stronghold. It is quite time to beat a retreat; and, laughing, and gathering her needlework in her arm, one end blown out over her shoulder like a white flag of distress, while a flying scud dashes in her face, the girl suffers Urquhart to help her up the rocks to a higher ledge. There they stand in safety, watching the great waves flinging themselves about the broken pinnacles, in a very snowstorm of spray, tossed wildly here, there, everywhere, on every airt at once.

IV.

THE breeze has begun to freshen, and to brush out the soft, bright rings of hair about her temples; but Milicent is far too absorbed to notice it. Leaning idly, with hands folded on the gate, as she appears, she is in reality hard at work. She is trying the nice task of balancing; and the scale that holds her own desires will weigh down heavily, for all her striving to pile up the contrary one.

As she stands there, her back turned on the old gray house, the harbor lies spread out in a silver-blue cross under Milicent's eyes. From just this point, the light-house island in the harbor seems to be joined to the opposite Long Island shore, with Westport curving round one arm of the cross, and round the other the white cove of Freeport on Long Island. If she had moved a little to the right or to the left, Milicent would have lost the impression. But as it is, that cross lies before her: and somehow watching it vaguely seems to steady her in the task which she has set herself.

There is a little pucker of thought on her usually smooth brow, and she is too absorbed to see that Thomas is coming towards her, his fishing-pole over his shoulder, and the inevitable basket of fish in his hand.   He is returning to tea, and he approaches so noiselessly over the close-woven turf that Milicent is unconscious of his presence, until:

"Who is it you are watching for?" he asks, stopping before her.

"I am not watching for any one," she answers; at the same time moving in order to make way for him to pass through the gate, — an implied permission he avails himself of, but goes no farther.

"Bah! tell me a girl can stand quiet for a full half hour, unless she is waiting for some one, or knows she is looked at," he stops to say.

"Notwithstanding that you do not believe me, I still tell you I am not looking for any one," answers Milicent, coldly.

"Not for that fellow Urquhart?"

"Not even for him."

"May I ask" — Thomas changes his tone to a polite one — "what are your intentions in regard to this stranger?"

"I have none" —

"I acknowledge there is enough to turn your head," he interrupts.   "If he finds fishing good sport, flirting also is pleasant pastime for these summer weeks, before the fellow's acquaintances will return to the city, and life there be at all worth living.   Permit me to give you a word of warning.   Urquhart's kind don't think much of marrying.   A little love-making, to pass the time with a pretty girl seemingly a few degrees better than a fisherman's daughter" —

"Many degrees worse," interrupts Milicent. "You, at least, need not try to blind me as to my position."

"It might be a much harder one."

"Harder! It is unendurable!" cries Milicent, impetuously.

"'Is your little body aweary of this great world?'" he quotes, as if amused by her vehemence.

"Weary to death! If I could only get rid of it all!" cries Milicent, throwing up her hands with a passionate gesture.

"Not rid of the world! You do not wish to die? Bah, child!" he adds, coolly; "it is not that your life is so hard, but you are so impatient of it. If you would take things quietly, you would find everything easier to you."

"Would poverty be pleasanter if I took it more quietly, as you advise, or Aunt Ursula kinder if I were meek and patient? Would your panacea save me from an hour's work, or make us warmer or more comfortable when the winter comes?" asks Milicent, bitterly.

"I bear all these, and do not fret under them," he answers, smiling.

"You do; but you have made your life, and so you must abide by it: while mine has been the work of others."

There is a sudden flash in the fisherman's eyes when Milicent speaks, which she does not see, for she is not looking at him. But fortunately it has died out before she adds, with a little shrug of her shoulders, meant to show disdain for her last remark : —

"After all, if I had only a chance to see some of those pomps and vanities Aunt Ursula has such a great contempt for, I have n't the slightest doubt that I should find there is something pleasant in life, in spite of drawbacks."

"You little fool," Thomas says, half good-humoredly, half pityingly. "Do you think you would find it such an easy game? You who can't bear a rough word from your aunt, how would you bear it if, while you were playing the queen, some one made an ill-natured remark about you? You would break your silly heart with mere rage and vexation. Every part of God's earth is made for some use ; and just such rough, out-of-the-way spots as this are as cities of refuge to some poor hunted mortals."

"It is not the place I complain of."

"Well, there is a way out of your difficulties, if you will marry Stephen. He will not starve you, literally nor metaphorically ; and so you will be comfortably rid of all the evils you complain of."

Milicent droops her head, her face in a flame.

"I will tell you what I was doing when you came up," she says, hurriedly. "I was thinking that it is a month ago this very evening since I asked Stephen to give me a month to decide when I would marry him. And now I will tell him I will marry him, on one condition."

"Milicent, are you mad!" exclaims Thomas, his eyes flashing threateningly.

"*You* need not be personally implicated," she continues, not heeding his anger, and lifting her head resolutely. "But I am determined not to marry Stephen with a lie in my hand."

"Pray when did you come to this virtuous decision?"

"Only this moment, since your own words have shown me the utter selfishness of my conduct, if I marry him to escape from my present life. Not that I have not had many misgivings and doubts before now," she adds, hastily. "There are some persons so true themselves that one dares not be false to them : and Stephen is one of these."

"I thought you loved him. I did not know you were only overcome by his virtues," says Thomas, contemptuously. "Of course you need not marry him if you do not wish to do so. No one is bent on forcing you. Only, as you have a chance to better your life, and you do not choose to take it, you need not hereafter make a moan over the inevitable."

"You should not complain," says Milicent. "I was perfectly silent until you chose to stop and question me."

"Softly, softly! One would suppose I had taken an unwarranted liberty in giving you advice. I don't know that Stephen will not find it a bit of good fortune to lose you, since you have no self-control."

"Then you must think me right in refusing to make his life miserable," replies Milicent.

"I am not bound to look out for Stephen's interests. I fancy he could manage you in some way, if he married you. It is only your side of the matter that I have been considering; and I still hold to the opinion that you are silly to keep to poverty, when you could get a fair competency. Besides, the truth and honesty you seem to set such store on are not altogether current in this world, and many might suspect them to be counterfeits."

"But," says Milicent, throwing back her head, and looking boldly into his eyes, "I have a great desire to obtain those baubles, honesty and truth, and unfortunately they are not heirlooms."

Did Milicent intend to rouse that sudden flash of anger? Certainly she quails under it, and shrinks back when Thomas comes menacingly towards her. Yet she could no more have curbed her words than she could have stayed the tide which is fast covering the rocks.

Poor little Milicent! Helpless and weak, and yet fighting against the inevitable, as the strong would not dare to do. If she would only bend her shoulders to the burden, she might in time grow used to the strain upon her strength, and so walk firmly and without pain. But, instead, she is rebelling, and saying she will have none of it.

What Thomas might have done in his ungovernable rage Milicent never knows; for there is Stephen calling her name. She was never so unutterably glad to hear his voice before; never felt as now, what it would be to give him the right to protect and care for her. She pushes through the gate, and without a word slips her hand into his arm, and walks away with him, never glancing behind her at Thomas, who has taken up his basket, and is turning towards the house.

"What was it, Milly? Did Thomas frighten you?" asks Stephen, wrathfully.

"I was frightened for a moment. It was my own fault. I had no right to say to him what I did," confesses Milicent; and Stephen does not question her as to what she regrets having said to her aunt's fisherman.

They walk on together, over the brow of the hill looking down on Green Cove. When they reach the cliffs, Milicent stops, and seats herself on one of the detached stones. Stephen throws himself on the rocks at her feet.

There falls a silence, broken only by the eddies of the withdrawing tide, that gurgle round the rocks with a soft, lapping music, certainly the sweetest Nature gives us. It soothes the girl, and takes away from her that sense of something happening which had disturbed her. Is not everything the same as before she made her resolution? How many times she has been here with Stephen, as now, upon this long breakwater of the Cove, and looked across these bastions to the sweep of Greenhead cliffs, as they stand in the white surf, the shades of evening mingling with the yellow light that flecks the grass, and tips their black-green crest of fir and spruce. How many times! Why should there come any change?

"Yonder is Urquhart's boat," says Stephen, who is looking seaward. "How fond he is of being on the water!"

"It is only because the sea is a novelty to him," answers Milicent, carelessly. "He would grow weary of his boat if he stayed here very long."

"I do not think so. He is genuinely in love with the sea. No doubt, if he had not more money than he well knows what to do with, he would have been a sailor. By the way, Milly, I have asked him to spend part of next summer with me. You don't object?"

He says this a little anxiously. These weeks have thrown the three together intimately. Milicent has been constantly on the water with the two men; Miss Ursula having for so long looked upon Stephen as the girl's best protector, that she never questions how the holiday hours are passed, if only the allotted amount of needlework and knitting be accomplished. At her gate, Milicent would dismiss her cavaliers; Urquhart, for one, having no desire to go farther. But there is not a day he does not manage to meet her out-of-doors; and Stephen has some shrewd doubts as to whether it is really the fishing which is the inducement to so long a tarrying. If Urquhart, however, is beginning to be lover-like in his attentions to Milicent, the girl laughs at the slightest show of sentiment, and is much inclined to rally him on his fastidiousness, — her ideas of manliness having been formed on an experience of a hard, exposed life, which would kill most men not inured to hardship from childhood. Urquhart, on his part, is amused by Milicent's hostility, and takes delight in rousing her disdain. Perhaps, as he told

Stephen, he has found too many smiles during his not very long life, and a frown is a new sensation. Be that as it may, Stephen would prefer that the two should be better friends ; or rather, it may be, that the yacht and its owner should sail away to fish in other waters. But next summer it will be different; and if Milicent does not object —

"I object! Certainly not. Why should I ?" she is asking.

"Because next summer Urquhart will be your guest, if he is mine," replies Stephen, looking up at her and smiling.

"You have not told him so?" asks Milicent, hastily.

"No, but I shall soon. Milly, our month is out to-day. I have passed weeks of expectancy, which would have been intolerable if I had not been quite sure you wished me to wait."

Milicent is not looking at him, but out on the sea where Urquhart's boat is sailing. "Some words are so difficult to say," she begins, in a slow, measured tone.

"These ought not to be difficult, Milly, when you remember how long I have loved you, and how happy they will make me."

"But it is something quite different from our marriage that I wish to speak to you about. Stephen, if I had made a great mistake in my life, would you advise me to confess it, or to live on as if I had not made it?"

"That depends very much upon whether you would like to speak of it or not."

" But if some one else were involved, — some
one else's happiness, — have I a right to keep silent ? "

The whole current of her thoughts and desires
has been violently changed in the last hour ; and
it is difficult for her to judge whether her decision
would be a wise one.   She forgets that it is hardly
generous to make Stephen the judge.

"I cannot imagine your keeping silence. I have
never found you in the least reticent," he says, not
catching the tone of anxiety in her voice.

" Thanks," she says, a little hurt, but unwilling
to show it ; " but frequently I fancy our best friends
do not quite understand us. I think it would kill
me, Stephen, to know you trusted me implicitly,
and that I deceived you, even if I did so from a
mistaken idea of making you happy."

"I do not see how you could deceive me, Milly.
I have known you so well and so long : ever since
you were a small child," is his confident rejoinder.

" And you have known everything about me,
Stephen ? "

" Everything.   Much more than you think."

" Tell me some of the things, — something more
of my life than I suppose you know," she says,
with eagerness.

" I know that often you weary of your work,
and long to be out in the sunshine when Miss Ursula wishes you to be employed in-doors.   I know,
too, that she is not always kind, though I think she
does not mean to hurt you.   And," here he lowers
his voice, and looks away from her, " in the winter,

when the weather is rough, I fear the house is cold,
and the coarse diet you are forced to put up with
is neither plentiful nor proper for you."

" But that is never for very long," says Milicent,
smiling. " For a load of wood is sure to come
from the cottage, as well as something nice to eat.
Is this really all you know of my life ? " she adds,
anxiously.

" Is it not enough ? Cannot you think what I
suffer when I am sure you need so much, and I
could rid you of all your troubles if you would only
let me ? "

" Could you rid me of all, Stephen ? I know
you are generous enough to do so at any personal
cost ; therefore I must be the more careful for you.
But how long have you known so much about us ?
Poor Aunt Ursula ! She has been trying to look
as if she were used to all hardships, and did not
mind half starving. It is foolish to think to have
secrets from one's neighbors. But when did you
discover so much about us ? "

" When I first loved you, Milly."

" And that has been more than a year ; two
years this autumn," she says, thoughtfully.

" It has been much longer than that. I have
loved you ever since we were children, and made
sand-houses on the Pea-Jack beach together. I
used to be in a fury with Miss Ursula when she
sent you into solitary confinement for wetting your
dress, when we waded for dulse; and I often
thought if I were a man I would punish her for
her cruelty."

" But I was only doomed to imprisonment until my dress dried ; for my wardrobe was not so full as good Queen Bess's. I was an ungrateful little wretch, and used to trample down your sand-houses if they were at all more perfect than mine. Ah, Stephen ! with all the hardships and trials of those days, how I wish we were both children again, building in the sand ! "

" I hope both of us have a better foundation to build on now," answers Stephen, trying to speak lightly.

" No ; no better. It is still shifting sand we are building on, that any tide of fate or storm of circumstance may trample down ; and it is best you should know it."

" Know what, Milly ? I am sure I do not understand you."

She does not answer him, and he turns to look at her. She is gazing intently at him, as if watching the effect of her words upon him. " Stephen, would you care so very much if I told you I must not marry you ? "

It is the subtlest change which comes over Stephen's face, — a change like the slowly deepening shadow of a cloud that sweeps just then across the sea. There is the briefest pause, and then : " Would I care, Milly ? That does not seem to me half so important a question as why you must not."

" There is something which holds me back, something — so that I dare not promise " — she begins, in a slow, measured voice, as if she were compelling herself to speak.

" Some person, Milly ? "

She does not answer at once; and then says evasively, " It cannot matter very much what it is, if it separates us."

" I am not so sure of that. It would make a great deal of difference to me why I had to part from you," says Stephen, firmly.

" Would it make it any easier to you to know that I am unworthy to be your wife ? "

" That would be small comfort indeed," he answers, smiling, as if relieved from a great fear.

" What would make a difference to you ? "

" Nothing, unless some one stood between us, and " —

" Some one does stand between us," answers Milicent, quickly, — "some one does stand between us."

That cloudy shadow deepens on the sea, and Stephen's face, turned towards Urquhart's white-winged boat skimming just beyond it, changes, as if the light were suddenly shut out.

Milicent, watching him, and seeing the change, but not the cause, says very low : —

" It seems so very hard that we have so little control over ourselves that we can never be free from the consequences of a wrong act. And the worst of it is, that the innocent are punished. He had nearly the whole world to choose from, when he came here ; and that he should have blindly chanced on this one spot, and so worked harm to you, through me " —

She breaks off suddenly, startled to find how

much easier it is to confess the whole truth to him, than to keep it back.

"If I could only tell you all," she says, "if I were free to tell you, you might find excuse for me. I never wished to deceive you, and living at the cottage seemed like going to heaven, to me. And it looked like stabbing you in your sleep, just to break with you, and give no reason. But," she adds, looking down and twisting her fingers nervously, as her hands lie clasped in her lap, while a faint blush mounts slowly up into her face, "it was only to-day that he said anything which made me sure how wickedly and deceitfully I have behaved to you."

"No one else would I permit to say such things about you, Milly," says Stephen. His voice is low and quiet: apparently he does not mean to press her with questions such as she has been bracing herself to resist.

Milicent's eyes grow dim, as she gazes out before her where a gauzy veil drawn over the distance has hidden Urquhart's boat. The far moan of the fog-horn at the light-house shows the fog is lurking in the Fundy, though it keeps off here. To Milicent's present mood there is something inexpressibly dreary in that sound, the three slow moans echoed by rock and water. And how will it be when she will have to hear it through the long, long stormy evenings in the old home, with no vista of the cottage beyond?

If Stephen had her horror of those lonely evenings, could he give her up so easily?

Yet when she glances askance at him, she sees, calm and firm as he is, that this thing is not easy to him. If she could tell him everything, if she were not hampered by a promise, would he ever give her up?

But she is hampered. She can do no more than put her hand out timidly and touch his sleeve, as he leans heavily forward on the rock which forms the arm of his chair at her feet.

He does not turn to her quite at once; and she falters : —

" I can see now how wicked it was. It is easy to say I would rather have died than have to tell you this; but indeed it is the truth."

" I would rather have you on earth, Milly, with ever so small a chance of hearing of or seeing you sometimes," Stephen says, wishing to soothe her evident distress and bitter self-reproach. " You must not think I find it difficult to forgive you. You are much harder on yourself than I shall ever be on you. But, Milly, you must promise me not to talk so wildly to any one else. Having known you from a child, I know how impetuous you are, and that you were never inclined to make self-excuses. But any one else might misunderstand you. So you must promise me to be more careful."

" I will promise," replies Milicent, with a pathetic little smile. " But I hope never in my life to have to feel again such self-condemnation."

" You do not wish us to be as strangers to each other, Milly. I could not bear to give up seeing you altogether, at least as long as we are neighbors."

"We shall always be neighbors, unless you weary of the life here, and go away from us. If anything unforeseen should happen, and I should have to leave, I will be sure to tell you. There is nothing to prevent us from going back to the dear old time before you told me you wished to marry me. Stephen, if you could go back so far, I would be so glad!"

"A man cannot walk backwards, Milly."

"And the future is so difficult and uncertain. May I come to you if I lose my way and am sore perplexed? For, Stephen, I have no other friend but you to counsel or to help me."

"I will always help you to the best of my ability, Milly," he says.

He looks up at her as he speaks, and sees her eyes fixed upon a skiff which is impelled by the vigorous strokes of a pair of oars.

A great jealousy overcomes Stephen. What is there about this Urquhart that has in a few short weeks accomplished what he in almost a lifetime has failed in? Certainly he, Stephen, has been more in earnest, and has striven harder. Yet some gain what they wish for so easily that they seem born conquerors; and others, braver, truer-hearted, with a far better reason for success, fail miserably.

"You will not mind my leaving you, Milly?" asks Stephen, beseechingly.

He desires to be generous and not pain her, and yet he cannot meet Urquhart just now.

"No," she says, holding out her hand to him. "I will not keep you any longer. I should have remembered how late it is. If I were only sure you can forgive me!"

"Be very sure I do. You must not torment yourself with a fear that I do not. The next time we meet, it must be in the old, old way."

He cannot say more to reassure her, for Urquhart is within calling distance, and is shouting to him to come and help him beach the skiff. But Stephen pretends not to hear, and walks away over the cliffs, and through the fields to the cottage; the same way Milicent returned that afternoon in June, when they sat together under the lilac-bush, looking out upon the sea, and upon a future brighter than Stephen can hope to look forward to again.

Urquhart's voice calling to Stephen first draws Milicent's attention to him. She had been gazing so far before her that she had failed to recognize what was quite near. If she had seen that it was Urquhart rowing towards them, she would have kept Stephen. Certainly, she had given him the impression that she was watching Urquhart, and so added another pang to the wound she had already made.

Before Urquhart can beach the skiff and spring on shore, Milicent has walked away. She can hear Urquhart's footsteps behind her, evidently trying to overtake her: but she will not look round nor slacken her speed, which she could not have quickened unless she actually ran away.

"Please, Miss Milicent, wait a moment," calls Urquhart : and she has to make a most unwilling halt until he comes to her.

"What is the matter with you and Stephen?" is Urquhart's unlucky question. "You both seem bent upon putting the greatest possible distance between you, in the shortest possible time. I feared you had both grown deaf, for I have been shouting to you for the last ten minutes, without gaining the least degree of attention ; but now I am convinced that there has been a small quarrel, and with the luck that good, innocent people usually meet with, I am in consequence to be the sufferer."

Milicent turns slowly and reluctantly to answer Urquhart; and as she does so, Stephen also turns to look at her. He is a good way off, crossing one of his own fields, so that he cannot hear her cold reply to Urquhart's greeting, nor can he see from her face, as Urquhart does, that he is not welcome. The rest of Stephen's walk home is far more painful, after his hasty glance, than it would be if he were a close observer.

As for Urquhart, Milicent is so preoccupied that he is sure she has had a quarrel with Stephen. Scarcely a serious one, for Milicent shows nothing of a woman's sure signal of distress, — tears. Neither is there any anger in her eyes, nor spice of the evil one, which Urquhart affects to admire ; but a far-off, wistful look, as if she had seen something she will never see again all the days of her life.

At the gate, Urquhart says good-by, and Milicent goes slowly to the house. She is not thinking of Urquhart, who turns to look at her. Nor is she thinking altogether of Stephen. Before her is her unsightly home, the windows all ablaze with the reflection of the setting sun. The burnished panes do not beautify the house ; indeed, they only heighten its ugliness. Milicent has just then a vision of the cottage embowered in vines, — the cottage she has refused to make her home, choosing rather this mass of ugliness. It has been entirely her own act. She has not given Stephen the decision whether to lose or keep her. She herself has rejected the sweet and taken the bitter. This sacrifice on her part has not pleased any one ; and she feels no great elation at simply doing right.

When Milicent goes into the kitchen, Thomas is sitting there smoking his pipe, and Miss Ursula is busied in preparing tea. The girl lingers a few minutes, idly gazing into the fire ; then turns to go into the hall on her way up-stairs.

" Tea is nearly ready," announces Miss Ursula.

" I do not care for any. I am going to bed," answers Milicent, in a weary tone.

" Fine acquaintances give dainty appetites. There is nothing here to pamper one," says Miss Ursula, who has seen Urquhart at the gate, — a sight of whom, for some reason she does not explain, always makes her temper sharper. "I only hope you will not lose your loaf and keep your hunger. Stephen seems to me to be failing in patience of late."

" I wish he would fail utterly. One never feels

half so sorry for impatient people as for the patient ones," returns Milicent.

" Then you ought never to complain of any lack of sympathy," remarks Miss Ursula, dryly.

" Let the child alone," says Thomas, knocking the ashes from his pipe. " Such a thing as pity we might afford to give her ; but then it is jewels she craves. Did you keep the two costly ones you were so anxious about an hour or two ago?" he adds, addressing Milicent.

" Yes," she answers slowly, " I kept them."

He is watching her from under the shade of his hand, as he rests his elbow on the arm of his chair. The girl has laid her hand on the table, as she pauses to answer him ; and the lamp flares into her face, a little pale and very weary, as of one who has fought her battle and been worsted by the victory.

The gloom in his own face deepens as he looks ; and then he shrugs his shoulders in a sort of bitter skepticism.

" At a great sacrifice," he says. " One has only to look at you, to know that. I hope your jewels may repay you, and also that you may manage always to retain them, since you value them so much. But do not parade them too ostentatiously."

" Rest easy," says Milicent. " No one could guess I have them."

Miss Ursula, who in moving about the kitchen has but half heard, and not at all understood, this fragment of conversation, now puts the tea-pot on the table. But Milicent's appetite has not returned, and she goes up-stairs.

Thomas was right when he called her jewels costly. No one knows better than she, what she has paid to retain them ; and the hard part of it all is, she is sure she will feel the poorer, not for now only, but for all her life.

V.

> " But I have known the lark's song half sound sad,
>   And I have seen the sea, which rippled sun,
>   Toss dimmed and purple in a sudden wind :
>   And let me laugh a moment at my heart
>   That thinks the summer-time must all be fair,
>   That thinks the good days always must be good ;
>   Yet let me laugh a moment, — may be weep."

MILICENT walks over to the cottage one afternoon, and stands for some time looking over the low picket fence; safe from meeting any one, for she knows Stephen is away.

Her quick eye detects a change in the pretty lawn, an evident want of care about the whole place. The vines over the porch are untrained, and long branches of honeysuckle trail over the grass.

The girl is sorry, and half resentful, as she might be at the neglect of a loved one ; and she feels, as never before, how much the expectation of one day calling the cottage home has been to her.

It is the old story of the outcast peri at the gate, she tries to tell herself, rallyingly. She has lost her Eden. The outside life looks very dreary to the poor impatient child, as she stands there facing it. Year after year stretches out before her, a long, dull road without a turning ; a daily routine of work, of trial, of penury.

She stands at the shut gate a long time, with a

weary look in her face, a dull pain at her heart:
before she turns and takes the path across the
fields to the shore. She walks away slowly, — so
slowly that the sun has set when she at last clambers down from the cliffs, and reaches the lower
range of rocks forming the irregular plateau nearer
the level of the sea. The rosy glow of the sunset
is still lingering, and the long northern twilight
makes it very far from night.

Suddenly, as she for a moment leaves the rocks
for that foothold of a path which curves out behind
Green Cove, Milicent comes upon Urquhart, who,
with the oars of his skiff upon his shoulder, is in
the act of descending to the Cove, where his boat
is beached. He comes forward eagerly when he
sees her, and begs that she will let him take her
out.

Though the girl does not care very much for his
or any one else's society just now, she has a decided
longing to be afloat on the water ; so she consents
to go with him.

Urquhart has had the yacht's small boat rigged
up for sailing when he does not care to take the Undine, that requires at least two men to handle her.
But to-day there is no breeze, and he unsteps the
mast, intending to row out some distance, and
when the tide is running in, to let the boat drift
back with it : as the sea-birds nesting on the island
fly against the wind when outward-bound, to have
a fair wind on their weary homeward flight.

When they are all out together, Milicent generally prefers taking an oar and letting one of the

men steer; but this evening she seats herself in
the stern, evidently intending that Urquhart shall
do the rowing. He pulls out vigorously, scarcely
aware himself of how much energy he is putting
into the work. He is seated facing Milicent,
where he cannot avoid looking at her; and the
stroke of his oar is keeping time with his thoughts,
which are surging up in almost painful rapidity.

Urquhart's position is a dangerous one for any
man; but the more so for him, because Milicent
is so unconscious of his admiration.

If she had ever shown coquetry, or even a desire
to make him attentive to her, Urquhart would
have been on his guard, and so would have escaped. But it is her entire indifference to anything he says or does that piques, while her
beauty and even her fitfulness impress him. Absorbed with her own trials and perplexities as she
has been of late, her woman's quick vision has
failed to detect what Stephen's slower sight did
not miss, — that Urquhart is in love with her.
It is just as well she has not seen it, or her self-
love might have been wounded by also seeing that
he loves her unwillingly.

Urquhart has been a wonderfully successful
man, so far in life: money, a handsome face, an
easy, cheerful temper, and a happy regard of consequences, which is of itself a preventive of much
disaster. Heretofore, he has had much of the
honey of life, without a drop of the wormwood and
the gall; and with the perversity of human nature,
has complained that so much sweetness is cloying.

He came to the little fishing-village to learn, as he thought, something of the rougher paths of life ; but in reality he was in search of a new sensation. And he found one, in this out-of-the-way spot, when he found this girl, who at every meeting is a fresh surprise.

All Milicent's out-door plans include Stephen: and by the help of his presence (for every one knows there is safety in the mystical number three, except in the matter of a secret) Urquhart has generally managed to keep on his guard with her, until this evening. So altogether, it is rash in Urquhart to go out thus with her in the summer sunset.

He is sure he has never seen her so beautiful as now. She has thrown off her hat, and is sitting upright, with the ropes of the tiller in either hand, yet looking with far more interest to the horizon where the clouds are piled — pale lilac, edged with a faint rose — than to the course of the boat as it pushes farther out to sea. "The western waves of ebbing day" are flowing with the peaceful ripple far beyond the island: and the girl has turned her back upon its foaming fringe of eddies, its ruined walls and pinnacles of rock, its sombre crest of wind-swept firs, and the gaunt gray house she knows is staring down upon her. What if she were leaving all behind, floating away and away, out on this sea whose shores are rosy cloudland ?

The discontent that sometimes dims her young face is gone ; in its place there is a soft, dreamy look, as if she sees something in the skies. But in truth the child is only thinking how pleasant it is to row away from all that troubles her; wishing there was no land, no home for her, but only an eternal sea.

She is not thinking in the least of Urquhart: the end of whose vigorous rowing is that he fights his way out of all the difficulties which have kept him silent for nearly a month. Having conquered, he quietly lays down the oars; and, stepping over the bench — which is now the only barrier between them, he is sure — he comes and takes a seat beside Milicent.

The boat is trimmed to float in with the tide towards the island. Steering is as useless as rowing just now: there is nothing to be done, but just what Urquhart has at last decided to do.

If Milicent had blushed, or had appeared at all conscious, if she had even turned her head to look at him, it would have been easier for Urquhart to speak. But she is sitting quite still, gazing straight before her, and evidently suspecting nothing of the tumult within him.

"Milicent, look at me. I have something to say to you," says Urquhart, laying his hand on hers, which are clasped together over the tiller-ropes.

She does as he bids her: quickly, with a startled movement, as if surprised by his words, his use of her name, or by his touch. "What is it?" she asks, drawing away her hands. "Why can I not listen without looking at you?"

But nevertheless she looks, and there is something in his face that puzzles her.

Suddenly she drops her eyelids, with a shy little motion of withdrawing herself as much as possible from him; and begins to play nervously with the ropes.

Urquhart smiles. "You have guessed before now that I love you?" he says. "You have known what has kept me here so long?"

"You said it was the fishing, and I believed you. You gave many reasons for your staying," answers Milicent, confining herself to the last question.

"A good many excuses. I have had really but the one reason for lingering. You are not angry with me for loving you?" he asks.

"Not angry; but it is very silly," she answers, with a vexed movement of her shoulders. "We were getting on so much better together, and I had really begun to like you."

"That is exactly what I do not wish you to do," says Urquhart, coolly. "I have no desire that you should get into the way of thinking of me as you do of Stephen. It may please him, but it would never satisfy me."

"You don't suppose I shall ever think of any one as I do of Stephen?" asks Milicent, flushing with anger at Urquhart's audacity.

"Do you mean to hint that there is anything between you, — that you are engaged to him?" asks Urquhart, quickly.

"There is not a thing between us," she answers very decidedly, yet at the same time looking away from him.

"I know very well that the poor fellow is in

love," Urquhart goes on to say. "I could guess it, if it were only from his jealousy of me. I don't mention it from vanity, so you need not be indignant"— for Milicent has made an impatient motion with her hands, as if to stop him. "If he is not jealous, why does he always go away when I come near you: or, if he can't get off, grow so silent and reserved?"

"I never notice that he does," answers Milicent, slowly drawing the rope through her fingers.

"He does, nevertheless. Poor Stephen! it does seem hard that all his sudden changes of manner, all his heats and cold, should not even be noticed. Verily, you women are cruel!"

"Not intentionally so, if you are thinking of Stephen. I would put my eyes out with my own hands, rather than see him hurt or offended by any act of mine," the girl says quickly.

"I am glad you have not noticed him, then: and I shall certainly not enlighten you any more on the subject, for your eyes are rather an important feature in your face, as they are very apt to tell more than your lips. Will you not look at me, then, and tell me it is not impossible for you to love me? I will promise to do my best to make you happy."

"That would not be so very difficult," answers Milicent, not by any means intending to be humble, but only honest. "I have had so few good things in life, a very little would suffice to make me happy."

"If you would only let me hold your future in my hands, Milicent, I would make it a perfect holiday for you. My poor child, do you think I have loved you all these weeks, and have not discovered what tries and teases you? You need not be frightened; there is nothing that is not natural in your discontent," Urquhart adds, laughing; for Milicent has turned to him with surprise in her face.

"What could you make out of my future?" she asks, with girlish curiosity.

"First, you must promise to marry me; I must have you for my very own, before I can bring you all I would. After that, we should take a longer sail than you have ever had in your life, for we should cross the Atlantic."

"Sail away," she says, under her breath, — "sail away, out of the past into the future! Leave everything behind us!"

Her tone is wistful, not regretful: so wistful, that Urquhart says eagerly, her words being the echo of his own wishes, —

"Sail away, out of the past into the future; for what will anything that lies behind matter to us? We will begin a new life in the Old World which is the new."

Her questioning eyes are on his, for all the blushing color in her face.

"You should see Paris, the good American's paradise," he goes on, coming down to details as he fills in the sketch in his own mind, "and London, if you cared to 'go home,' as you province people say. But my chief delight would be to have you to myself in some of those quaint old southern towns

on the seashore, where we could live unmolested
by acquaintances, and could be as much **on the**
water as we chose."

Urquhart is waxing eloquent, for he is building
up in words some of his castles projected in the
air, which have heretofore seemed rather vague,
but to which speech gives substance.　In a dreamy
way, Milicent is listening; the thought that here
is her escape comes bewilderingly.　Just here is
a turn in the dreary road which only an hour ago
appeared to stretch out before her illimitably.
Once beyond that turn, and what can the past be
to her or to Urquhart?　With Stephen, it would
have been different, of course; his life lies here
upon this island : and here there could be no gulf
fixed between the past and the future, if she were
his wife.　But with her and Urquhart, what lay
behind them on the island could be nothing, — nothing at all to either of them.　Having come to the
turn, she has but to take it, to find the past breaking sheer off, like those frowning cliffs she is now
watching ; and the wide ocean stretching out between it and the future.　And what a future Urquhart is painting for her admiration and approval!
An eternal holiday!　Whole years spent in traveling and sight-seeing!　An easy, free life, leaving
behind all cares, all anxieties!　A fairy-tale, where,
by a little talisman of a ring, everything necessary
would be at once provided !

Suddenly Urquhart stops speaking, in evident
chagrin.　As no response has reached him, he
naturally supposes he has been talking to deaf ears.

Then comes the thought that perhaps he has taken her too much by surprise; or that she is too shy to give him an answer.

But Milicent seems neither shy nor frightened: only lifts to him eyes like a child's opening in the midst of a dream.

"Do you know," she says, "that what you tell me sounds like a fairy-tale to me? You offer me much wonderful happiness, — and I have nothing to give you in return," she adds wistfully, looking at him as the enchanted maiden out of the fairy-tale might have looked at the prince who came to set her free.

And in truth he is as handsome as the prince in the fairy-tale; with some new glamour in his eyes, as they hold her own. Or is it that the golden haze from off the sea is blinding hers? They fall before his, — and he is saying eagerly, —

"You can give me yourself, Milicent. That would be untold riches to me."

Milicent laughs saucily, coming back to herself. "Then I will be liberal, and give you untold riches. For I suppose I must give you myself, if you marry me."

Urquhart is perplexed. What is this the girl is bestowing so carelessly?

He almost shrinks from accepting a gift she grants so easily.

"I warn you, it is everything I have, however," goes on Milicent, without a pause. "I have n't even a mat of my own hooking, or a net of my own making, a fisher-maiden's proper dower."

"I will take you as you are, and not quarrel with my bargain," says Urquhart, eagerly.

"But I must add one thing to it, — a promise. Will you make it?"

"A dozen, if you please."

"No, I wish for only one; and that I cannot think will be a difficult one. It is that after you take me away from here, you will never bring me back again."

"Do you mean you would not be sorry to know that you would never return here?" asks Urquhart, in surprise. "I confess I should be loath to say good-by to the island forever."

"I should not, in the least," replies Milicent, with much decision in her voice. "Perhaps some day, when I am quite old, I should not mind returning; for then I fancy one ceases to care for anything very much."

"If I must wait until you are old, I too shall have lost all desire to return," says Urquhart, laughing. "That will be an immense time, unless you take to gray hairs prematurely : which I warn you I do not intend to do."

"I fancy no one takes kindly to old age. Why should any one be prematurely old?"

"A great sorrow might make one so, or" — stagnant, uneventful life, Urquhart is going to add : but he remembers how very monotonous Milicent's must have been, and she has certainly preserved her juvenility.

"Do you know," she says, not noticing his broken-off sentence, "I have never been away

from here since I was a very small child. I do not
remember any other place. You cannot imagine
how much I long for a glimpse of some other kind
of life. But," she adds anxiously, " can you really
afford to travel ? Aunt Ursula says it takes a very
great deal of money."

" I think I may manage it, if you 'll promise
not to be too extravagant, and want all the fine
things you see," replies Urquhart, striving to look
grave.

He remembers how he has seen her count over
the few pennies received as change when Miss
Ursula has sent her to the village shop for a necessary purchase. He is about lifting her above such
sordid cares, and she will thoroughly enjoy the
luxury. He looks at her in her blue cotton dress
and the coarse hat plaited by herself from the
wheat-straw she has gathered in Stephen's field ;
and he thinks, pretty as she now is, how much she
will be improved by the accessories of dress that
girls delight in. But Urquhart does not care to tell
these thoughts of his. He would have Milicent
marry him for himself, not for his money. He
would no more have confessed the state of his
finances, than he would have told her how often
he had determined it was better for him to go away
silently, never telling her he cared for her: until
a half hour ago this brilliant scheme of taking
her abroad flashed upon him. He is a sensitive
man, and shrinks from the thought of having Milicent talked of, and watched, and wondered at, by
his " set." He is willing to give up country and

friends for his young love; he is not willing to take her, in all her ignorance and girlish downrightness, into what he calls his world. But now he has hit upon a plan which will leave her untrammeled for a time, and unconsciously to herself break her into the ways of the world.

Having to capture his bird warily, Urquhart's love-making must be rather cool. It seems almost a bargain between them: though this is very far from his thoughts. That she should be willing to leave everything she is used to, and go where he chooses to take her, has, it must be confessed, the appearance of great devotion on the child's part. Thus he never thinks that if he had offered to marry her, and take her some few miles away to live, she would certainly have refused him.

"Milicent," he says suddenly, looking into her dreamy face, "do you know you have not once said that you loved me?"

"I would never have promised to marry you if I disliked you," she answers, with an expressive little shrug.

"But I want more than an assurance that you do not dislike me."

"Very well, I will give you more; I like you."

"Like is not love," says Urquhart, sententiously, at the same time not looking well pleased.

Milicent opens her eyes very wide as she lifts them to him. She never told Stephen that she more than liked him; and yet he had been content to marry her on such an admission. Why should Urquhart wish for more than satisfied

Stephen ? Is it something so very much to be desired, this love ?

"What is it to love?" she asks, gently. "I will
do my best to learn, if you will only teach me."

And Urquhart is charmed with the ingenuous
promise. It seems just now the sweetest pastime
in the world, to teach this fresh young heart to
love.

Love can certainly grow from as small a seed as
faith : the germ is there, Urquhart is very sure,
and there would need but a little cultivation to root
it well and strongly. The sweet flowers and fruit
would be for his own gathering, in that fool's paradise he has now fairly entered.

They can feel the keel grating softly on the
strand. The tide has been more watchful than
they, and has floated them into Green Cove, safe
past the rocks on either hand. They have reached
the land sooner than Urquhart expected; and twilight has so nearly faded into night, that he cannot very well propose pushing out again on the
water.

After all, he is very well content with his evening row. He has gotten rid of the constant struggle with himself to keep silent: which, whenever he
was alone with Milicent, he was not at all inclined
to do ; so that now that he has committed himself
without recall, it is a great relief. And Milicent
has promised to marry him.

When the boat is beached, Milicent would have
sprung out on the shingle without assistance, as is
her wont. But Urquhart takes her in his arms

and lifts her, leaving a light kiss on her cheek as he does so. She is frightened and angry. "How dare you!" she exclaims, blushing furiously, and struggling to free herself.

Urquhart is half amused, and a little angry.

"I thought I had won as much right as that, when you promised to marry me," he says coolly, as he releases her.

"You ought to have asked a fisher-girl in your own country to marry you," answers Milicent, scornfully. "It may be a fashion with them."

"I thought it was the fashion with all lovers," Urquhart says, not able to restrain a laugh at her vehemence, "but I promise not to offend again. The next time I will wait to be asked."

Milicent makes no answer, but turns and walks away. Urquhart cannot follow her at once, as the boat is not fastened, and he must not let the tide float it away. He is sure Milicent will be at the house before he can secure it properly; but he is determined not to call out to her to wait for him, and also determined not to hasten his movements.

He regrets this loitering, however, when he finds her waiting for him where the path to the house turns off from the cliff. Perhaps her ire has had time to cool, and she thinks it just as well not to quarrel outright, the very first hour of their engagement. If she does, Urquhart agrees with her; the rather, as he looks at her shy, blushing face.

"I wonder if Miss Ursula will see me this evening?" he asks, thinking it would be wise to have all preliminary ceremonies over.

"No, certainly not," answers Milicent, hastily. "It is far too late. Aunt Ursula never will see any one after dark, and especially a stranger."

"But that is just what I wish to tell her I am not," says Urquhart, laughing. "Hereafter she will have to consider me a part of her family. You don't think she will make any objection to our engagement?" he asks a little anxiously.

"Objection! Of course not. Why should she?"

"I am rejoiced you have no father to be petitioned; I begin to feel a little nervous at my expected interview with your aunt. It is somewhat presumptuous to ask a man for his daughter. Aunts, I fancy, do not see it in the same light; all women being tender towards a love-affair."

"I do not see what concern it is to a father any more than to an aunt, if the girl herself wishes it," answers Milicent, shortly.

"Unfortunately, the father is not also in love; and men are more apt to go into particulars than women. I have not much fear of satisfying Miss Ursula."

"You need give yourself no trouble on that score," says Milicent, with decision. "I shall tell Aunt Ursula we are engaged, and that will be all that is necessary. I am not going to ask you in to-night," she adds; for they have reached the gate. "To-morrow you may come."

Though thus dismissed, Urquhart still lingers, leave-taking being always a pleasant pain to a lover. When at last he is gone, Milicent, as usual, passes round to the door of the kitchen (the hall in front of the house is never lighted artificially), where she finds Miss Ursula.

A small oil lamp does the whole duty of illuminating the great bare room, for the summer fire of small wood barely succeeds in cooking the pan of fish upon it. A table near the centre of the room holds a dish, on which Miss Ursula is piling some baked potatoes; and a pitcher of buttermilk, flanking it, adds to the suggestion that there is a meal to be partaken of.

"Have you had tea yet?" asks Milicent's clear young voice, as she enters the room.

"What is the use in having tea when there is no one to eat it? I do not know at what hour you will be coming in, after a while," answers Miss Ursula, feeling the just irritation which irregularity causes the housekeeper.

"Let me turn the fish for you," proposes Milicent, seeing Miss Ursula moving towards the fire for the purpose. "I have been out on the water, and did not know how late it was."

"It is no hour for you to be on the water," returns Miss Ursula, not offering to relinquish the cooking of the fish.

"It is darker in here than it is out-of-doors, so it seems later than it really is," says Milicent, with one of her impatient shrugs. "Aunt Ursula, I have something to tell you that perhaps you will be glad to hear. Mr. Urquhart wishes to marry me, and I have promised" —

She stops: it is not easy to go on, with Miss Ursula's back to her, and no sign that she is listened to.

There is a pause, until her aunt breaks it as coolly as if the subject in hand were quite a matter in the abstract : —

" How many neat drawings we make of the lives of others, only to have the pencil taken out of our hands, for them to make such scrawls for themselves as any child might be ashamed of ! "

" Yes, but wait until you hear the end. We are to go abroad, and not return until I wish to."

Miss Ursula was in the act of turning the fish : but instead, she turns herself to look at Milicent, who certainly appears very well satisfied with the news she has given.

" Was it anything you told him that made him offer to take you abroad ? " asks Miss Ursula, sharply.

" Certainly not," answers Milicent, coldly. " It was his own proposition. I had nothing to do with it."

" Oh, I see ! He wishes to hide you, until he is not ashamed of you. A Parisian modiste and traveling : both will be vastly improving to you, no doubt."

" Do you blame him for his desire to make me presentable ? I do not, if it will spare me discomfort or humiliation," replies Milicent, quite calmly.

" Or save himself," suggests Miss Ursula. " Men are much more apt to think of their own sensations than of others'."

And then she adds, as if to dismiss the subject altogether, " Stephen was here this evening. He

seemed sorry to miss seeing you. What fools we
are to set our hearts upon anything in this fickle
world!"

Milicent turns to Miss Ursula, with a troubled
look in her eyes; but just then there comes the
sound of a man's footstep outside the door. "I do
not want anything for tea but this," says Milicent,
helping herself from the dish of potatoes. "And
Aunt Ursula, if you will tell him" —

There is a marked sound of entreaty in Milicent's voice; and she leaves the kitchen hastily.

Urquhart's love-making has not robbed her of
her appetite; for she gropes her way to the front
door, as the most unfrequented spot, and, taking a
seat on the steps, eats her unsavory supper, and
seems to enjoy it, though she has not brought a
grain of salt to season it. Then she rests her head
on her lap, as a sleepy, tired child might do, and
falls into cogitation.

Her first thought is of regret: Stephen was
looking for her while she was listening to the love-
making of another man.

This comes as an actual pain to her, and she
torments herself with questions. Will he care
very much when he hears she is going to marry
Urquhart? Would it not be far better for him,
in the end, if she went away? He would be sure
to forget her the sooner, if he could not see her
every day; and she could not possibly leave, unless she married Urquhart. This is rather wild
reasoning on Milicent's part. Certainly she has
lost sight of her own dread, — that Stephen, for-

getting her, might one day bring a wife to the home which was to have been her own.

For some time Milicent sits on the doorstep, with bowed head, not thinking of Urquhart, but of Stephen. What will Stephen say?

She is so in the habit of going to him to have all doubts and difficulties solved, that it never occurs to her that some decisions must necessarily be terrible tests of honesty and unselfish love, and therefore burdens never to be shifted from our own shoulders.

When she rises at last, and goes up-stairs to bed, she has come to a strange conclusion: she will tell Stephen of this new phase of her life, of what Urquhart has offered her: and if he desires she will break her engagement. So much she owes her old friend and playmate: if she does not marry him, she will not marry any one else against his will. He might never know half the sacrifice she makes: her wish is to spare him all the pain she can; her determination, that he shall decide how she can best do it.

Having come to this childish conclusion, she goes to her room, and presently falls into a dreamless slumber, with no visions of either lover.

Youth and old age are said to touch each other, and in nothing is their contiguity so plainly shown, as in the ability they share, of falling into an untroubled sleep over their perplexities and griefs. An old man shuts his eyes on an intrusive thought, and forgets it; a child — and Milicent is hardly more — will cry itself into a smiling slumber.

VI.

<blockquote>
" Let us make no claim,
  On life's incognizable sea,
  To too exact a steering of our way,
  If some fair coast has lured us to make stay."
</blockquote>

WHILE Milicent, on the doorstep of the old gray house, with her face hidden from the starlight, turned her thoughts away from the bright future Urquhart had pictured to her, and took her resolution that Stephen should be the arbiter of her fate, Stephen, seated on his porch, smoked his evening pipe, trying to enjoy the beauty of the scene; and then he went over his work for the morrow, planning what he should set his laborers to do. But all the while, Milicent's face was before him. She would never sit beside him on the porch, listening to plans and hopes for their future, as she so long led him to believe she would.

Stephen had gone over to the old house that afternoon, as soon as he returned home. He had been called away suddenly upon business; and as he had had no opportunity to see her before he left, he thought she might be curious to know the reason of his absence. It was a hard task he had set himself, — that of an attentive friend, where he had been the ardent lover.

Not finding Milicent outside the house, he had

gone to the kitchen in search of Miss Ursula. As usual, she was busy in some menial employment. She seemed to have a knack of discovering disagreeable drudgery, which, if she had been a believer in the sacrament of penance, one might suppose she was using to help her heavenward.

"Is Milly at home, Miss Ursula?" he asked, after bidding her good-evening. He did not apologize for interrupting her: which in point of fact he did not, for she went on with her homely work.

"No, I have not seen her since dinner. I thought she had gone to the cottage."

"She did not leave any message, if she did. I hope she was not disappointed by not finding me."

"I cannot say. It is difficult to know what pleases her. She needs looking after; but she will not bear it from me, and there is no one else who will interfere with her. The young must always go their own gait, and think they see the road to its ending; and when they stumble, they blame the road, and not their recklessness. There is no use in my crying a warning. But I did hope you might smooth the path for her treading, poor child, and not give her up so easily."

"I, Miss Ursula? I never gave Milly up. She is the best judge of what she wishes. I could never have forced her to care for me, by keeping her to her promise to marry me. I do not see why we should fear evils for Milly: she is young, and life may have many good things in store for her," he added, hopefully.

"If she would only be contented, and not strive to grasp more than she can hold. A safe home at the cottage is what I have long wished for her."

It was so seldom that Miss Ursula expressed interest in Milicent that Stephen was surprised, as well as touched. He might have asked why she felt unusually anxious for her niece's welfare, not being at all assured how far she was in the girl's confidence : when he caught sight of Thomas coming to the house.

"Is it Milicent you are looking for?" asked Thomas, with primitive unceremoniousness, which would have shocked Urquhart, but from custom had no such effect upon Stephen. "She is rowing on the bay with Urquhart. She ought to know it is too late to be out with a stranger."

Stephen made no answer, though the remark was addressed to him, Miss Ursula having returned to her labor inside the kitchen as soon as she saw Thomas approaching. Stephen did not care to discuss Milicent with her aunt's fisherman : who was right, however ; for as Stephen walked home by the cliff, he saw Urquhart's boat making great headway, being propelled by vigorous strokes from its owner's oars. Stephen could even make out, though the distance was great, Milicent sitting in the stern. He would not watch them, but passed on quickly. But just as he reached the path which led into his own field, he turned, and was rewarded by seeing Urquhart lay down his oars, and striding over the bench, take his seat by Milicent.

It was a little hard on Stephen to have their

love-making going on under his eyes. Bitter enough to be forced to give up the hope of ever having Milicent as his own ; but to give it up to a stranger, who had not known her as many weeks as he had years, was adding both wormwood and gall. Miss Ursula's fear for Milicent's future suddenly took possession of Stephen. How were they to know that Urquhart was what he represented himself ? — a gentleman somewhat daft about fishing.

But when Stephen had turned his back upon the bay, and could no longer see Milicent and Urquhart sitting together, he knew he had done Urquhart an injustice. There was nothing in the least suspicious about him. He was refined and frank, very liberal, and, Stephen believed, honorable. If Milicent loved the man, Stephen could not honestly see that there was any objection to the match.

And that she did love him, Stephen had no doubt. It was the only barrier she could possibly have found to her marriage with himself, — this newly awakened love she had discovered in her heart for the handsome stranger.

The face of much in life looks brighter to us for leaving the night behind, and letting the morning sunshine in. It may throw light upon some clew for which we have been groping in the dark, to unravel a perplexity; or it may show us there are some smooth and easy reaches in the steep road we have been fearing over-night. But to Stephen, who has no perplexity left to unravel, and who knows how hard and unlovely the lonely road must stretch up to the very end, the new day means merely sunny skies that seem to have no sense of anything going wrong just under them.

The sun, — who is always in haste to run his course on a summer morning in the north, — is pushing level beams across the ripened grass in the field behind the cottage, till it looks a golden-ruddy sunset sea, as the wind tosses and ruffles it into mimic waves; and all the swaying blades that have caught and still hold a jewel of the dew flash out, as sown with gold and diamonds. Scheherezade need not have looked over the sultan's palace-garden wall to find Aladdin's jeweled garden, Milicent is thinking, as she stands in the road close to the fence. Stephen, who is in the field giving directions to the mowers, chances to turn, and sees her standing there.

"Is anything the matter?" he asks, going towards her, and showing his anxiety by his abruptness. "It is an early hour for you to be out."

"No, there is nothing the matter, — at least, nothing in the way you mean," she replies quietly. "I have come to ask you what to do. I have no one else in the world to go to. Besides, you promised."

"I will help you all I can, Milly; you may be sure of that," answers Stephen, cheerfully; though he has strong previsions as to the matter to be advised upon. She would never have come to him if what she had to say had not been of all importance to her. He is sure Urquhart has asked her to marry him, and she is a little fearful, perhaps, of saying yes, unless some one sanctioned it. It does not even seem strange or out of the way that she has come to him. Miss Ursula is scarcely one to whom a girl would care to go with a love-tale : and Milicent has no one else save him. Therefore he is bound to put aside all thoughts of himself, and think only of her happiness. He never suspects for a moment what her errand really is, however.

" Aunt Ursula said you were over at the house last night," begins Milicent, finding it a little difficult to broach her errand as abruptly as she had intended.

" I was sorry not to see you, for Miss Ursula seemed to think you started to come here," answers Stephen, never hinting that he had seen her in the boat with Urquhart. She should tell her story in her own way.

" Yes, I did come over : but not to see you. I knew you were away. I met Mr. Urquhart as I went home by the beach, and he asked me to row with him."

It is so quietly said, that Stephen begins to accuse himself of unreasonable jealousy : when Milicent adds, in her downright way, coming at once to the point, " He — Mr. Urquhart, I mean — has asked me to marry him."

" And you have promised you would ?" asks Stephen, a little sharply.

" Yes. And he has also promised to take me abroad to live, and not to bring me back unless I

wish to come. That is just what I want most,"
Milicent adds, still keeping to facts.

"I am sorry your old home is so disagreeable to
you, Milly," says Stephen, reproachfully ; and yet
he half fears he has helped to make it uncomfortable.

"It is not on your account that I wish to go,"
says Milicent, quickly divining his thoughts.
"There are some things at home" — She stops,
looking away from him.

"Were these things your only reasons for promising to marry Urquhart, Milly?"

"They were some of my reasons," — slowly.

"But not all.   You love him, Milly?"

She does not answer him at once, though her
eyes fall under his gaze, and a blush comes into
her face. "I like him," she says at last, finding
Stephen waiting for a reply.

"*Like* him, Milly?"

"I did not come here to answer such questions,
but to tell you " — begins Milicent, throwing back
her head with an impatient gesture, and blushing
hotly. But a look into Stephen's pale, set face
stops her.

"Yes, I remember," he says quietly. "You promised to tell me if you were going away. Is it to be
so soon?   Are you in such haste to go?" he adds
bitterly, though he is trying not to show he feels it.

"I did not come over to tell you what you might
hear soon enough. What I came to say was that,
though I — what do they call it when a girl promises to marry? Engaged? — I engaged myself to

Mr. Urquhart last evening, I am ready to take back my word if you wish. I have n't forgotten all you have been to me, nor all I owe you. And though I cannot marry you, I 'll not marry any other, if you do not wish me to."

" I cannot be happy if I know you are not," she goes on hastily, finding she gets no answer. " I am not altogether selfish, though Aunt Ursula says I am ; so if you will only say what you would rather I 'd do, I will abide by it."

" Is Urquhart's love so little to you, Milly, that you could give him up for a wish of mine ? " asks Stephen, hurriedly.

" Stephen," she says, looking up at him, her eyes glistening with unshed tears, " I cannot bear to do anything that displeases you, or makes your life a bit more lonely. I would rather you should decide what I shall do."

Milicent must have understood very little of the love Stephen feels for her. She may have thought it made up of the same stuff as her own : a mixture of a child's trusting affection and a girl's friend-ship. She could not have dreamed how he has longed for her, how he has suffered when forced to give her up. If she had, she might have shrunk from putting her fate so completely in his power.

And yet her instinct is not at fault. She stands awaiting his decision as she has a dozen times be-fore in her life : though never, perhaps, with the same anxiety.

There could be nothing quieter nor calmer than the two appear. A passer-by might have imagined they were discussing the veriest trifle, — that is, if he thought of anything but the pretty picture Milicent makes as she stands there on the road, her arms resting carelessly on the top-rail of the fence, her voice lowered to a subdued tone, not to be overheard by the laborer mowing the small hay-field but a few feet from them ; while Stephen, on the other side of the fence, is seemingly intent on digging a hole with the end of his stout walking-stick. Alas for Stephen ! He is digging much more than that useless hole ; for is he not burying out of sight his last hope of making Milicent his wife ?

She has not asked him to decide which is best for her, but for himself ; not for her happiness and content, but for his own. He cannot guess what her sacrifice might be, though he knows very well what is his own. And so he puts into one grave his hope and his temptation.

"I must not decide this for you, Milly." he says, at last. " You can tell much better than I, what would be for your happiness. It ought not to be any harder on me to see you Urquhart's wife than to know you can't be mine. So if it is only of me you are thinking, be very sure that whatever will make you happy I'll like best. Only, Milly," he adds, seeing she has taken her arms from the fence, making a slight movement as if she had received her answer and was preparing to go, " don't marry Urquhart unless you are very sure you love him. It is hard lines for a girl to be married, unless she has the sort of love that makes her feel all burdens light, in comparison with the chance only of losing her lover."

"I'll mind, Stephen," Milicent promises. "I suppose all lives have their troubles; only some are harder to bear than others. I shall always have one," she adds, sorrowfully, "go where I will, and live as happily as I may: and that is, that I seem to have hurt your life. There may come a day when you may see it all differently, and know I did you a kindness in not coming here to live."

"I doubt if that day ever comes," answers Stephen, quickly; then gently, "Milly, you must look upon me as a brother now; and if you need help, you must promise to come to me as you have to-day."

"I have promised that once before," replies Milicent, without hesitation. "I shall never depend on any one as I do on you; so if ever I have need of help, I will be sure to come to you."

"You will depend on Urquhart. I did not mean to put myself before him. But brothers, you know, can often do what lovers would like, but cannot."

"I understand you," says Milicent, reaching out her hand over the fence to bid him good-by.

"Shall I not walk home with you?" asks Stephen.

"No, I had better go alone. Your breakfast must be ready by this time. I did not come to be unnecessarily troublesome."

Stephen is about to tell her she could never be troublesome to him; when he remembers she is Urquhart's betrothed, and it would be better for him not to show her even those small attentions she has long been accustomed to, from him. She might meet Urquhart on her way home, and neither would care for a third party. He must learn to think of her as belonging to another man; and of himself as no longer necessary to her.

So Milicent sets out for home alone, carrying with her a much lighter heart than she brought. She is glad Stephen has not asked her to give up Urquhart. It is much better for Stephen that she should be away: and it is ten times better for herself. To spend the rest of her life as a holiday, going where she pleases, — that is something, certainly, to look forward to. Oh, yes, she is very glad Stephen has not asked her to stay in the old house, that looks more like a great prison than ever, in this morning sunshine.

She turns her back upon it, when she has passed within her own gate, leaning on the topmost bar, and thinking all these thoughts. Miss Ursula's voice soon brings her out of them ; but later in the day, when all that tiresome stitching, stitching is over, she is there again, in the same attitude. Thinking, — or perhaps she is dreaming so ; for she starts as one suddenly awakened, when Urquhart finds her there.

She says nothing to him of her early walk ; so he has not the mortification of knowing that Stephen has been the arbiter of his fate, — Stephen, who, he is sure, knows much more of the raising of potatoes, or the market value of cod-fish, than of the nice questions of love or honor.

It is a question of the latter, Urquhart is now come upon. Though Milicent has told him that

Miss Ursula feels very little interest in their engagement, and does not pretend to exercise the slightest authority over her actions, yet he is determined to ask her permission for their marriage. Milicent is not only very young, but she is also ignorant of the world's ways ; and it seems scarcely honest to take her promise, and have so little exacted from him on her part. Such, at least, are Urquhart's views; but when he tells Milicent he wishes to see Miss Ursula, she laughs at him, and it is not until he insists upon her calling her aunt, and looks grave and decidedly hurt, that she shrugs her shoulders most uncivilly, saying, " Aunt Ursula won't thank you for the trouble you will give her."

It is in the room called by courtesy the parlor, that Urquhart waits for his interview with Miss Ursula, — a great bare room, almost blinding with the glare from the many shutterless windows. It is scrupulously clean ; not a spot to be seen, though the searching light reveals even the corners. As to furniture, it is scant indeed; only a table, and barely chairs enough to seat half a dozen people. There is nothing to give the room a home-like look, or even the air of ever being used. A book or two, or a few flowers, even a woman's work-basket, or a trifling ornament, — anything to hint of a feminine love of decoration, — would have taken away from the appearance of great poverty.

There being nothing to see, except a fine view of the sea from the windows, and nothing to do to wile away the time, Urquhart's patience is very soon exhausted. It seems to him an interminable while before he hears steps in the hall ; and then Milicent comes in, followed by Miss Ursula.

Urquhart is struck with the extreme dissimilarity between aunt and niece: Milicent so slight, almost childlike beside Miss Ursula, whose stature is increased by the severe style of her dress, so scant that there is not an unnecessary plait or fold in it. She looks as if she belonged to that most peculiar order of religionists, the lay-sisters of a convent, who, though often reared delicately, voluntarily take the hard, disagreeable life of a menial, either to gain a painful admittance into heaven, or to fulfill an earthly vow that of itself is bitter and humiliating.

"Milicent tells me you wish to speak to me," says Miss Ursula, as soon as she comes into the room, vouchsafing Urquhart no other salutation, though she does motion him to a chair.

He is far too wise to submit to being seated on one of these, stiffly set back against the wall, where he would feel like a school-boy in disgrace. So he draws the indicated chair up to the table, by which Miss Ursula has taken her place. After that one act of self-assertion, Urquhart scarcely knows how to proceed ; for he is embarrassed by the consciousness that Miss Ursula is watching him keenly, and at the same time does not intend to help him out in the least, by a judicious remark or even a question.

Fortunately, Milicent comes to the rescue in her

downright, imperative way. It is absurd, in her eyes, for two people to sit looking at each other, if either of them has anything of importance to say. So she remarks to Miss Ursula, by way of giving a bit of information which might be of service, —

"Mr. Urquhart has only come to repeat what I told you last night, Aunt Ursula. I told him it was quite unnecessary to trouble you; but I fancy it is customary and civil in him to ask your permission, or he would not take so much pains to do so."

"You have told him that I have nothing to say about your marrying, — that I have neither the power nor the wish to interfere with you?" Miss Ursula asks Milicent, very much as if the young girl were sponsor to Urquhart, and were making the promises for him.

"Yes, I have told him, though perhaps not in those precise words," answers Milicent, as coldly and measuredly as Miss Ursula herself.

"Then I suppose you have also told him that there has been no objection made to your marriage by any one," says Miss Ursula, still speaking to Milicent, and ignoring Urquhart.

"But that is not what I came to speak of," Urquhart interposes. It is decidedly awkward to be left out of the conversation; and besides, he has come there with an intention, and is fully determined to carry it out.

Miss Ursula looks at him when he speaks, but makes no remark; so he goes on: —

"That your niece should take me on trust is not

surprising. But it is only natural and proper that you should wish to know something of me, before you willingly trust me with Milicent's future happiness. Unfortunately, I have nothing else to bring you but a few letters from men whom, if you have never known, at least you may have heard of; and also some vouchers which will show you that if Milicent outlives me there will be a sufficient provision for her comfort."

Urquhart has taken some half dozen letters from his pocket, as he makes this speech; and lays them in a pile before Miss Ursula. But she brushes them away with her hand, as she says, —

" It is not at all worth while for me to take the trouble to read these. How could I know anything of your correspondence ? "

" They are from prominent men in the States; those who are well known by many who have no personal acquaintance with them," Urquhart begins.

" Fame travels slowly to these parts, and I never read the papers," Miss Ursula says, bluntly. " As for any future provision for Milicent, it is as well to tell you that there is no form of poverty, except absolute beggary, which she has not felt; so that she will not be hard to satisfy, and she can be safely left to your own notions of justice, even if they be ever so limited. I beg your pardon if I seem uncivil," — for Urquhart is scarlet with suppressed wrath, — " but we set very little store on social standing, in such a primitive place as this."

" But you can't object to reading my letters, for

Milicent's sake. I shall feel utterly uncomfortable, if you know nothing whatever about me, and take me entirely on trust."

" You will have to be taken on trust, after all," replies Miss Ursula. " I have no doubt your letters are most satisfactory, especially as far as your character goes. If not, you would not be so eager to show them. But you are a young man yet, and such certificates are to be believed only when we are in ripe old age, or after we are dead. Many a proud ship has a weak plank that is never discovered in a calm sea, nor until the storm comes and it founders, to the surprise of many. If Milicent is bent on marrying you, she must run her risk, as every other woman does."

Urquhart begins to gather up his rejected correspondence, silently. He wishes he had taken Milicent's advice, and not insisted upon seeing Miss Ursula. Yet how could he have foreseen that certificates of respectability and wealth would be utterly scorned?

" Have you a mother ? " asks Miss Ursula abruptly, as soon as Urquhart has put the unfortunate letters into his pocket again.

" No. I was so unhappy as to lose my mother before I could remember her."

" Nor father ? "

" He died the year after my mother."

" Have you no sisters nor brothers ? "

Urquhart shakes his head.

" No relatives who have a right to feel an interest in your marriage ? " she questions.

"I have no near relations. Some distant cousins, perhaps, who would be glad to claim the same blood if I should die intestate," answers Urquhart, shortly.

"Then no doubt you have some friend you ought to consult."

"No. I had a guardian, but I have outgrown, some years ago, all right of interference on his part."

"Then of course, as we ask no reference on your side, you will care for none on Milicent's. Any of our neighbors can testify as to our being poor. As the world uses the term, Milicent is well born; that is, her family was originally of good standing. I have only my word to give you, however. I have no correspondence to offer as proof that what I say is true."

"I do not wish anything of the kind on Milicent's account. It is of Milicent herself only, that I have thought," replies Urquhart. "I only desired to show you, through my letters, that I am not a mere penniless adventurer. I am sure I ought to feel flattered that you do not care to read them."

Miss Ursula has waited with undisguised impatience for him to finish. "If I might only give you a caution, and were sure you would profit by it, I should be glad," she says. "It is very simple, — only that you had better go away at once, and have nothing to do with us. Milicent will get over your desertion. She is young, and so must necessarily be shallow of feeling."

She does not wait to hear what answer he would

make, but leaves the room at once, without even bidding him good-morning. Again Urquhart hears her step on the bare floor of the hall; then a door slams, and there is a sudden cessation of all sounds.

"Do you intend to follow Aunt Ursula's advice?" asks Milicent, from the window where she has been standing, rather pale and very still, a mere listener since she had made known to Miss Ursula what was Urquhart's business with her.

"Not unless you wish to send me off," answers Urquhart, smiling, and not looking at all anxious nor unhappy.

"But perhaps you will go away?"

"Not until you are ready to go with me. Being still somewhat young myself, I do not believe in Miss Ursula's doctrine about the shallowness 'of youthful feelings. Indeed, I flatter myself that you would grieve over my going."

"I should certainly be disappointed."

"Only disappointed?" asks Urquhart, hurt and surprised by the cool admission, when he was in search of something far warmer and more tender.

"What would you have more? Does not the word cover every evil in life? Every failure must be a disappointment. I can't think any other word comparable to it in real sadness," says Milicent, quietly.

"Then you shall never have to say it. I shall take care that you have no disappointments in life," Urquhart declares, more tenderly than wisely.

Milicent comes a step nearer. She clasps her hands over the back of Miss Ursula's chair, that stands between them. Her color has faded again, the dimples are gone from about the rosy mouth, and there is a troubled line upon her brow, as she says slowly, —

"Oh, are you *sure?*"

"Sure, Milicent?"

"That you want me — *me?* Just me? — and that nothing else makes any difference?"

Urquhart laughs; there is a ring of triumph in the sound. Is not she learning already the lesson he promised yesterday to teach her?

"Just you, Milicent. Nothing else makes any difference."

He is coming to her: but she draws away, her color returning again.

"One likes to be honest, and not take more than one gives. I am afraid I am more of a gainer in this engagement of ours, than you."

"Not if I gain your heart, Milicent."

"If either of us knew what it is worth!"

"Its value may increase," says Urquhart, lightly. "Love is said to bring out all the innate goodness of the heart. Hence all lovers are for the time, at least, religious."

"But I 've heard they are somewhat given to idolatry. It must be pleasant to have a household god, even though it is a forbidden thing," says Milicent, laughing; and then, thoughtfully, "Aunt Ursula was wrong, then. She said I was making a mere scrawl of my life."

" I fancy she is not infallible. Milicent, I can understand very well, now, why you were so anxious for me to promise not to bring you back here. Miss Ursula, if I may be permitted to say so, must be slightly uncomfortable to live with."

" Oh, Aunt Ursula is not half as bad as others," returns Milicent, quickly.

" As others? What others?"

" Other things. I don't think you would understand, even if I told you," answers the girl, a little sharply.

" Try me, and see if I cannot. Perhaps I am not so stupid as you give me credit for being."

" Want of experience is not stupidity, though sometimes it makes us very ignorant. I suppose you know very little about poverty, which is a terrible bugbear of mine."

" I have no personal knowledge," admits Urquhart regretfully, as if he would fain have, for her sake. " I never knew the value of money before now, when it will increase your happiness."

" Aunt Ursula says very differently," begins Milicent.

" As I told you before, I don't think Miss Ursula infallible. But what does your sage aunt say?"

" That money is of but little use in making one happy, and sometimes even comfortable. She has known a very rich person die of starvation."

" Then that very rich person must have been bent on self-murder," says Urquhart, laughing.

" No, it was some disease where it was impossible to swallow.   Of course no one is exempt from illness."

" But, Milicent," asks Urquhart, a little anxiously, " you are not altogether mercenary? You like me a little for myself?"

" A little," she answers, smiling.

" And if I were poor, you would still be willing to marry me?"

" Oh, yes, certainly I would. That is," she adds, still smiling, " if you would be sure to take me away from here."

" You are not afraid to go with me, Milicent?"

" No, not in the least. Why should I be?" she asks in surprise.

" Because you know really so little of me. You had better read these letters Miss Ursula scorned so. They will tell you something, perhaps," he urges.

" No, Aunt Ursula is right. The past can be nothing to us, as we live in the present; and your letters can refer only to it."

" But my past is sure to color my future. To tell the truth, Milicent, if I had a sister, I would not permit her to marry a man she knows so little of, as you of me, unless she allowed me to make inquiries."

" If you had a sister, you would know by this time that she would do just as she pleased," retorts Milicent.

" I know you women are frightfully reckless. Not that I have any intention of imposing upon you," says Urquhart, smiling.   " I am hugely flattered by your trust in me. Nevertheless, I am sure that if you had a father " —

" What would my father do ? "

" He would read those letters Miss Ursula scorned to touch."

" He would do nothing of the kind. We are not suspicious in our small community. If a fisherman has good luck, it is not polite to ask him where he sets his nets."

" Because you suspect him of infringing on some fishing-law, then. Be wary, Milicent. I never knew a woman yet, who would not argue both sides of a case, if you gave her sufficient time ; or, if not, adroitly change sides," says Urquhart, laughing.

" Therefore I 'll not argue at all, but flatly assert that I intend to abide by Aunt Ursula's decision."

" The risk is on your own head, then, if you find me sailing under false colors. I give you a fair chance to inspect my papers, and you refuse."

" Let us go to the cliffs," proposes Milicent, abruptly ending the subject.

" You should have let me propose the walk," he says gravely ; and then, seeing her blush and the angry flash of her eyes, he adds, laughing, " You silly child ! as if the cliffs are not as much your reception-room as this parlor. If there is only wind enough to sail, however, I shall like that better than walking."

There is just enough to swell the leg-of-mutton sail of the yacht's small boat, which to-day again is beached in Green Cove. It is with a beating heart that Milicent lets Urquhart hand her to the stern, and takes the tiller-ropes once more, while he pushes out from shore, and springs in after her. Is it a dream, that twilight hour yesterday? Has nothing at all happened only they are just sailing out upon the water, and the sun is going down in rose and lilac, as it did last evening?

VII.

THE summer is past; September is blooming about Stephen's cottage. The apples lie in rosy heaps through the small orchard, the only one on the island, in its sheltered nook behind the low spruce-wood. In one corner, an ox is lumbering through the unusual task of walking round and round in a short dizzying circle, turning the cider-press, which creaks with its load of fruit. The earth is preparing for her long winter's rest; and Stephen, like Joseph of old, is hoarding her treasures in his barns, against the future. It gives him little pleasure to know that Nature has been unwontedly liberal in her gifts: for these are not now for Milicent. Only last year she liked his cider —

"Why is it that everything tastes good to a boy?" asks Urquhart, who is sitting on the gate, watching the gyrations of the patient ox. He has walked over to taste the new cider, which, from his recollection of boyish enjoyment, he expected to be delicious, and which proves to his more mature taste insipid, as well as dubious as to wholesomeness. "I remember drinking quarts of just such apple juice as this," he goes on, "and not only thinking it fine, but I have lived to tell the tale:

which in my judgment is the more surprising fact
of the two. If our palates were not cultivated, as
well as our minds, we would relapse into utter bar-
barism."

"No doubt it was the mode of imbibing the
cider which made it fine," replies Stephen, amused
by Urquhart's disgust. "If you had a straw in-
serted into the bung-hole of that barrel, you could
give the apple-juice a better test."

"Not unless it were forbidden. Stolen waters
are sweet. There is a certain zest about secret
pleasures, if only cider through a straw."

Stephen looks annoyed, and says hastily, "That
is a dangerous doctrine."

"Perhaps so, unless we confine it to cider. I
rather think you have hit the truth, and it is the
quantity that makes it unpalatable. Indeed, I suspect most things are better taken through a straw.
It prevents a surfeit, and that has been my chief
evil thus far in life."

"Did you come here in an invalid state, in search
of an appetite?"

"Metaphorically. But I did not expect to find
my cure by means so charming and delectable as
I have."

"You mean Milicent."

"Exactly. I had always the deepest pity for
Adam, as the one man in the world with only the
one woman for companion. Just fancy it! At
least it was not my idea of paradise. But lately
I have come to quite a different conclusion, and
think his love-making must have been amply suf-

ficient for his happiness, especially if his Eve had as many moods as my Eve's, which I occasionally think adequate to half a dozen of her sex."

"I am not so sure you are a fit judge of the peculiarities of our first father's position," says Stephen, pushing aside, a little viciously, a stone he has been turning over with his foot. It gives him a sharp pain to hear Urquhart discuss Milicent. "You like fellowship with men so much, that you seek the fishermen when I am not to be found," he adds.

"But Adam could always get at his Eve, as there was certainly no Aunt Ursula in Eden to look forbidding, and make him feel awkwardly in the way. You cannot tell," continues Urquhart, shifting his seat somewhat in search of comfort on the rail, — "you cannot tell, because you have never tried it, what a different sensation it is to make love on the bosom of the ocean under the blue sky, or in the pauses of a whirling dance or the crush of an overheated ball-room. I did not know ' I love you ' could take such varied meaning from varied surroundings."

"Do you mean you have ever said that before — before you came here ? " asks Stephen, finding sudden difficulty in naming the familiar name " Milicent."

"Many dozens of times. Ever since I left off petticoats I have had a Dulcinea. I do not think Milicent need be jealous : for such a mild type of the disease was no guard against my taking it in its most violent form."

It is sacrilege, in Stephen's opinion, for Milicent to be one of many loves. With him she was his first; and she will, he is very sure, be his last. Urquhart guesses something of his thoughts, for he says, —

"I believe it is a well-ascertained fact that first loves come to naught. I am convinced, Ferguson, that one of the genuine Flora MacFlimseys would fascinate you, looking at her with your honest, rural eyes, as my little fisher-maiden has bewitched me. It is novelty and great extremes that touch the fancy."

"I could not possibly admire a woman of the world," says Stephen, decidedly.

"Nor did I incline to rusticity a few months ago : and now I wonder at my want of taste. Depend upon it, a handsomely dressed woman, with pleasant, easy manners, would make a vast impression upon you; and they are to be found in our cities by hundreds. Whereas, such a gem as Milicent " —

"I have been too long used to Nature and her ways, to admire fine dress and fine manners," breaks in Stephen, with a little asperity, thinking of Milicent in her blue cotton dress.

"It is a fact that they are at variance, — nature and millinery, I mean. But don't taste cider through a straw, and compare it to manufactured wine," says Urquhart, coolly; adding somewhat abruptly, " Come with me to the beach, Ferguson. That ox can keep on waltzing without your watching, and I want your opinion about something."

Urquhart gets down from his perch as he speaks, remarking that a sofa is a more comfortable seat than a fence-rail; another hallucination of his boyhood forever disposed of. And Stephen, supposing that the something to be the subject of consultation is the yacht lying at anchor in the harbor, leaves the cider-making in charge of a hand, and goes with Urquhart.

Some weeks before, Urquhart had sent to a lady friend for a box of dresses and millinery, dainty things for a lady's toilette. He wrote as if the articles were a commission he had undertaken: whether for a trousseau was not very plain. Altogether, Urquhart's was a very diplomatic note, prodigiously inclined to mislead; certainly giving no hint that the pretty things were meant for a gift, which he very much hoped Milicent would see no impropriety in receiving. Indeed, he was not nearly as uneasy upon that score, as upon the risk he ran in giving such general directions where particular ones were needed. Urquhart was very proud of Milicent's beauty. He was a judge of good style, he was sure, and understood something of the secrets of the becoming. He had a great desire to see Milicent as she would look as his wife; indeed, as his betrothed, he would have liked her to dress better than the girls in the village.

When he knew the important box was well on its way, he ventured to broach the subject to Milicent; and, to his great relief, she only treated it merely as an unnecessary bit of generosity on his

part, and made no demur about accepting it. So
now it had arrived, and had been taken to the
house, and even smuggled up-stairs to Milicent's
room without Miss Ursula's suspecting it; and
Milicent has promised Urquhart to meet him on
the cliffs in one of the new dresses. This is what
he wishes Stephen to see.

It is a pity Urquhart could not have watched
the child's delight as she unpacked the box, hastily
emptying it of its contents, the name and use of
much of which she could not even guess. The
bed, the chairs, the floor, were strewn with the
prettinesses which have an effect so enchanting
upon Eve's daughters. Milicent, whose experience was confined to the few shelves of Mrs.
Featherstone's small shop, had had no idea such
perfect shades and colors were to be found out of
the sky, — Nature's palette, where she is wont to
experiment in mixing hues.

The box was soon emptied; though not until
Milicent had grown a little weary of admiring and
pondering the use of much of her new finery. Then
came the reaction : she began to feel strangely sad
and oppressed. A great dread overwhelmed her,—
a dread of the big world, and of what might be re-
quired of her in it. The thought might never have
occurred to her, if she had not suddenly found herself in possession of so much of the world's pomps.
Such fine dresses must of necessity belong to a
fine lady; and Milicent had never given a thought
to that phase of the new life before her. Certainly
it had no part in her conception of enjoyment.

To seek new scenes and sights, with new adventures by the way; to sail in the Undine on unknown waters; to row on foreign bays, instead of on the only two she knew,—Urquhart of course bearing her company —

Suddenly a low sunbeam casts itself into her lap, bringing opal tints out of the silk that lies across it. Milicent looks up quickly: to see through her western window that the sun is setting.

Urquhart is already on the cliffs, waiting for her.

She rises hastily, and begins to dress. She must not be so late that he might lose patience and come in search of her. She has her own reasons for discouraging his visits after sunset. Perhaps Miss Ursula disapproves? — or the miserable lamp may be an objection? Girls have whims and false shames; and Milicent has her full share of both.

She chooses the simplest dress in her new collection, for her trial-toilette, — a silk the color of a dove's wing, — and pins a knot of poppy-colored ribbons amongst the lace at the throat, to give more effect to the quiet shade. It is of the harmonizing of the colors she is thinking: she does not stop to look at the effect upon her face in the glass. It takes her no longer to dress in the rustling silk than in her blue cotton, and she does not stop to try on any of the pretty ornaments strewn over the small dressing-table. Her next action is peculiar. She tilts her looking-glass — no larger than a common-sized window - pane —

against the wall, setting it on the floor ; and after a few trials to get at the precise angle of vision, she turns her back to the glass, keeping her head well turned to see behind her. It is an uncomfortable as well as a disappointing effort, to catch sight of her first train. Backward and forward goes Milicent, striving to catch in her bit of mirror the soft sweep of the silken folds. She might have been taken for a child playing lady, as she passes up and down the great bare room, perfectly absorbed in the unwonted splendors of her train.

Suddenly she remembers that Urquhart is waiting for her. She softly opens the door of her room, and looks out into the hall. There is no one to be seen or heard on that story. She gives a quick, anxious glance at the wonderful amount of fine things scattered over the whole room. There is no time to gather them up, and no hope in the world of getting them into the small box from which they were unpacked. The only hope is that Miss Ursula will stay down-stairs : if she should make an unwonted visit to her niece's chamber, Milicent cannot help smiling at the astounding effect all these pretty pomps and vanities would have upon unsuspecting Miss Ursula. But she must trust to luck ; so, drawing her skirts tightly about her, that the silk shall make no tell-tale rustle over the bare boards, Milicent runs quickly down-stairs, across the hall, and lets herself out at the front door.

She is fortunate also in meeting no one on her way to the cliffs. Once there, she will not fear being seen by any of the village people; it is the general tea-hour, and nothing less than a strange sail in the offing would bring any one out-of-doors. Urquhart is waiting for her, and — yes, she is very sure, and a little ashamed; for she had not looked for Stephen.

The two men are walking up and down a great flat octagon of a rock, as if pacing a fisherman's quarter-deck, which is said to measure two paces and a turn: and their backs are toward Milicent as she runs over the rocks to them, the rustle of her silk lighter than the little rushing eddies round the pools at their feet.

Milicent feels very much as if she were on some madcap masquerade in her new finery, and wonders if she will be easily recognized? She did intend to play her part bravely, and to be received as a fine lady should be. But she begins to be hot and uncomfortable and awkward, and blames her new dress for the unwonted sensation. So when the two men turn in their walk, she is standing just before them, blushing as red as her ribbons, and yet looking at them with eyes eager to read approval in theirs.

She ought to be satisfied; for it is plainly to be seen that, though both the men are taken by surprise, they like the pretty vision.

But on Stephen's face the look of wondering admiration dies out as quickly as it came; and for the first time in her life Milicent feels she has lost his sympathy.

The look she takes for apathy is the blank certainty that he has lost his little friend as well as sweetheart, in the fine lady Urquhart would fain make her.

But Urquhart's eyes show neither apathy nor a sense of loss: but rather the greatest satisfaction. Before him stands Milicent just as she will be when she is his wife. He has often painted a mental picture of her arrayed as he is accustomed to see fair women ; but now he has to confess his brightest dreams failed utterly in doing her justice.

In his great delight, he has caught both her hands, and draws her to him. "Stephen, is she not beautiful? Will not all the world wonder where I got my bonny bride, when I show her?"

"You will have to say you fished me out of the sea," she puts in, laughing. "I warn you, I do not intend to admit that I came from a small fishing-village of an island not to be found on a map of respectable size."

"Of course only the sea-foam could have made our Venus. Stephen," continues Urquhart, eager for sympathy in his rapture, "where are all your theories that nature only is to be admired, when you see what Paris millinery has done for Milicent?"

She turns again to Stephen, as Urquhart speaks.

"You do not like it. You may as well say so in plain words, as look it," she says, with a little quaver of disappointment in her voice. "You would rather see me a fisher-girl, with a basket on my head, than dressed like a lady."

"I never saw you in silk before. It is very pretty," says Stephen, gently touching the dress.

"And you will never see her in anything else hereafter," adds Urquhart, curtly. "No matter, Milicent; he knows nothing about it. I do, and I consider you charming."

"Of course you like me in the dress, as you bought it for me," returns Milicent, with what Urquhart thinks unnecessary frankness. "But Stephen evidently does not admire it."

"Hang Stephen! What is it to him?"

"You are far too fine, Milly," says Stephen, rallying a little under Urquhart's evident wrath. "To my thinking, your cotton dress suits the cliffs and the sea. I shall be afraid to move an oar when we are boating, for fear of splashing you with salt water."

"I shall not wear the dress boating," replies Milicent, reassuringly.

"We will not have our Cinderella going back to her ash-heap and old gowns," Urquhart interposes.

"I did not mean to be unkind, Milly," says Stephen, feeling much more the girl's hurt face than Urquhart's heat. "The dress no doubt is very grand, and you do look pretty in it. But I am used to a different Milicent, and the first sight of you made me feel you had gotten far away from me. You have, you know; I should be used to the knowledge by this time. You are not going on the water, you say; so you will not need me now, and I am wanted at home."

Stephen turns to go, and neither Milicent nor

Urquhart asks him to stay.   If he is hurt, he does not show it, but hurries away across the fields.

"Ferguson is decidedly impertinent," says Urquhart, as soon as Stephen is out of hearing.

"Because he thinks differently from us?" asks Milicent, with a slight shrug of her shoulders.

"He has a right to differ" — Urquhart is somewhat mollified by her use of the pronoun — "if he honestly does so: which in this case I do not believe.   But I cannot see why he should criticise what you wear."

"Only if people will ask questions, they naturally expect answers," suggests Milicent.

"Which is unfortunate, if the answer conveys an opinion utterly worthless.   Fancy Ferguson an oracle of fashion!   I confess I am glad your future life will be far removed from his influence, or he might be using it in a more important matter than the style of your dress.   You have contracted a habit of turning to him for approval: when you are separated, I have an humble hope that in time you will regard *my* opinion as something worth."

Urquhart speaks very coolly and decidedly, with the evident intention of making an immense impression.

"That will depend on the opinions themselves," answers the girl, a mischievous dimple coming and going about the demure mouth.   "No one can judge of the best without naturally making a comparison."

"Of course the comparison must be with Ferguson's opinion. I am greatly obliged to you for giving me the opportunity to ask what might have seemed an impertinence at another time: why you prefer me to Stephen? He has told me you could have been mistress of the cottage if you had chosen."

"Did he tell you that?" She has dropped her silken train on the rocks, forgetting the risk the color runs from contact with salt water; and stands looking after Stephen as he crosses the slope against the sunset. "Only an angel would do for Stephen. I am not half good enough for him," she says, after a moment of silence; and there are tears in the girl's eyes as she speaks.

"And I must put up with a woman! After all, I am rather glad I am not so superlatively good that I must needs have an angel for my wife; for, to tell the honest truth, I should not know what to do with her," says Urquhart, restored to his accustomed good-humor.

"Of course not, for how could you lecture an angel? — and I think you like to do that occasionally. Besides, an angel is above caring for your pretty dresses and gewgaws, all of which I admire so much. Only it was frightfully extravagant in you to be so lavish with your pretty things," says Milicent, smilingly.

"And you liked them all?" he asks, pleased with her approval. "I was afraid Ferguson had set you against them. But you must not permit him to, for they are vastly becoming to you."

It is later than usual when Milicent comes home

this evening. Miss Ursula had complained of headache, and had gone to bed early. Milicent gropes her way through the dark hall to the kitchen; for though the moon is up, she needs the unwonted luxury of a lamp, as her room was left in confusion. Miss Ursula never makes any provision for light when Nature gives the moon, any more than when she gives the sun.

Thomas does not seem to regard the rules of the house; for he has the only lamp, and is busy doing something to his fishing-rods by the light of it. Fortunately, there is a candle to be found in the closet, and no keys are used in Miss Ursula's housekeeping; so Milicent goes softly across the great kitchen, in the hope of not disturbing Thomas. She forgets her dress of silk is making a rustle, with her unwonted train.

" Come here, Milicent," Thomas says quite suddenly. "Let me look at you."

She comes forward, slowly, reluctantly, with the unlighted candle in her hand, and stands before him. Thomas takes the candle, lights it, and coolly surveys her with its feeble aid; lifting it above her head, or lowering its tiny flame, to throw as much light as possible on her pretty figure.

Milicent stands quite still, never moving a muscle under this scrutiny of his, though the hot blood that surges scarlet to her temples tells that she resents it.

" Where did my bonny bird get her fine feathers ? " asks Thomas at length. " Not from Mother Featherstone's shop, I dare swear."

"Mr. Urquhart has sent me a whole box of them," says Milicent, in a vain attempt to answer indifferently.

"So he has begun to dress you, has he?" Thomas's bronzed face is as flushed as her own, and he puts the candle down on the table with an unsteady hand. "Most men wait until they are married, for that; and even then they like it so little, that the bride manages to have clothes enough to take her through the honeymoon."

"Does she?" asks Milicent, vainly trying to keep a sob out of her voice. "I wonder where my store of clothes would come from?"

"Not from your Aunt Ursula's purse, certainly," answers Thomas, who has recovered his usual coolness. "She is not in favor of this new choice of yours. Women are always partisans, and she is all for Stephen. But I say to her, if the bird wants to fly, it is silly to cut her wings; for she will be sure to think what you call needful restraint is persecution. Yet now I must warn you: if you wish your aunt to keep quiet, you must not turn fine lady until you really are one, and get miles away from here."

"I do not see why Aunt Ursula will not let me wear my pretty dresses, as I have them," says Milicent, looking down on the shimmering silk. "As I am a lady, why should she object to my dressing as one, if it costs her nothing?"

"Dresses! The fellow is at least liberal. By all means, wear the pretty things, for they are vastly becoming. But I may as well tell you that if Urquhart had considered you his equal in the social scale, he would never have presumed to give you them."

An utter silence follows this remark; not even a fold of the silk dress rustles.

Thomas must have been very sure of the effect of his advice; for he adds, " Keep to the cotton dress, Milicent. There is nothing certain in this life, they say, except death and taxes; and if Urquhart chooses to jilt you, it will be awkward to doff the silks and go back to cheap prints. Indeed, if I were you, I would keep one of my cotton dresses, as King Cophetua's beggar-maiden might have kept her rags: a rod to hold over your lord's head if he does not array you finely enough. He would not like his so-called friends to see you in the gown he wooed you in."

" He might use it as a rod over my head, unless he found a more effectual one," says Milicent, quickly.

" So he might; and if he is wise, he 'll try to find something to keep you humble. One might think these dresses were meant for just such a lesson, if he knew how proud you are. But evidently he has not a suspicion."

" How could he, when I am so ignorant, I don't even know when to be proud?" says Milicent, with tears in her eyes.

" He 'll not put that down to a personal defect: only to your education. There, don't cry about it. There is no harm done, only you 'll be wise if you don't wear the things."

He turns back to his fishing-rods, as if they were really of more importance than Milicent; and does not speak to her again, though she lingers awhile before she goes up-stairs.

She has to clear a place on the poor chest of drawers for her lamp; and then takes up the dresses from the chairs and bed, not to observe and admire them, but to fold and put them back into the box. At first she folds them carefully; but she soon grows impatient of the work, and sweeps them ruthlessly, all in a mass, into the box. She has some trouble in pressing the lid down, and she would willingly have driven in the nails, but for the noise in what is the middle of Miss Ursula's night.

Not that Milicent is in the least dread of her aunt; but that the wound to her pride is too deep for her to care to lay it bare.

VIII.

" I THOUGHT you would have worn some of your pretty things, if only to please me," remonstrates Urquhart, when the next day he comes over to the house, and Milicent meets him in her usual dress.

" Why should I ? " she asks, with a shrug.

" I gave a reason.   To please me."

" A man should be above such paltry pleasures," she says, lightly.

" Above being pleased by seeing you look pretty ? Yet I acknowledge there is something I would admire in you, besides your beauty. May I venture to tell you what it is ? "

" If you choose," she answers with a little yawn : which, however, her tone belies.

" I would admire, and also be grateful for, a little yielding to a request of mine."

Milicent looks at him rather steadily. " Then you must let me rely on your never urging me to do what you would not approve in others."

" Do you think I would urge you to do what I disapprove of ? " interrupts Urquhart, hotly.

" That depends upon whether you approve of yesterday's gift to me, — whether it is one you would have offered to any other girl of your acquaintance.

Yet why should we quarrel over a box of millinery?" she adds, with a contempt for his expen-
sive present, in which Urquhart rejoices, as in
many more of her small ignorances. Just now
he is uncomfortably in fear lest she should press
home the question whether he would have given
his heap of millinery to any of his city friends;
and he is only too glad to find the very low esti-
mate she puts upon it — too small for a discussion.

"Why, indeed, should we quarrel over a trifle?"
he says, with alacrity.

"I showed you last evening," Milicent goes on,
not heeding his cheerful interruption, "how I shall
look when I am dressed as girls in my position
usually are; and you seemed satisfied."

"That is too feeble a word. I was charmed."

"I will keep to my poor gowns while I am on
the island, where I am as out of place in the others
as a sailor in 'longshore toggery," she says with a
smile. "Your pretty things can wait until — until
I am married. Till then, as Stephen wisely said,
it would be foolish to tramp about here, decked
out as a fine lady, — foolish and inconvenient.
Whereas, in this dress" —

"In this dress you have no excuse to urge why
you shall not go out sailing with me now."

For he knows very well Milicent will find no excuse in the southeasterly wind, which might have
dismayed some fair yachtswomen he had sailed away
from at Grand Manan; but which only brings the
sea-sparkle into this girl's eyes, and the wild-rose
color to her cheeks.

As they cruise about, outside the harbor, they can see how the wind drives the breakers in, against the outgoing tide, which, with its rapid rush through Grand Passage, repels them in long, heaving billows, that have not time to break until they are pushed back beyond the black point of Peter's Island : when they join again, in white and angry ranks, that rush on to the narrow pass, to be again repulsed. On the Long Island shore is the same rush : the breakers, like huge white-maned sea-things, chasing each other into the cleft point.

Then comes the pause, so brief here, a breathing-space between the falling and the rising tide. The steady surge of the tide-rip in its long white line shows when it turns ; and Milicent immediately proposes to pass into the harbor, and to sail the whole length of the village, past the high knoll which looks down on the white street and over the Bay of Fundy. " You said you had not been up there, but in a fog ; and now it is so clear, we 'll have the best view of the setting sun from there."

But who can count upon a sunset, even when the first red tints are deepening in the west ?

Or who can count upon an hour's sentimental journey with Milicent ?

" Look, there is a trawler coming in, and it not yet Saturday ! " she cries, as they skim into the passage. " See the two boats floating after her. It is old Angus — no, but some one from Freeport yonder in the cove. See, she is sailing over there. Very well : I don't know why old Angus should have had such luck again ; it is n't long since he came in before the week was up, with such a fare of cod, — a hundred and fifty thousand pounds aboard his schooner!"

"Why, what a little fisher-maiden is lost to the island when the Undine carries you away! I dare say, now, you understand this trawling?"

She nods. "A hook on every yard or so of line, sunk straight, and anchored at each end" —

"And know the whole tribe of cold-blood relations by sight, — cod, hake, haddock, pollock; which of them was marked by her grimy finger-tips, when they slipped out of old Dame Nature's hand?"

She nods again. "If you should have spent all your substance on traveling, and should have to turn fisherman in earnest, — only not here," she interrupts herself quickly; "in — in the Mediterranean, for instance — Do they have coddies there?"

She leans forward, laughing; then with a sharp cry, —

"Oh, look, look! The child! He is caught in the tide-rip — he will certainly be drowned!"

The shifting of the sail just there shows them both what it had hidden: a crazy boat with a small, fair-haired boy in it; far out in the Passage, caught in the swirling eddies which look so smooth and glassy, and which are so treacherous.

It is the hour when the tide is running in through this strait between St. Mary's Bay and Fundy. Many a stout fisherman, ignorant of the currents, and entangled in them just here, might lose heart.   But the child, unconscious of the perilous net spread for him in those smoothly circling lines, is calmly paddling about; and only when his oar is wrenched out of his small brown hands, by the invisible power, he gives a cry, more of astonishment than fear.   It rings out over the water, and blanches Milicent's white face yet more.

At her quick gasp, Urquhart turns to look at her, for an instant removing his eyes from the boat yonder.

What is it her eyes say to him?

It is in answer to them that Urquhart, his lips set, and a half-resentful fire in his glance, seizes the tiller-ropes out of her cold hands, and runs the boat into a pool in the ledge.   Without a word, he lifts her out upon the rock ; and before she knows what he would do, he has pushed off again into the stream, he has crowded on all sail, and is flying before the wind into that tangled net, winding now closer and closer about the helpless boy.

One moment Milicent stands there, the tide gliding by her so fast that these very rocks where Urquhart has left her seem to heave.   The next moment she has sunk on her knees, unconscious of movement, though her trembling limbs refuse to support her ; unconscious of prayer, though her hands are clasped before her ; unconscious of self, and only gazing out, with all her soul in her eyes, to those two boats,—the one caught in the tide-rip's circling sweep, the other skimming towards it, with the wind in the full sail.

One moment : then she brushes her hand hastily

across her eyes. What blurs them so that she sees not two boats, but only one?

Two? Yes; the other upturned, drifting, its white wing spread drenched and helpless in the water.

There is a cry, a shout from land. The girl, her whole soul in her straining eyes that never move from yonder point upon the waters (though she can see nothing but two boats that float keel upward now),—the girl hears nothing consciously: knows nothing, till across that blue expanse there shoots a dory, with a man bent to the oars.

Her white lips part then. "Stephen! O Stephen!" and then it is easy to say, "O God! O God!"

For human help makes us believe in God's.

If Stephen lifts up his head to look at her, she does not know. All she knows is that he can thrid that net of waters as none other can : and that, a moment more, and he has lifted a limp and dripping burden into his boat.

And now it plies about there — to and fro, to and fro. Is any one entangled in the rigging of the overturned sail-boat?

A dimness as of thick gray mist closes round Milicent.

She has not swooned away; but somehow she knows nothing, until there is a step upon the rock, and Stephen stands before her.

She does not know she is still kneeling; she does not move, but looks up half blindly into Stephen's face.

It is very pale and grave, as he lifts her to her feet.

"Come away, Milly. The worst is over. He will live."

" He — will — live " —

"They have brought him to, at last. He opened his eyes just as I came away."

She stands trembling, clinging to his arm with both her hands; but his tidings have brought back a tinge of color to her face. Or is it the reflection of the sunset's lingering glow, that reddens the brown rocks where she stands, and goes rippling with the treacherous currents over Grand Passage?

Stephen, looking down into her face, draws a hard breath. So! all her thought is for this Urquhart, this stranger —

" I knew you would save him," she says, softly. " *You* would save him, if any one could. They have brought him to — and he has asked for me ? "

" No — that is — I do not think he has had time to understand."

" But you will take me to him," she says, clasping her hands over his arm. And then, the light coming into her eyes and the color with a rush into her upturned face: " It was a brave thing and a noble, Stephen — to fling away his life, to save the child's. You will take me to him, and let me tell him so ? "

Stephen is silent an instant. Milicent, suddenly looking up questioningly into his grave face, remembers, with a pang. Has she hurt Stephen, with her eagerness ?

But he is saying, —

" Urquhart is at Mrs. Featherstone's, Milly."

" Yes. Well, that is quite near."

" And the boy was Mrs. Featherstone's."

" Dickon? Naughty little Dickon, who never will keep out of mischief! Poor little fellow, no doubt he has learned a lesson now."

" A lesson he will need never more, Milly. Come, dear, you had best let me take you home now. Urquhart will be able to follow, after a time."

But the girl is looking at him with wide, frightened eyes.

" Never more, Stephen? He — he is *dead?*" And then, with a piteous cry, " Oh, and I let him almost throw away his life for nothing, — for nothing! Let me go to him, Stephen, — let me go to him ! "

Stephen hesitates. The drowned boy lies in the room through which Milly must pass to reach Urquhart, — Milly, who has known so little of death, and yet has a dread, a shrinking from it, beyond words.

She seems to divine what is passing through his mind. She looks up at him with a ghost of a smile. " The child he would have died to save," she says softly. " Oh, Stephen, he must be so sorry, so sorry! Poor little Dickon! You will take me to see him ? "

The short walk to the cottage on the hillside is in silence. Stephen feels the thrill that runs through Milicent, as she rests her hand more heavily on his arm when they near the gate, and see the neighbors clustered about it. Most of the men are away at the fishing; but the women are out, in eager knots, that take Stephen's memory back to the day when the boats came in after the storm, and brought the Undine with them. Is Milicent thinking of that, too?

He cannot tell: she is hurrying along, with her eyes fixed on the cottage in a straining sort of way, as if seeing nothing nearer. Once or twice her foot has slipped on the pebbled path between the fish-flakes, as if she might have fallen if he had not led her on. One woman would have stopped her for a bit of whispered gossip over poor Widow Featherstone's sad loss, and the brave young gentleman; but Stephen puts her quietly aside, and leads the girl up the two or three low front steps.

The cottage stands, like its neighbors, with its gable to the street. One large bow-window is all ablaze with flowering geraniums; the other, on the opposite side of the front door, is set out with lollipops to tempt the village children; with a roll or two of gay prints; a scarlet japanned tea-chest; a slanting box of sugars; a knot of ribbons and artificial roses overhanging all, from some sort of an erection in the midst. But it is not into this, the village shop (successful rival of the Boston trader's on the pier opposite), but into the corresponding room across the box-passage, that Stephen is now leading Milicent. He would fain have taken her in some other way; but the room where they have laid Urquhart has no entrance save through this.

At first Milicent is passing through blindly, as it were, suffering Stephen to guide her, and only looking down blankly on the diamond-pattern of the strip of home-made carpet she is treading. Then suddenly she glances up, and her shrinking eyes take in the whole scene.

The ruddy afternoon glow fills the room: there are no shutters to exclude it jealously from the house of mourning. It creeps in at the side-window, through the screen of gay geraniums, and flits cheerily about, until it reaches a table drawn out from the wall, — a table where lies something, long, and still, and stiff, beneath the straight white folds of a sheet.

The mother is seated on the farther side of it. She does not heed the tearful women round her; she does not see Milicent, who has withdrawn her hand from Stephen's arm, and stops short, startled and trembling.

The mother is not trembling. The child might have been asleep, for all the sign she gives. She sits there as she might have sat beside his crib, not so many years ago, smoothing the sheet slowly and slowly over the still form, as she might have smoothed the coverlet above her slumbering little one. But she is not looking at it. With stony blue eyes, and round, dazed face, out of which the ruddy bloom has fled, she is staring straight across the dead child's body, to the opposite wall: to the picture of the late Captain Featherstone's tomb.

To Milicent, that picture, with its weeping-willow and its drooping mourner, might be merely a dismal thing to shiver over ; as to Urquhart, it has been something quaint, for a kindly laugh. But Mrs. Featherstone must find something more than just a work of art to be proud of : for her lips are moving, though no sound comes from them.

The ink of the lines written on the imaginary tombstone of the man who lies under the sea is not yet brown with time ; some one standing on that side of the room, and observing the direction of Mrs. Featherstone's eyes, reads them off, in a high-pitched tone of exhortation : —

"Death reaps the field,
And fishes the sea,
And carries from both
To the Far Countrie :
For the Lord of the sea and the land to keep,
Till the Trump wake the sea and the land from sleep."

But the mother gives no token that she hears ; and one of the women says, in a troubled way, " Pity the neighbors have taken the children off. If the poor soul could turn to, and take a hearty good cry, it would be the best thing for her."

" For it 's just a vale of tears," one placid body improves the occasion by observing, as she lifts the corner of her apron to wipe away an imaginary drop, — "just a vale of tears, and it 's not for us to set store on anything in it, and to make us idols " —

" There, there ! " A sharp-faced woman, the hard lines about her mouth grown tremulous, pushes past the speaker impatiently. " When the good

God gives one of us an innocent like that to love, it's if we didn't love it, He'd be angry with us. See here, you poor thing, I've fetched you in a cup of tea you had already set out. Just try one cup." Then, putting her hand on the poor, empty one that is slowly stroking down a fold of the sheet, she answers Milicent's wondering look by a significant glance down at the cup she holds: a child's mug, gilt and flowered.

At her touch — or perhaps the fumes of the tea rousing some association which words fail to reach — the mother turns and looks at the mug in her neighbor's hand.

"I set it out for him," she says in a low, strained voice. " The lad loved tea like a sailor, bless his heart, — like his father — and I'll never make another cup for him " —

As at that thought, she bursts into a passion of tears. And indeed, descending to bathos as it may, is not that the thought in every stricken mother-heart, — no more work for the little one, no more tender cares ?

" And he loved the sea so ! " she cries between her sobs, — " the cruel sea that has no heart in it ! The lad was never content with a firm floor and no offing ; let me head him on what course I would, he'd have been a sailor, like his father before him. And to think it's these two years we've knocked off the sea, — and now to lose him by it, like his father ! "

As the poor woman covers her face, sobbing, Milicent's cold hands turn back a corner of the

sheet, and she stands and looks down into the face
of the child for whom her lover might have died.

Poor little Dickon! That long, still form is
not like his. But this face, with the wet curls
about the dimpled, sunburnt cheek —

Poor little, merry-hearted fellow — he might be
lying here asleep!

Milicent stoops, and lays her warm lips to the
cold, calm brow. And with that strange touch
thrilling through and through her, she lets Stephen
lead her to the inner door, and open it for her.

She hardly knows that he has not followed her
in, she has gone so quickly forward, and is standing at the foot of the couch where Urquhart lies.

He does not open his eyes at once: when he
does, and sees who it is that has come in to him, he
closes them again.

Milicent waits a moment; then she almost whispers, —

"It is I. Do you not know me?"

He opens his eyes again at that, and looks
across at her, where she stands blushing before
him, and smiling — with a quiver about the lips
fresh from kissing the drowned boy her lover
nearly died to save.

"Know you? Yes, I know you," he says bitterly, at last. "Why do you come here to me,
Milicent? Would you have come just so, if I had
died the death you sent me to?"

She stares as if she cannot understand. Then,
very slowly, —

"I — sent you to?"

" You sent me to,—without one word, one breath, to hold me back from the death's-errand your eyes bade me go upon. Mind you," he says, raising himself on his elbow, further to emphasize his words, — " mind you, I should have gone, in any case. God forbid that I could have stood aside, and seen that child swept to its fate alone. But that you — you who knew the danger even better than I — you who should have had a woman's heart in your breast for your lover, — that *you* should have sent me to my death, without one word, without one sign that you would care to hold me back " —

" Come, Milly." It is Stephen's voice that speaks to the trembling girl. " The doctor is here. They sent across to the Cove for him ; he is just coming in." Then quietly to Urquhart, as if he had not heard what was just passing on his entrance : " He is coming to see *you*, Urquhart : but I am not sure that Milly here has not the greater need of him. I found her kneeling on the rock where you had left her, more dead than alive."

She does not seem to hear his words : but Urquhart's " Milicent ! " draws her to him.

That is the doctor's voice, speaking in an undertone in the outer room.

Milicent draws her hands swiftly away from Urquhart, and turns her wet face round upon Stephen : and they go away together.

But Stephen knows that he has given her back to Urquhart.

IX.

An undulating bank of green, against the sky; a tiny harbor deepening between jagged black fangs of rock, foaming as the waves fling over them; the island edged with black where the sea laves it; and, above, the russet-brown trap-rock rising in flights of steps and blocks, and here and there a broken shaft, to the grassy summit. A low crest of spruce and fir darkening this —

"Is this your Birthday Island, Milicent?" asks Urquhart, when, after a couple of hours' run before the wind, Stephen makes ready to take in sail. "I had no idea it was so large a bit of land as this. Are you sure it is devoid of water?"

"There is not a drop of fresh water on it, so luckily it can never be inhabited," says Milicent. "There is no inch of it Stephen and I have not explored; you see, every one of my birthdays we keep here, like this one, by a gypsy tea-party. But you run no risk of suffering from thirst; for I have a kettle of water, and intend to make a famous cup of tea, which you will remember all the rest of your life."

"Nevertheless, I wish I had brewed a bowl of punch, or brought some claret. Tea is but poor stuff," says Urquhart, with contempt for the mild beverage.

"Not as I brew it," declares Milicent, good-humoredly. "It makes a wonderful difference, to boil the kettle out-of-doors. Wait until you taste the cup of tea I will give you."

The girl is radiant with excitement and happiness. The day is perfect, the wind in the right direction, the yacht in charming order, and Miss Ursula's unwonted good-speed had sounded like a sailor's cheerful whistling for the wind. The devotion of the two men, each inclined to vie a little with the other in attentions to her, is enough to turn a wiser head than Milicent's : though it has its natural drawbacks, as appears when Urquhart, who was skipper of the yacht, finds himself quite useless on the island. Only Stephen can drive three sticks in the ground in the most approved way, to suspend the kettle gypsy fashion; the water being far too precious for experimental hanging. Stephen can best decide where the fire should be built, so that it should be sheltered from the wind, yet have sufficient draught. As the hamper is his own, packed by himself, he is certainly the proper one to unpack it. So on the old principle that every dog will have his day, Stephen is having a remarkably good one.

To satisfy one person is not difficult; two may tax the wisdom of a Solomon. But Milicent is young enough, and daring enough, to make the effort with a belief in her own success. She flits about, seeking discoveries of something hidden safely away the year before, for future use; or making allusions to events of some precious expedition : allusions which have to be explained to Urquhart, when they sound trite, and scarcely worth the trouble of repetition.

Perhaps Urquhart might have borne with equanimity the fact that there is a large part of Milicent's life with which Stephen is very closely associated, if she had not declared him awkward and decidedly in her way, and ended by blandly advising him to make himself comfortable under the shade of a fir-bush, until she had prepared the tea, and had time to wait upon him. Urquhart could not deny his awkwardness; no doubt he was doing more to retard than to help ; but while Milicent is carrying her fox safely, her goose is in mischief.

Urquhart has thrown himself down on an uncomfortable rock, his face turned seaward, pretending to enjoy a cigar, but in reality chafing and irritating himself because he was born without eyes in the back of his head.

When Milicent comes to him, and with a little rustic courtesy announces tea, he does not look at her, nor move in the smallest degree; but goes on smoking, and watching the gulls flying landward.

"Come and see how nice everything is," urges Milicent, flushed and pleased with her rural housekeeping.

"Thanks," says Urquhart, still not looking at her. "I am not in the least hungry."

"But something might tempt you. We have chicken, duck, a fish-pie" — and she runs over glibly quite a list of dainties, which do sound appetizing after an early lunch followed by a long sail. Urquhart is hungry, — quite famished, he would have said, if his ill-humor had not overcome his appetite; but he sits quite still, observing the perturbed flight of the gulls.

"Are you ill?" asks Milicent, anxiously.

"Not in the least."

"Has anything happened to you?"

He shrugs his shoulders at this question, but makes no reply.

"Of course, if you have no appetite, I cannot be expected to offer you one," flashes out Milicent. "But I should think that on my birthday, and the last one here, and when I have done everything" —

"You might do more than you do," says Urquhart, at last looking up at her, with some qualms of conscience when she reminds him that it is her birthday.

"I thought something lay astern of your loss of appetite," declares Milicent, with a laugh. "Please do not propound riddles. What is it I have done, or left undone?"

"I really do not mind being called awkward and useless, for I have not the slightest talent for housekeeping, like some men I know." Of course he means Stephen. "But that is scarcely sufficient ground for you to leave me alone for a whole hour, while you spend it in flirting with Ferguson over a tea-kettle."

"It has not been a half hour, if the sun is correct." Milicent glances at the luminary, and then adds gravely, "How can you be so foolish? I have been trying to keep Stephen from remembering this is his last birthday feast. Hereafter I must look to you for them."

"You are always doling out your attentions scrupulously; so much for my share, and then a justly even measure for Ferguson. Now, Ferguson has nothing in the world to do with you."

"Hush!" she says, quickly. "He may hear you."

"If he does, it will make no difference, especially as I intend to tell him the same thing myself," replies Urquhart, not lowering his voice a tone.

"What will you tell him? That you object to my doling out to him a little friendship, when he has been so kind? Why should you be so miserly, when I have given you " —

"What have you ever given me? Only your liking, you told me once."

"But that was some time ago. Time brings change — sometimes," says Milicent, sententiously.

"And I have gained a little by time and its changes?" asks Urquhart, leisurely.

"You forge ahead rather fast," says Milicent, laughing and blushing. "Yet this I will confess," — seeing his face fall: "I think it is much nicer to love than to like."

"At last you have learned it!" exclaims Urquhart, with effusion, as he springs to his feet.

But Milicent as quickly moves away towards the

table-rock where tea is served, and where Stephen is patiently waiting for them. "That is right," she says, nodding saucily as she looks over her shoulder at Urquhart. "I was very sure you were hungry, languishing as you seemed to be."

Urquhart thinks the tea Milicent has drawn the best he ever tasted; but Stephen detects a slight flavor of smoke, — a flavor not generally approved by tea-lovers. The tea-room is perfect: this small green island set in a waste of aqua marine; out farther, beyond soundings, the water a deep blue. Behind them, the few houses straggling up the island ridge at home show sharply cut against the lilac sky; and the sun, round and glowing like a blood-red moon, is just ready to dip down into the ocean, out of sight.

Urquhart has happily recovered his good-humor, and all three are merry over the gypsy meal; until at last Milicent declares there is not a drop of water in the kettle, and that they must be preparing to return.

"What a dreadful waste a feast is!" she remarks as she makes ready to repack the hamper.

"There spoke Miss Ursula's own niece," declares Stephen, laughing. "Cannot you manage the 'remainder biscuit after the voyage'? The feast is yours, you know."

"And have the soup made of the chicken-bones to-morrow?" suggests Urquhart.

"Many a true word is spoken in jest. That is just what Aunt Ursula would do, if I put the chicken back into the hamper; and it would be a

very good soup.   But I have a desire to make an
end of our feast, not to have a second edition of
it to-morrow, — just as I have heard of friends
breaking the glasses from which they have drunk a
toast.   Very extravagant, no doubt; but sentiment
is generally a spendthrift."

" It will be a tremendous waste," says Urquhart,
leaning on his elbow at her feet, and laughing up
at her as she stands with the heaped plate in both
hands, the sunset shining in her eyes and in the
bright, breeze-roughened hair. Afterwards, to both
men will come back, with added meaning in it,
the picture she makes there, against the glowing
background of the sea.

" But what shall I do with it? Stephen, do you
remember Aunt Ursula used to tell you, when you
wasted the bread she gave you, because it was not
buttered, that some day you would wish for a piece
of bread? I feel horribly like Aunt Ursula at
this waste, and recall all kinds of ill omens to the
wasters."

" Let the gulls have it, Milly. They are always
needy beggars," suggests Stephen; and then he
adds, " What a stir. they are making! They
ought to be roosting, instead of keeping up such a
noise."

" There must be a storm coming. At any rate,
we ought to be off. I will have the china packed
by the time you have the yacht ready."

" A storm!" exclaims Urquhart. " What are
you thinking of, Milicent? I never saw a clearer
sky, nor less sign of a change in the weather."

" The gulls are wiser than we. Besides, the sun is setting ominously red. We can manage to get up a blow at short notice in these waters. Please make haste, Stephen," urges Milicent, uneasily.

" There is no use in starting until the tide turns, for the little wind has almost died out, and will hardly help us. Do not mind the gulls; they are foolish birds," says Stephen, cheerfully.

" Proverbially so. Will you smoke ? " Urquhart proposes to him.

The two men stroll off, leaving Milicent to repack the hamper. When she has finished, she comes and seats herself by Urquhart, who takes this his first opportunity to whisper in her ear some soft words of thanks as well as approbation, for her confession that it is better to love than to like.

It is a confession he would not often entrap her into making. Milicent has her moods, sometimes of the imperative ; but there is always the brightest sunshine after a storm. Never a cold, murky sky, well named sullen, depresses Urquhart's love. Capricious clouds and fitful gusts, he is very sure of ; an electric shock at times ; but in the end they prove beneficial to his atmosphere.

As an on-looker (which Stephen has taught himself is his only part now, after what he believed to be Milicent's confession of love for Urquhart, that day she said the cottage must not be her home) Stephen might very well have thought Milicent cared most for him. If when what to Stephen seems a lover's quarrel rises like a small cloud between them, as it blows over, Milicent would be very gracious, and would meet Urquhart nearly half-way towards a reconciliation, she never goes meekly the whole way, and says she is sorry, as she does with her old friend. Her old friend, Stephen says to himself, bitterly; convinced that there is less friendliness in her feeling for Urquhart, and that the past is a sealed book he dares not open, save in dreaming over it alone.

Stephen has stretched himself on the grass, a little way from the two, and has his eyes shut, so they think he is asleep; that is, if they think very much about him. For Milicent is absorbed in listening to Urquhart's low-spoken words; sometimes whispering back to him, until he is persuaded that the birthday festival is not at all a failure, as he once decided it.

Suddenly there comes a soft "rip-rapse, rip-rapse," against the rocks; and Stephen, who is very far from being asleep, and who has only good-naturedly kept himself out of the way, knows that the tide has turned. Presently an odd, sobbing sound in the freshening wind causes him to open his eyes, and spring to his feet. As the sun dips down, the wind is rising, and that is a ragged brown cloud which is driving before it.

"There is a squall coming, but we had better catch it here," Stephen says to Urquhart, who is observing nothing farther from him than Milicent.

"It seems very far off, and night is so near. You remember we have no moon."

"There will only be the danger of a thorough wetting, even if we remain here all night," replies Stephen.

"Milicent could not possibly remain here all night. It is absurd to propose it," says Urquhart, with heat.

"That is a very ugly cloud, Stephen!" exclaims Milicent, who has been intent on looking up some small articles, and packing them, so has just rejoined the two men. "What had we best do? Is it safe to start?"

She naturally turns to Stephen for advice; for he is not only the better sailor, but he knows perfectly the weather-signs which nature hangs out for the mariner's guidance.

Her reliance upon Stephen's judgment irritates Urquhart, who answers shortly, —

"We will be compelled to start. A capful of wind won't hurt us."

"'Blow risks!' Mr. Urquhart would like to be nautical enough to say," puts in the girl, slyly.

"The tide too is in our favor," he hurries on. "We'll get in before the storm breaks. We must be quick, though. Come on, Milicent, don't stop," he adds, authoritatively; for she has started forward to put out the smouldering fire.

"I cannot run the risk of having the trees burnt," she explains. "A few minutes can make no difference."

Stephen is at once at her side, and tramples out the fire; while Urquhart mutters an impatient as well as an evil-sounding ejaculation, and strides off to the yacht. He feels no particular sentiment for the island, that he should scruple to consign the trees to the flames.

A moment afterwards, Stephen shoulders the hamper, and Milicent follows close behind him.

"He has not the least idea of the danger we are running," she is saying, as she hurries after Stephen.

"It is his boat," replies Stephen ; and he might have added, his sweetheart.

"What nonsense! If we are drowned, who cares who owned the boat?"

"Urquhart does not like my interference ; that you can see for yourself"—begins Stephen.

"How slow you are! One would suppose you had nothing more important to do than to talk," says Urquhart impatiently, but to Milicent, not Stephen.

"The most important matter is to save our lives," replies Milicent, quite coolly, rejecting Urquhart's hand stretched out to help her into the yacht. "I have no intention of going on board."

"You cannot possibly spend the night here. I could not think of permitting you to do so," says Urquhart, again extending a helping hand.

Still Milicent hesitates ; until Stephen says, "We have a chance to get home before the squall breaks. At any rate, we know it is coming, and will be prepared."

Urquhart has put both hands in his pockets, in great wrath ; and walks to the stern of the yacht, where he stands with his back to 'the island. A moment afterwards, Milicent joins him.

"Are you not going to help Stephen ? He needs you," she says, curtly.

But if Stephen needs help, Urquhart does not want advice. " What is the use in taking in every rag?" he asks, finding Stephen making all taut and fast. " You might as well give her more help from her sails. If Milicent were not on board, I would crowd on everything, and show you the Undine's temper."

" It is well, on your own account, that Milicent is on board, then," answers Stephen, quite coolly. " That cloud will bring a change of wind, and the less canvas you have to show, the better. You have seen nothing of our storms as yet: to-morrow you will have had another experience."

" I have sailed in many seas. One can't always have a ' ladies' wind.' I hardly fancy your storms are unique. It appears to me our best plan would be to make a dash for port, — not get ready for a storm miles away as yet."

" At any rate, we do not need two skippers. The yacht being yours, I am under command," says Stephen at once.

He is relieved to find that since Urquhart takes the whole responsibility he is less inclined to be foolhardy and venturesome, and that he only puts out a small show of canvas. But even that flutter of white makes Stephen uneasy. He would much rather have the Undine meet the storm under bare poles. Yet with that singular shrinking from interference with another man's rights, which men show in all professions and business, Stephen leaves Urquhart to his own devices, and goes to where Milicent is sitting.

"You would be far better in the cabin, Milly," he tells her.

But the girl shakes her head decidedly.

"No, Stephen, no. Alone in there?"

"Two hands may be wanted here, Milly."

"Then you must keep me too. Ah, Stephen, do you think I could bear it, to leave you here, if the storm should really come? I should be fancying all sorts of horrors in every wave, in every gust of wind."

"Since when have you turned coward, Milly?"

But he opposes her no longer: only, before he takes the tiller from her, he brings a tarpaulin, and begins to wrap it round her.

"Wait until the storm comes, Stephen; it is so heavy," pleads Milicent.

"It is here already, Milly."

Stephen is right: the storm is upon them. He has hardly finished speaking, when the great drops are pelting down out of the gathering blackness overhead. They wet the two men in an instant. There is a vivid flash of lightning and a burst of thunder from that overhanging cloud, which appall Milicent, unused to thunderstorms: until she is glad to hide her eyes under the tarpaulin's fold. When she shrinkingly peers forth again, the gust of rain has passed; but the wind has increased in fury, and she can just dimly see, through the lowering darkness, that Urquhart has had perforce to take Stephen's advice, and is furling even the close-reefed foresail.

Milicent's presence has not prevented a trial of

the little yacht's temper. Buffeted by the waves, and driven by the wind, which Urquhart's small show of cloth made more dangerous, the Undine is about as manageable as the fisherman and his wife found their beautiful changeling. All that can be done is to let her lie breasting the heavy seas, under bare poles.

The wind changed to the northward of east, when the squall blew up; and under the pitch-black sky the great waves are bearing the yacht like a toy away to the southwestward, — away from home, and down into the howling solitudes of the Atlantic.

Pitch-black the night is, overhead, as the long hours go by; and all around, the moan and rush of foaming swirls, closing about, and threatening to bury the Undine. With every moment, she dips and ships a flood over her bow; and when she sinks her stern, the waves that chase her leap as if to spring over the rail. It is as if those great waves were toying with the fragile thing: playing with her as a cat plays with a mouse, before dealing the death-blow.

Once or twice, Stephen has glanced across in the direction of the cabin: would not Milicent be safer there? But how would she bear, alone, the Undine's laboring, her frantic plunges, baited as she is by all those clamorous waves? "No — no" — she answers breathlessly, when Stephen, by dint of shouting, conveys to her what he would have her do.

There is a moment's pause; and then:

"Urquhart shall take care of you there, Milly,"

he makes her understand, whether or not she
catches half the words.　"One is enough to watch
the Undine here."

But the girl only repeats her passionate refusal;
and indeed, would she be safer there? It is a
question none could answer; while no doubt to be
shut into the cabin, with the skylight closed and
the companion shut, would be like lying in one's
grave at the day of doom, while the whole earth
quakes and trembles above and around. At least,
so it seems to Milicent's shuddering fancy.

So the three keep all together where they are.
It is impossible to talk; they do not even see each
other; all that they can see, and dimly, is the
threatening foam as it flies past them, almost overhead, and confounds them with the sense of their
own helplessness and hopelessness. It is hard
enough for the two men; but for Milicent —

"Milicent" —

She cannot hear him speak to her; but she is
glad to feel her lover's presence in the darkness
which has come on with such appalling suddenness.
Urquhart has thrown his arm around her, and
holds her fast, so that they shall not be separated
even in death. Stephen also is close to her, — as
far as life apart.

Stephen's hand clenches with a grip upon the
tiller, and steadies itself there.

In all this blackness of darkness, there is but
one cold ray of comfort reaches Stephen : that no
one could live long in such a sea as this. Death
must come after a very brief struggle, he is sure,

even for himself: and he is the strongest of the three. And there is no marrying nor giving in marriage, in that safe harbor they seem bound to. He will no longer have to stand aside and make way for Urquhart. There will be no more heart-burnings and jealousy, such as he is undergoing now: for in the darkness and fury of the storm, he knows Milicent and Urquhart are clinging to each other, and neither is altogether wretched, even with death so near. Stephen would willingly die to have those arms clinging to him.

But he puts away these thoughts from him with a great dread. Would not Milicent suffer an un-told torture, even in a short death? Little Milly, his playmate and only love! Is this to be the end of all her prettiness and charm, that have made the only two men she has known love her?

He sees her struggling in the hungry maw of every wave that is turning up, livid and foaming, out of the wide-reaching darkness. He hears her sinking wail in every far-drawn soughing of the wind, that only falls back to gather strength anew. Little Milly, — and he cannot save her, cannot even die for her. While this Urquhart —

But Stephen is a strong man; stronger than he that taketh a city: he puts that thought out of his mind. Milly — and Milly's God, who only can deliver her.

So the moments go by, each black with the shadow of death. But one there comes, with a special horror of its own. It is when the Undine quivers with a fiercer wrench and jar: when the

11

tiller rests slack in Stephen's grasp, and he knows
that the rudder is gone.

Then he leans forward impulsively, and reaches
out his hand. "Milly" — he says. But the wind
has snatched his voice away, and the girl does not
hear; and it is Urquhart's wet sleeve that his out-
stretched hand has touched.

Light dawns on the darkest hour, it is said ; and
after that, little by little, the wind draws off, the
fury of the sea begins to die away. The stars
struggle out through clouds that veer about; and
presently these trail away, and leave the skies clear
for that cold shining. And though the sea still
works tempestuously, there is no more danger ; the
storm is over.

The storm is over, though the wind is still fitfully violent; for how could it lull itself at once
into a perfect calm, when it had been for hours
lashing itself into the wildest fury ? Neither can
the passionate, eager heart soothe itself by a mere
longing, into the saint's tranquillity.

Whither will the Undine now be driven ? And
where are they ? The great Atlantic gives them no
hint, as she rocks them on her broad bosom.

Urquhart is hopeful enough. They cannot have
been driven very far to sea, he thinks : the Undine is in good condition ; and they have the stars
to steer by. Stephen's hand still grasps the rudderless tiller, which he keeps fixed in the grooves,
that the others may not guess its uselessness. Let
the cheerful morning sun light up their situation,
before Milicent must know it.

"Must we drift so helplessly? The wind seems to have veered, in clearing," says Urquhart, with a glance at the pole-star, as the clouds clear away.

But Stephen only returns, "Wait for sunrise;" and Urquhart, who is candid enough to know the other has proved himself the better sailor of the two, has nothing to answer, and sits silent at Milicent's side, while Stephen follows his lead in pointing out the constellations to her.

"See, Milly, there comes out Mooin the Bear; and there are the Hunters after him, pursuing him to his Den in Berenice's Hair. I was just thinking of my hunting-days among the Tusket lakes, when my Micmac guide and I lost the trail, and found it by following the Hunters."

"The Hunters?" repeats Urquhart.

"Ay. You see, the Micmacs know that bears have no tails to speak of, but are apt to have a following of hunters. These all have their names; and one of them has his kettle: see, the small star yonder. Milly, do you think that now the stars are out, and the storm is over, you could get a little sleep in the cabin?"

It is still too dark to see the face she turns up to him as he speaks; but the gesture is eloquent enough. She has confronted death too lately, to bear solitude.

"Let me stay. You know I am well wrapped, and — and indeed, indeed, I could not stay alone."

Urquhart is of opinion that Ferguson needs rest, and that he himself might as well steer awhile (with Milicent's help). But Stephen does not take the hint: to the suppressed indignation of Urquhart, who does not know what reason Stephen has for declining to relinquish the tiller.

Under the circumstances, there is not much speech among them. The waves have the hour to themselves, while the stars flicker in their dying struggles, and are put out, one by one; and the morning-star is risen, and the day begun.

Milicent has many thoughts to keep her silent. In her efforts to reassure Urquhart's anxiety that night, she forgot much of her girlish shyness, and unwittingly gave him a deeper insight into her feeling for him than he would have discovered in months of ordinary intercourse. Indeed, she might have opened her whole heart to him, and made some startling revelations, if Stephen had not been there. For the future is very doubtful; only the present is theirs; and all that she had deferred for a future telling, she would have wished to speak now. Only, what she would have said is meant for Urquhart's ear alone — a death-bed confession she tells herself that she can make as well in heaven.

Stephen's grave voice, when he does speak, irritates Urquhart with the fear that it may hint to Milicent of their danger. Urquhart never dreams she understands as much of it as he himself, but asks no questions where she is not at all sure of true answers.

But it is Stephen alone, who through these dark hours faces the situation in all its horror. Where will the rudderless Undine be driven? What chance is there of being found? And how long could they survive, with neither provisions nor water? Alas for the remnants of their feast, of which they cheated frugal Miss Ursula's soup-pot, to feed the gulls. Miss Ursula has proved herself an oracle: and the unbuttered bread he once scorned, Stephen would now have been thankful for, to store away for Milicent. Death in a new and more dreadful form is before them.

Stephen shudders at the thought that one of them must survive the others. Not Milicent, he prays. There is a fiction in law, that a woman under such circumstances dies first. Stephen clings to it, as if the law were gospel. Even there, the great unselfishness of his love is shown; for it would be harder for him to see her die than to die himself. His present foreboding is a Nemesis cruelly punishing him for his almost fierce joy in their first danger. His fears are for Milicent: for himself, he dreads life much more than the death that may be very near him.

The morning comes very unexpectedly to Milicent and Urquhart: for Urquhart's watch had stopped; and though he had frequently wondered what time it could be, Stephen, who knew each hour by the stars, never hinted of this knowledge, as he did not wish Milicent to discover how long they had been driving before the wind.

The sun rises red and angry out of the sea. It points out the new anxiety, which Stephen can no longer keep from Milicent: it shows her that the rudder is gone, and the Undine helplessly adrift.

And yet, for all, after the first shock of that

surprise, it is impossible, at least for Milicent, not
to catch hope from the bright face of this new
day, that after the long northern morning twilight
shines on them at last.   From the first pale yellow
" rose of dawn " beginning to show itself out of
the darkness in the east, where the stars struggle
and struggle and die out: to the flames of the full
sunrise, spreading slowly, and deepening from east
to west and north and south. until the whole wide
sea takes up the radiance, wave after wave leaping
to catch it, and falling back with rainbow crest
and burnished hollow, in the level-drifting beams,
—from first to last, as Milicent watches it, hope
dawns the brighter within her.

In truth, it is hard to be afraid of the sea now ;
that joyous, dancing, rushing sea, the sunlight
flashing on and through the leaping waves, that
bear the Undine over the green hollows and the
frothing crests.   Stephen is making shift to use an
oar for rudder, thus partly to avoid the rough sport
those same merry-seeming waves might otherwise
make of the yacht : while the sun mounts higher
and higher, and three pairs of eyes are scanning
the great wilderness of water, in search of a welcome sail.

After all, it is Milicent who first sights a " three-
masted Yankee " ; a schooner, happily bearing
down towards the yacht, so that there is but little
difficulty in hailing her.   In less than an hour, the
three are standing on her deck, their adventure
well over ; the Undine made fast to the stern by
a rope, and looking far less battered and misused

than they who had ungratefully doubted her sea-
worthiness.

The rough sailors are kind and hospitable, and
soon have tea made, which is as nectar to the cast-
aways, though sweetened with coarse brown sugar.
Milicent's hard up-bringing has its advantages
here. She came out of the fold of the tarpaulin,
thanks to Stephen's forethought, perfectly dry;
ready, after her fast, to enjoy without squeamishness the sailor's hard-tack and salt pork. In the
captain's little cabin, with the port-hole shut, and
the green water rushing past it as the schooner lies
well over, Milicent afterwards throws herself down,
and soon sleeps the dreamless sleep of the weary.

Stephen and Urquhart have borrowed from the
sailors' kits while their own clothes are drying: and
they speedily discover that the nearest coast is
Maine; that the schooner is bound for St. John;
that they were a hundred miles from there when
they were rescued, and if this wind holds out, they
will be in the harbor in the afternoon. All very
pleasant to know, after such a night of anxiety.

Milicent's birthday will be an anniversary long to
be remembered by all three. Together they have
passed into the very shadow of death, and together
they have come out unscathed. For this they
might give a general thanksgiving: yet each one
has a special one. Urquhart, that he is at last
sure Milicent loves him; Milicent, that she knows
her own heart; and Stephen, that his wild wish
was not granted him, and Milicent is as far as
usual from being an angel or a saint.

X.

WHEN Milicent comes on deck, the harbor lies before her, aglitter in the evening sunlight. The round, fortress-like Partridge Island is passed. The city, with its background of green highlands, is rising, tier above tier, on its peninsula of rock thrust forward into the Bay of Fundy: Courtenay Bay to the right, and to the left the St. John River sweeping snow-drifts of foam along the tide, from the falling rapids in the gorge through which it tears its way.

The scene is a novel one to Milicent; she is pleased as a child with a new toy. The gayly flagged ships; the sturdy tugs darting here and there, with shrill whistle and loud puffings; the ferry-boat crossing to the Carleton side —

Milicent follows this last with her eyes, which sweep up the green heights of the Carleton suburbs, to the old martello tower, which she instantly pronounces (erroneously, but Stephen does not care to correct her; let the child enjoy her little romance) to be the old French fort defended by Charlotte de la Tour, under the French domination, against her husband's rival compatriot, Charnizay.

"Look!" the girl cries to Stephen, "it was there she drove away the ships of Charnizay, besieging her. And when he came again, by land, with her handful of men she kept his troops at bay for three long days; until that Easter morning, a traitor sentinel let them scale the walls, and forced her to surrender. And then the wretch, — Charnizay, I mean, — what must he do, the wretch, but in his rage at having granted terms to a woman backed by such a mere handful of a garrison, he broke them; and he made her stand, a rope about her neck, to see the execution of her whole brave garrison. It broke her heart, you know: she died a few days after."

As he watches her shining eyes upon it, Stephen is glad he did not set her right as to the fortification; since, of the old French fort of nearly two centuries ago, the site is all that now remains; and even that is beyond Milicent's range of vision from the schooner's deck. And she would not have had time to get over her disappointment, before Urquhart, who has been talking to the skipper, comes back, where she is standing with Stephen.

"Get your hat, Milicent," he says. "The captain has offered to send us ashore in his yawl."

"I have n't any hat," she answers. " I tried to save it from being crushed when Stephen wrapped me in the tarpaulin; but the wind took it out of my hands. It is the only thing lost, so don't look so worried."

" I can't see what is to be done, unless you wait here with Stephen until I go into the town and get a hat for you," Urquhart says, in a questioning, undecided way.

" We had better get away from here as soon as we can, Urquhart. The captain is going to unload at once, and Milicent will be in the way."

" But how can she go without a hat ? "

" Of what consequence is a hat, in comparison with getting her away from here ? " Stephen says, knowing from experience much more than Urquhart of coasting vessels and unloading.

" It is of a good deal of consequence to Milicent, who does not wish to be stared at as a buy-a-broom girl."

" Oh, I don't care in the least," declares Milicent. " One who has just faced death does not mind her fellow-mortals' gaze."

Still Urquhart is not satisfied.

" You don't suppose any one is going to remark on Milicent's being hatless," says Stephen, laughing at his squeamishness. " Two rough-looking fishermen and a girl with them, landing from a schooner, will never attract any one's attention. We are n't fine people, to be stared at."

There is something in this. They would never be taken as belonging to a class among whom to be bonnetless, even by accident, would be an impropriety. So Urquhart leads the way with Milicent, when the captain tells him the boat is ready.

They must row themselves, for he has no man to spare; and they are to leave the yawl in charge of a boatman until the captain can send for it.

"I could not think of steering. I should be run down by one of those pert little tugs," Milicent declares, as she takes her seat.

"Nobody asked you," remarks Urquhart. "You would have every rat on the wharf screaming to us at the novel sight of a woman steering. Stephen will have to pull two oars."

"I don't like the position of the Undine," says Stephen, after at least five minutes' steady but silent rowing. "Twice, since we left the schooner, has she escaped being run into, as by a miracle. She would be much safer in dock."

Urquhart looks around uneasily. Certainly the yacht's position is a precarious one. "We can't afford to lose her," he says. "She is our best chance of reaching home. If Milicent would not object to waiting for a few minutes on the pier, we could row back and tow the Undine to the dock."

"But Milly will object," replies Stephen, quickly.

"I shall do nothing of the kind. I will not have the yacht run any risk, through foolish fear for me."

"We will not be gone fifteen minutes," Urquhart assures her. "We will keep in sight of you, and you will be perfectly safe by that pile of boxes."

It proves a nook so very secure, that when Urquhart has placed her there, Milicent declares she

does not object at all to being left, and they need
not hurry on her account.

"But we will, though. Just show a white flag
if you are in distress, and we will be with you at
once. Come on, Ferguson: the sooner we are off,
the sooner we will return."

But Stephen lingers to be sure Milicent is not
afraid of being left; until Urquhart drags him off,
while she is saying: "What can happen to me? I
don't intend to move from here; and I am rather
too large to be taken off forcibly."

Indeed, as Milicent says, she knows nothing to
be afraid of; and she is infinitely interested in the
scene around her. Everything is a novelty to her
rustic eyes: the odd, low-swung wagons, with their
piles of goods; people running here and there, as
if they had not a minute to spare; even the wharf-
boys and the hack-drivers, those intolerable nui-
sances to respectable travelers, amuse Milicent by
their eagerness, as they stand in line, with beckon-
ing whips in hand, along the slope of the wharf:
for the Boston steamer has just come in.

There is a railing along the top of the wharf,
and a line of spectators gathering there, looking at
the landing of the travelers. The tide has fallen
its twenty or thirty feet, and the bridge of the
wharf swings down to meet it; and upon either
hand of the steep incline by which the passengers
mount, as they come ashore, the wooden walls
tower up, green with seaweed and white with barnacles. Between them sweeps the stream of pret-
tily dressed women, prolonging their visit to the

seashore by this fashionable rush up through the
Provinces; gorgeously adorned nurses, half wild
with their efforts to keep from sudden death re-
fractory children, who have no fear but of doing as
they are bidden; men in absurd costume, gotten
up, it is supposed, for comfort at the seaside. Is
the gay steamer a pest-house they are all eager to
escape from, so remorselessly are they crowding
and pushing?

It is all a grand panorama to Milicent; and
though, with the arrogance of youth, she criticises
the appearance of the women, on the whole she is
not sorry to think she will some day or other be
like them. It is the children who appear to her so
odd and overdressed; uncomfortable little mortals,
compared with the sturdy, ruddy fishermen's bairns
on the village street at home.

Milicent has seldom looked prettier than now,
as she stands leaning against the pile of boxes, her
great, earnest eyes taking in all these new scenes
and impressions. She is far too interested to feel
uncomfortable. Indeed, she has forgotten her own
existence: and her face, a perfect April sky, —
now clouding and tear-gathering, and a moment
after bright and laughing, — is a pretty study for
those who have an eye for this kind of picture.

" What a handsome girl, — but horribly bold! "
the ladies say as they pass poor unconscious Milicent. " Think of standing alone in all this crowd,
with no hat on ! "

" What, hide her pretty face? Not she! The
men will know her the next time they see her,"

comes the spiteful answer from one whose head-
covering is hardly worn because of the angels : they
keep so aloof from her vicinity.

The men know much better what a really bold
woman is like.

Though some of the fortunate ones, who have
no luggage, and no customs-officers to look after,
nor any of their women-kind with them, collect in
a group uncomfortably near Milicent, she gives
little heed to them, as there is nothing picturesque
nor amusing in their appearance. If she were
listening, she might discover that they are discussing her. Her hair, her eyes, her wild-rose bloom,
even her pose as she stands carelessly leaning
against the boxes, are freely commented on, much
as if she were a picture in an art-gallery.

Presently she looks towards them, but certainly
beyond them, and smiles and nods.

It is to Urquhart and Stephen, who are hurrying
to her. Urquhart sees the group of men ; and,
with a muttered expression of displeasure, strides
forward.

He is looking at and thinking of Milicent : or
he might avoid recognition. But in spite of the
growth of his beard, and his sunburnt face, as well
as his rough fisherman's suit, he is at once hailed
and captured as an acquaintance, yclept friend.
There is no getting away ; and Urquhart has to
shake hands, and explain that he has been yacht-
ing all summer, and has just put into St. John :
though he takes good care not to tell how he was
picked up at sea this morning, and whom he has

with him as companions, — neither in what waters he has fished, this pleasant summer through.

"It must be you she is nodding to, — that pretty girl minus a hat. Who is she?" asks one of the men, who thinks watching Milicent better pastime than questioning Urquhart about his travels.

"I rather think she is nodding to the man who was with me, making the Undine safe," says Urquhart coolly, not even glancing towards Milicent.

"Then you don't know her. I hoped you did. She is rarely beautiful."

"I thought you understood I have just landed," returns Urquhart briefly; and then answers some query as to his luck as fisherman.

The man who had assisted to make the Undine fast is just at Urquhart's elbow; but he hastens to Milicent.

"Are you very tired of waiting?" he asks.

"No, I have been very much amused. Fancy such fantastic dressing on the sea! I can't imagine how the women get on," says Milicent, forgetting her own disappointment when he objected to just such dressing on her part.

"I should n't think they could walk very far on the cliffs, with such heels to their boots; and there would not be much chance of their balancing themselves on the gunwale of a boat. But don't stand any longer in the sun, Milly. Urquhart will come as soon as he gets rid of his friends."

"But will he know where we are going?" Milicent asks, with a natural dread of separating in such a crowd.

" We 'll not go far; only out of the sun," Stephen promises.

Round on the other side of the boxes, they are not only out of the sun, but also out of view of Urquhart's acquaintances; and Milicent is just as much amused with the scene on the water as she has been with the panorama on the wharf. Before very long, Urquhart joins them.

"Why did n't you get a carriage? I am afraid they have all driven off," he says to Stephen.

" I hope they have. I would much rather walk," Milicent replies for him. "Did you see the way they dashed up hill? I should be frightened to death."

" But you can't walk without a hat," objects Urquhart.

" What are you going to do?" Stephen asks shortly, drawing Urquhart a little aside. He is not at all pleased with Urquhart's cool way of ignoring any knowledge of Milicent to his friends.

" I don't know yet. We can decide whilst we are driving."

" I think we had better know before. Milly might understand the dilemma. Of course none of your fine hotels will take two fishermen in."

" I think Milicent, and our having no luggage, will be our chief difficulty. Is there no chance of our getting away from here at once?"

" None whatever. You see, there is more amiss with the Undine than we thought at first. We shall have to hire a couple of men to sail her home when she is put in repair; and we must take the steam-

boat to Digby. Unfortunately, there is none until
to-morrow. Digby is our nearest point for home.
We can drive down the French shore; and from
there, with a favorable wind, we shall have but
two or three hours' sail across to Westport. The
Undine can come into St. Mary's Bay by Petite
Passage above Long Island, if she is ready for
us: if not, we can easily hire a boat to take us
across. But there is no means of getting away
from here until to-morrow."

"It 's unlucky. But of course it can't be helped.
At twelve o'clock last night, I would have been
glad to be cast on a desert island, so treacherous
I thought the sea. Miss Ursula must be slightly
worried."

"I don't believe any of the fishermen comforted
her, indeed. They have n't much faith in a brown
squall. But this is not deciding on our plans."

"Perhaps, then, we had better drive to the Dufferin. I was there before I went to Grand Manan,
and I know the proprietor. If you will let me out,
and drive on a little way, I will explain our position; and perhaps he can get the coast clear, so that
Milicent may be safely housed without being seen."

"It seems rather hard that we, who are doing no
wrong, should have to go to work surreptitiously,"
Stephen remarks, dryly. "I much prefer the ways
of a rough fishing village, where one is not so particular about the proprieties."

"No doubt you would: and you were angry that
I did n't introduce Milicent to that raft of idiots.
I never saw such a scowl as you gave them in pass-

ing.   As if I would permit her to be stared at, and commented on behind our backs!"

"I don't see what comments could be made, except that she has lost her hat," Stephen remarks, shortly.   "That was easily enough explained."

"Girls don't go roaming about with men not related to them"—

"I thought the squall was responsible for our being here," interrupts Stephen.

"But not for our going to the island.   The whole trouble has arisen from that."

"Then I wonder you did not object to it at the time"—Stephen begins, hotly.

"Nonsense: there was not the slightest impropriety in it.   You would n't have dragged Miss Ursula to your fête?   And if you had wished to do so, it would have been beyond your strength. Still, as things have turned out decidedly provokingly, we had better adopt the little fiction as old as Abraham, and pass Milicent off as the sister of one of us.   You may claim the relationship."

"Very well," Stephen says, shortly.   "Milly must be tired of waiting."

"Let me out at the Dufferin, and then drive round King Square.   Don't come back for me, but stop at the corner above, and I will come to the carriage," Urquhart directs the driver, as Stephen hands Milicent to her seat.

There is not much talking to be done by a girl who for the first time in her life finds herself in a carriage.   She clings to the strap a little breathlessly, when the horses dash up the steep incline of a street, as St. John horses have a knack of doing. But her momentary terror does not prevent her eager observation of everything. She turns from the forest of masts overhung by Prince William Street, to wonder at the broad edifice of creamy sandstone commanding the water with its dome and towers — a vast palace, it looks to her inexperienced eyes, knowing only the frame cottages on the island : until she is told it is the Custom-House. What a pile of buildings! and now they are glittering in the sunset, with rows upon rows of windows, tall and deep-set, the narrow spaces between them quaintly ornamented with crosses and diamonds done in bricks set cornerwise into the wall. Now and again, in the well-built, substantial streets, one comes upon a picturesque reminder of the great fire which a few years ago swept the city through and through, and smouldered in its ashes three months afterwards. Now it is a ruined mass built high upon a rock, with perhaps a flight of steps climbed by daisies and buttercups ; or a square, like a half-crumbled tower overgrown with vines. The living rock is cut through to form the level of the street; and here and there a fine house, perched high on its rocky base, sets its foot on the neck of its neighbor in the street below.

But it is at the shops that Milicent is all wonder and delight. Stephen laughs at her, insisting that at least the mode of trade in the village is more convenient, as everything to be bought is to be had in one small shop.

"Just as Mrs. Piggott thinks it is so much better to live in one room with her dozen children. It is so much handier for flogging the children, she told me one day."

Stephen thinks the children would prefer longer range; and Urquhart reminds her, for the third or fourth time, that she has no hat on, and must keep in the corner of the carriage, out of sight.

"Bother the hat!" Milicent exclaims each time; but submissively draws back into her corner, until she forgets, and looks out again.

The drive round the square is much pleasanter: Urquhart has gotten out, and Stephen encourages her to look. And now there is subject for new wonder: the trees of King Square, in the midst of which a fountain is playing, with a sound as of rushing rain. Milicent thinks the fountain a poor substitute for nature's hydraulics on the cliffs; but she recalls the balm-of-Gilead at home, with its scant, quivering crown of leaves; and fortunately Urquhart is not at hand to suggest that these trees might in their turn suffer by comparison with others. Then the carriage draws a little out of the way, to give Milicent a better view of the quaint old burying-ground, which Stephen points out to her as the gathering-place of many in that night of raging flame which swept over the whole city, and utterly destroyed a score of streets, leaving thousands no other home than this. Stephen was sailing up here in a Westport schooner on that terrible twentieth of June; and he had long ago told Milicent the story of the burning city on the rock, the lurid flapping curtains of the flames veering all over it; the sea aglow with the reflection, a red and brassy background for the boats and rafts of refugees: — one such raft-load, showing out black against the ruddy water, his schooner had picked up, as it was drifting helplessly out to sea, with its score of women and children.

The two are talking it over now, as the carriage moves on; and half-way to the corner, Urquhart comes across the green square, to meet them.

"The books were just crowded with names of people I know. The whole of New York and Boston seems to have been swept up here by the hot wave of this week. I could not possibly have kept out of their way," Urquhart says in a low voice to Stephen.

"So large an acquaintance must be something of a nuisance," Stephen returns, laconically.

"Of course it is. I wish you would stop your platitudes, and suggest something."

"That is n't as difficult as you think. There is a hotel I generally put up at: not a grand house, by any means. But I can recommend it as neat, and kept by a landlady who knows me and will make Milly comfortable."

"That will do finely. Why did you not mention this hotel before?"

"I thought you had better try your own way first, and see if it succeeded."

Urquhart and Stephen have both a direction to give the driver, and then they get into the carriage.

"I thought we were to stop here," says Milicent, who has taken a decided fancy to the square opposite.

"No, it was impossible for us to get in," says Urquhart; and Milicent fortunately does not ask wherein lies the impossibility. She soon forgets her disappointment, in looking at the shops.

Again the carriage stops : this time before a milliner's establishment; and Urquhart alights.

"Does he expect to find lodgings there?" Stephen asks, puzzled by Urquhart's shopping mania.

Milicent is not at all puzzled, but only says, "He had much better have taken me with him : " and begins to peer out of the window anxiously, without being reminded by Stephen of her hatless condition.

But Urquhart soon comes back, carrying a parcel wonderfully fastened at the four corners, which he casts into Milicent's lap, before taking his seat by her side.

"I hope it will do," he says, with very much the air that it will have to do.

Milicent unpins her parcel, and holds up to view a small French hat, which has the appearance of a large nosegay.

"It is ugly," says Stephen, very decidedly. "But it will do until you get home."

"When you will give her straw for domestic manufacture," returns Urquhart, sarcastically.

"It is a beauty," says Milicent, just as decidedly as Stephen ; "but it will not do at all."

"Why not? The milliner took a peep at you

through the window, and said it would just suit madame; and she is a French woman, and ought to know."

"But she only had a peep," answers Milicent, still regarding the hat half regretfully.

"Won't it be becoming?" asks Urquhart. "Put it on. Stephen and I will be your mirror."

"Oh, no doubt I would satisfy you both in it. But my dress would never do with it. It is flannel, and rather the worse for the sea-water."

"What does it matter, so that you have a hat on your head? That seems to be the main point," suggests Stephen.

"Perhaps you had better get a general outfit. I assure you it can be done in a few minutes," says Urquhart, eagerly.

"No, thanks," returns Milicent, with a blush for her once accepting a general outfit, as he calls it. "I suppose I must have a hat, but I can't trust either of you to select it for me. Just stop at a shop where I can find a straw one. Let me see: we passed the London House and the Victoria House; they both sound promising for anything one might want."

Urquhart gives the order. "Had n't the clerk better bring the millinery to you?" he asks.

"No, it is only a step; no one will see me if I am quick. You can sit still; Stephen won't mind going with me."

But both the men prefer going with her: and Milicent quickly finds a hat that suits her. The clerk tries to entice her to add a spray of flowers

to the trimming. "It will be such an improve-
ment," he declares.

"So it will, Milly. It is just as much too plain
as the other was too fine," says Stephen.

But Milicent shakes her head.

"White and red roses are quite fashionable,"
the clerk says, smiling as he holds up the pale tea
buds, and looks down at the eager, blushing face;
"and the pink will match your cheeks."

"Put on your hat, Milicent; we must be off,"
says Urquhart, sharply; and as he stops behind
to pay for the hat, the clerk infers that he is her
husband and grudges her the roses. He does not
suppose his compliment was offensive: indeed,
he imagines he was very polite in showing the
fisherman and his pretty wife his flowers, though
of course they were not his handsomest, not even
French.

Nor does Milicent understand why Urquhart
was so suddenly out of temper, and thinks it was
because she had refused to wear the French hat.
She was sorry, but she never thought of censuring
the clerk.

The hotel Stephen recommended is in a much
quieter part of the town, and of the kind generally
patronized by farmers and country shopkeepers.
It is irreproachably clean; and yet has an odor
of every dinner ever cooked in its precincts. But
it has one advantage, Urquhart gladly discovers:
which is, that, though kept by a woman, there are
none of her sex among her guests. Evidently the
farmers' wives have different tastes from their

husbands, and when they come to town prefer more fashionable quarters.

The landlady is delighted to see Stephen; and, being from the seacoast, she very soon understands the circumstances of their case, and the great danger he and his friends have passed through. She is inclined to be rather oppressive in her hospitality; but that is on Stephen's account, who is a favorite of hers.

After their late dinner, the two men leave Milicent in charge of the landlady, and go in search of a couple of coasting sailors who would attend to needful repairs, and sail the Undine to Westport. It is not an easy thing to find trusty men to undertake this; and not until after dark do they return to the hotel, having met with much annoyance, — which Urquhart soon forgets in a fresh grievance. The landlady reports that Milicent has gone out.

"Why, where could she have gone? Could there have been anything madder than her going out alone? She has n't an idea of the place," exclaims Urquhart, impatient with anxiety.

"Don't be afraid. Milly will find her way back. She is too much of a sailor, not to have some mark to steer by. No doubt she has gone to take a nearer view of the shops that fascinated her so, as she drove past them. You ought not to have bought her a hat, if you wanted to keep her indoors," says Stephen, laughing.

"We had better go and look for her," proposes Urquhart, shortly.

"I don't think we need; she would rather not, I fancy. Besides, she will be here in a few minutes."

"It is far too late for her to be out. I wonder she can be so silly."

"Rather set it down to ignorance," replies Stephen, gravely.

"Well, I must go and find her. If she comes in before I return, you can tell her what a fright she has given me," — and Urquhart hurries off.

Stephen may possibly be right, and Milicent has gone to look at the shops: or perhaps to King Square, where strains of music are now mingling with the fountain's plash.

Urquhart would not be surprised to meet her lingering somewhere there, listening to a band for the first time in her life, most probably. Prompted by this fear, he walks on rapidly, looking for her carefully; too carefully, — for he almost runs into the arms of some one who is crossing over from the Dufferin, and who proves to be one of his acquaintances met that afternoon on the wharf.

Urquhart has to stop and speak civilly; and before he can plead pressing business as an excuse for passing on, he has caught sight of Milicent turning this way from King Street.

Urquhart's desire is to get rid of his friend before Milicent comes opposite to them. There is good hope of his doing so; for she is lagging at every shop-window, and at her present gait may be half an hour in making the progress of half a square. But, unfortunately, she sees Urquhart standing there under the street lamp; and, thinking he is looking for her, she crosses over, smiling, and wondering if he has been frightened about her.

"Ah, there is the little girl I saw on the wharf this morning!" exclaims Urquhart's friend, much to his annoyance. "That is a face one can never forget, the coloring is so perfect, — and such sudden changes of expression! I was sure for a moment she thought she knew one of us; and then a pretty look of disappointment came over her face."

No wonder a change comes over Milicent's face, as she nears the two men, for Urquhart turns his back on her. She is very sure he saw her, and was ashamed of her; for Milicent has gained some ideas about dress and the fitness of things, in the few hours she has spent in Vanity Fair. So she passes by, with flaming cheeks, and bright, indignant eyes that are looking straight before her.

"Zounds, but she is a beauty!" Urquhart's companion exclaims. And he would have followed Milicent, and perhaps have made some startling discoveries, if Urquhart had not detained him.

Milicent's way lies round the next corner, and it is not very long before Urquhart has overtaken her.

"You had better take my arm," he says, very shortly.

"Thanks; I would rather not;" she answers, in the same tone.

Just then some one walks in between them, and they are separated for a second or two. When they meet again, Urquhart is peremptory in his desire that she shall take his arm; and Milicent, a little frightened at the crowd, obeys.

"I have been greatly alarmed about you, Milicent. What induced you to come out?" asks Urquhart, after securing her.

"I don't know what inducement there was for me to stay in," she answers, with much defiance in her voice. "I had no one to speak to, and nothing to do. It was certainly more entertaining out-of-doors."

"But scarcely as safe. You will find the habits here rather different from those you are accustomed to."

"I don't need to have you tell me so," breaks in Milicent, with an increased glow in her cheeks, and an endeavor to draw her hand away from his arm: which she does not succeed in doing, for he holds it fast. "I have discovered the difference myself."

"I am sorry for it, Milicent. It was careless in me. I should have warned you," says Urquhart, evidently troubled.

"I don't think warning would have helped me in the least."

"It would certainly have prevented your coming out by yourself," answers Urquhart.

"It certainly would not. I am not going to stay in a disagreeable, close room, just because you are ashamed of me."

"Ashamed of you! What are you saying, Milicent? I thought some one was impertinent to you!" exclaims Urquhart in surprise.

"And so some one was, and it has happened to me twice to-day," Milicent says vehemently, struggling to free her hand: which Urquhart permits her to do, as they have reached the hotel.

“What has happened twice to you to-day?” he asks, gravely.

“That you have refused to recognize me. All on account of your grand friends!” she adds, with a scornful shrug of her pretty shoulders.

“Is that all? But I could n’t help myself,” says Urquhart, laughing, and feeling much relieved.

“Could n’t help being ashamed of me?”

“Ashamed! Why, I was never prouder in all my life of anything that was my very own!”

The girl looks quickly up at him, a certain thrill in his voice drawing her glance. The light from a window, under which they have paused, shows her his face; and somehow, when their eyes meet, it is not easy to doubt him, even when he says, as if continuing: —

“But the only thing I could do under the circumstances was not to know you. You ought not to be angry with me, for I was acting for your own good.”

“But I do not understand how not speaking to me could do me any good.”

“And I don’t care that you should understand. I only wish you to believe me.”

“I hate blind belief,” she cries impatiently. “It is a mere weakness.”

“I think it requires a prodigious effort of strength on your part,” Urquhart says, laughing. “How are we to get on through life, if you are to have no faith in me?”

"I don't admit I have no faith in you. Only I would like to be certain that it was not my old flannel dress you were ashamed of."

"As if a flannel dress is not good enough for a fisherman's sweetheart! Did you think I cared for such a trifle? If I had any real cause to be ashamed of you, I would not marry you; but I won't refuse you on account of your dress."

He laughs as he speaks, and evidently expects an answer from Milicent.

But she seems satisfied with his assurance, and goes up-stairs to the parlor. He watches her until she is safely on her way, and then turns into the office to give some directions relating to leaving in the morning.

Stephen is in the parlor, reading the evening paper, when Milicent comes in. He was anxiously watching for her, until he caught sight of her returning on Urquhart's arm : when he took up the paper.

"I wish we had never come here!" exclaims Milicent, in a vexed tone, throwing her hat on the table, — a little too hastily, for it misses its intended resting-place, and goes spinning across the room.

Stephen goes quietly and picks up the much-abused hat, and then comes back to his seat, before he says : —

"I think this is better than risking death on the ocean, Milly."

"Oh, I forgot that! It is very ungrateful in me. I thought last night if I ever got to land again I would be so very different. So gentle, and so good. And I have been all day just as I always am."

"Which is n't such a bad way," Stephen says, gently stroking the hand that lies on the arm of his chair.

"It is n't grateful in me. Stephen, I am afraid I am of an ungrateful disposition."

"I always thought just the opposite. I have always found you grateful even in trifles."

"Oh, in word, but not in deed. I suppose I could say very easily, I thank God for sparing our lives. But if I had to give up something just because it was right, I would not do it."

"Yes, you would, if it were necessary," says Stephen.

"I would if I were forced to, if I could n't help myself. But I would never do as — as you would do, Stephen — do it quietly and without fuss."

"Yes, you would. When we feel very deeply, we don't care to be noisy about it. Where did you go just now? To see something pretty, I wager."

"And got a scolding for my venturesomeness. Stephen, why is it that people who live in the country are not fit to live in the city?"

"I should transpose that sentence," Stephen says, laughing.

"At home I am just like other people," she goes on to explain. "But here, I 'm different from every one. And such little things seem to put people out. And it is just horrid!" she ends energetically.

It is not a very clear insight into her troubles, that Milicent is giving Stephen, and he does not care to question her; so he says hopefully: —

"We 'll be at home to-morrow, and then you 'll not feel so lost."

"Do you know," she says, "I 've been wondering all day if they are sorry at home."

"Are n't you sure they are? I don't believe there is a heart in the village that is not sore for us."

"Yes, in the village. And Aunt Ursula is grieved for you, for she is fond of you. But it is different about me."

"She loves you better than you think, Milly."

"She does n't care very much for me: I am in her way more than you know. But I shall be glad to go back and do something to help her; and perhaps when I go away for always, she will miss me a little. I should like her to."

"It is a hard burden to bear, to miss those we love. But no struggling will rid us of it."

"I don't want *you* to miss me," says Milicent, quickly.

"You want me to be different from all the rest?" he asks, a little pained, but thinking he does not show it.

"You are, and always will be, different from all others," says Milicent softly, and laying her hand on his shoulder. "There is, and always will be, but one Stephen in the world to me."

Urquhart comes in just then, and sees Milicent's hand on Stephen's shoulder, and perhaps hears her last words.   Any one might have come into the room as well.   "Do you want any tea?" he asks, shortly.

He had intended to propose to her to walk after tea.   Under cover of night, he did not fear to take her.

"No, thanks.   I am going to bed," she answers. And as neither of the men presses her to stay, she says good-night, and leaves them.

Urquhart goes out, perhaps to meet his friends, who do not mind being seen with such a rough-looking fellow, when it is so easy to explain who he is.   He is too rich a man, not to be permitted a few vagaries.

Stephen spends the evening alone.   Urquhart did not ask him to go with him : perhaps he did not care to give any trace as to the whereabouts of his fishing-ground, and it was n't at all likely Stephen would refuse to say where he came from, for any whim of Urquhart's.   As he could not very well explain to Stephen why he desires to keep both Milicent and the little fishing-village from the knowledge of his acquaintances, he avoids both ex-planation and companionship, and goes alone.

Stephen naturally thinks, with Milicent, that many things are different in the city.   But not be-ing inclined to study manners and customs, he quietly smokes a peaceful pipe, chatting with the landlady, and the few farmers and countrymen who are inclined to keep moderately late hours, in conformity to city ways.

XI.

"Henceforth
The course of life that seemed so flowery to me,
Becomes the sea-cliff pathway, broken short,
And ending in a ruin."

THE next morning the travelers make an early start for home. Milicent laughs merrily at the slip-shod, sleepy appearance of the streets, so gay and full of fine people the evening before. Here and there a baker's wagon is opening its queer, low, cupboard-like back door, to dole out bread to early customers; but the shops look somnolent, with their windows like great eyes fast closed. Every now and then, the sun peers, with a white face like the moon's, out of the dense folds of a fog pushed for an instant aside, only to be drawn down again. There is not much to be seen of the harbor, save the masts rising up like spectre-ships out of dim nothingness; or a fishing-weir at low-tide left bare on the Carleton side, a straggling V of bushy brown boughs driven upright into the brown flats. Back and forth, and in and out, the sturdy tug-boats are darting; to Milicent's amusement, as she sits on the deck of the Empress, looking on.

Stephen stands talking to a knot of men, across the deck; Urquhart is beside her. His friends having decided last night that they would not cross the Fundy in a fog, and there being thus no danger of a rencontre, he has fallen easily into Stephen's views as to the return trip.

And indeed what could be more enjoyable, than to sit thus on the deck with Milicent, and share her fresh young wonder and delight in the busy scene around her?

It is very busy and crowded, to the girl whose thoughts now and then flash back to the tiny piers of the fishing-village, which once seemed bustling enough. This grove of masts reminds her of the dead belt of spruce-trees on the headland, which the fire had swept by, with its blasting breath, once on a time, and had left them standing wan and melancholy against sea and sky. But this remembrance lasts only an instant: there is the bustle of lading; and the throng, or so it seems to Milicent, upon the wharf. The Boston steamer passes; and now the Empress is feeling her way out of the harbor; and the fog shuts down on Milicent's parting view.

The sun, however, burns the fog up before the opposite coast-line is reached, and Milicent watches the land grow before her, with a thrill which a more experienced traveler might have missed. Little Bryer Island has no history; or if it had, its people have forgotten. But here, two centuries and a half ago, how the earliest French colonists' hearts must have beat high on entering this safe haven from stormy seas, — never dreaming that the waves of war would roll this way, and sweep them from their settlement at Annapolis, or Port-Real, as their descendants still call it. But how they could have passed by Digby downs, to settle at Annapolis above, it would be hard to know.

For Digby is so beautiful, as the Empress steams through the Gut, the gap in the North Mountain range, cleft for the Fundy, which here sweeps into a broad blue basin set about with hills. Hard by the strait, and where Ben Lomond in his fir robes stands benignantly to ward off Fundy fogs, pretty little red and white and brown Digby under its cherry-trees climbs the promontory between the Raquette and the Joggin — Indian for Snow-shoe and Mitten, the shape of which the water takes, on either side, spread out in blue amid green slopes.

Half the population of Digby, and all the summer sojourners in the lovely little watering-place, gather on the long pier to watch the coming and going of the Empress. Milicent, in recalling the scene a day later, will look back with a sort of longing, as one who, swept along over the cataract, looks back at the smooth stretch of water gliding on merrily up to the very brink.

For it is all so bright and sunny and cheery: the lines of the North Mountain; the village streets climbing the downs in terraces, bowered in trees that bring a blush to Milicent's cheek for her poor balm-of-Gilead at home; the dancing blue water, with the Empress gliding away, the white-winged fishing-boats swooping to the waves, and the Indian canoe paddling in, to set its queer square sail and take on board the young squaw and *ho-dé*, or little one, who have been selling baskets and moccasins on the pier, and saying a few words to Milicent, beginning with the soft Indian "*Bazouli*," and ending with "*Adieu*," learned probably from their French priests.

Milicent and Urquhart loiter on the pier, until Stephen brings the carriage for the drive down the French shore, just opposite Bryer Island, where the Undine is to meet them. It is a long drive; but they choose it instead of the long waiting for the evening train: the rather, as Milicent's eyes widen with something like terror, when for the first time she watches the engine panting to and fro, bringing its passengers and freight for the Empress to the foot of the pier.

They change horses at Weymouth, a village lying like the Sleeping Beauty in the Wood, on her rumpled couch of hills, her loosened silver girdle of river trailing off across her lap. They have driven on, down St. Mary's Bay, now distant and now nearer: when presently the road becomes one village street, — one street of seventy miles' length, that stretches on with here and there thin spaces where some *habitant* has added field to field about his house. Elsewhere, the cottages straggle, one after the other, along both sides of the road, which keeps the undulations of the coast, green hay-slopes to the right and left, with ripening grain-fields turning golden in a snow-drift of buckwheat, and the dark of the fir-wood behind. Under the verge of the billowy-green bank lies blue St. Mary's Bay, edged by Long Island, where the North Mountain range dwindles into steep, red-brown, wooded cliffs, sheer to the water's brim. Dwindles and dwindles, until at Greenhead, on Bryer Island, it plunges beneath the Atlantic.

Here and there, where smooth pebbles have been strangely built up by the waves into a sea-wall against their own encroachments, a beach thrusts out a long, brown arm, with a pier in its grasp, or a skeleton ship, half-built, its gaunt ribs standing up against the sky. At Church Point, three iron crosses, surmounting a structure of brown and withered firs, mark where, on Corpus Christi Day, green boughs and flowers point the line of procession — the French Walk — from the church to the seashore. First walks the priest, bearing the Holy Eucharist, with banner and crosses, and followed by a throng of white-robed children and white-veiled girls, scattering flowers, and supported by two lines of the devout. Hundreds and hundreds, chanting as they go, they reach and pass the Holy Stations, turn back again from the sea, and reach the church and disappear within its open doors.

Sometimes the priest in charge here is French; sometimes Irish, with an Irishman's ready wit in exhorting or rebuking. Such an one may be chatting with you on the roadside, as you stop to deliver his mail, when one Pierre, well known for a wife-beater, comes up to him. "One moment, Pierre," he says in English, knowing the man understands it; then turns to you, as if continuing the conversation: "As I do be saying, this man Peter, in the old country, him that was well known for a

wife-beater, died at last, and his wife mourned for
him, though he was no great of a loss. One evening, she comes praying at the grave of him, and
to humble herself like, she ups with her skirts, and
goes down on her bare knees, — right on a nettle
growing there. 'Och, Peter, Peter,' she says,
'though 't is dead and gone ye are, the sting 's
there still.' "

The coachman tells the story, with a glance over
his shoulder for Milicent's approval. In the old
mail-stage days along this road, he was accustomed
to look out for the entertainment, as well as the
safety, of his passengers ; and stored away, for ready
use, many an anecdote anent the stage, with himself always handling the reins. It was he, and no
one else, who was driving the crowded stage to
Yarmouth one pitch-black night, when the wind
was blowing fit to tear the luggage from the rack
behind, and one Mr. Campbell incessantly requiring to be assured of its safety there : until a fellow-
passenger condoled with him that he had not been
born an elephant rather than a camel, that he
might have had his trunk always before him. And
it was he and no one else, of course, to whom, when
driving the American lady-traveler out of Digby,
along the tide-drained chasm of Bear River, she re-
marked that she had never known, before she came
to Nova Scotia, what an addition water is to a
river.

As he tells the story now, the day is waning ; in
the barnyards stand the oxen, staring idly as the
strangers pass ; yonder blue is alive with the white

sails of homeward-flitting fishing-boats; and the
fields ring out from time to time with cheery
French voices, as the hay is gathered in. The sun
drops behind Long Island; the carriage rattles
down the one road-street of its final stopping-place.
Milicent is welcomed into the cottage "hotel" by
some bright-eyed, gentle-mannered Evangéline,
who inquires whether she has "travellé par le rail-
road;" while Stephen and Urquhart walk across
the hayfields to the seashore to see if the Undine
has come or is coming in.

But there is no sign of her. Instead, the fog is
creeping up, and neither wind nor tide gives any
encouragement to the hiring of a boat to-night.
There is nothing better to be done, than to wait
until to-morrow for the Undine.

There is a legend of a traveler astray in the
forest, who, in the silence round about him, hears
the morning-bells ring out, leading him on until he
comes upon a village sunken in fair meadows. A
village of the olden time; out of whose cottages
stream a procession of mediæval saints and sinners,
whom he follows (beckoned on, perhaps, by a swift
glance from some pair of bright eyes), until all
vanish under the church porch. Vanish, — holy
bells and heavenward spire and quaint village, all
gone as a dream; and the traveler stands rubbing
his eyes, staring in bewilderment upon the blank
of quivering greenery before him.

Oftentimes there is a grain of modern truth in
those old legends; and just here, on the French

Shore of Clare, it seems to Urquhart he has found it, when, the next morning being Sunday, the blessed bells ring out, and lo! the old-time gathering at the church-door.

If among the groups there waiting is no white-capped, red-juped Evangéline, there is more than one in nun-like black, with gold cross on her bosom, and the graceful black silk kerchief tied three corner-wise over her head, the straight fold drawn forward till it slightly shades the face, the ends tied in a true French knot under the chin. Perhaps only Evangéline, with her clear-cut features, her warm olive and peach bloom, and her soft bright eyes, brown as the sloeberry, would look her prettiest under that quaint head-gear. But there is more than one Evangéline here.

Inside the church, it is difficult to believe one has not entered into the midst of a congregation of religieuses. A black-robed multitude, a thousand kneeling as one: not a sound, not a breath from them breaking the silence. Only the swinging of the censer chains by one of the four white-tunicked altar-boys; the tinkling of the altar-bell; the rustle of the priest's silk vestment, thrown over his shoulder with the great cross broidered like a banner on his back; the murmur of his voice at his Latin, and the chanting of the sweet, fresh choir-voices in the *Agnus Dei*. The darkening of the spacious nave with all that black concentrates the light about the altar, white and gilded, with its twinkling candles and brilliance of fresh flowers. Milicent is on her knees; and presently a shivering sob escapes her. Stephen, who is next her, leans slightly forward to screen her. He is very sure he understands : it is the reaction after the long strain ; the sudden, overwhelming sense, here in the outer court, of how nearly the gates of the other world had opened to her on that night upon the sea.

Yes; but if he had known the thought which choked the sob? Is life as solemn a thing, after all, as death? Dying, she would fain have told her lover all the truth about herself; will she, living, venture to withhold it?

Urquhart knows nothing of her conflict. No doubts are troubling him ; he has seen far finer churches, with more glow and glitter, and is not paying over much attention here, until the Latin is put by for the French. In that, the priest exhorts his people to the keeping of the Assumption as the national Acadian fête, to the improving, *temporellement, moralement, et spirituellement,* of the Acadiens : — a word of warning thrown in, as to the danger of being tempted to stray from the true faith, by intercourse with Boston, for instance. Boston ways and fashions are called to mind, perhaps, by Milicent's new hat in a front pew, conspicuous among the kerchiefed heads. Unconscious Milicent, who misses Urquhart's amused glance.

The Undine is well in sight, white upon blue St. Mary's Bay, when her passengers come out of church ; and they are soon waiting for her, pacing up and down the beach under the overhanging hayfields.

Presently Milicent stoops, with a little, eager cry, for a handful of dulse flung up by the waves at her feet.

"Who knows — perhaps it came from home," she says. "How far away it looks, a mere blur on the blue!"

She is balancing herself on a bit of rock on the edge of the water, as she gazes wistfully across. Urquhart follows her eyes, half jealously.

"Don't forget," he says, "it is going to fade out altogether from your horizon, one day very soon."

She looks round with a frightened blush. But Stephen has walked on towards the landing place; so after a pause she remarks confidentially to Urquhart : —

"Do you know, I am very sure I shall prefer Venice to any other city in the world ? "

"Why Venice ? " he asks.

"Because, as there are no carriages there, one is not forced to drive."

"It will be safer for you, as you will take the gondolas, and not frighten me with the idea that you have lost yourself, as you did yesterday evening."

"Lost! " exclaims Milicent, in infinite scorn. "As if one could possibly be lost in such a place as St. John ! With some one or something to set one right every few steps, one cannot rightly be said to be lost. It was much more like it, when we were drifting over the wide Atlantic, the black sky as much a howling wilderness as the black sea.

But when the stars came out, and we could tell at least the north from the south, it was not so very dreadful. I was never in my life so glad to see anything, as that north star."

" I must confess the sight of the schooner was a much greater relief to me than the stars could possibly be. The Undine seemed a mere cockle-shell when you were not quite sure you were not on mid-ocean. The relief you feel when safely over such an adventure is so great, it is almost a repayment for the anxiety."

" I am not sure I felt anxious to that extent," replies Milicent. " Even now, I do not shrink from the recollection as from something altogether horrible. Some day, perhaps, we will both look back to it almost with pleasure."

" It will be, then, when we have something worse than death to face."

" I did not think there was anything worse than death," says Milicent, with a shudder.

Urquhart sees it ; so he says lightly : —

" Venice, shall it be, then, Milicent ? "

" Ah," with a long, happy sigh, " how much I have to see ! — and I shall see all, really, really ? " — looking up at him wistfully.

Can anything be more delightful than to have the world to show to this fresh little girl? As Urquhart answers her glance now, he forgets what he may have wished some day or two ago : he would not have her one whit less unsophisticated and worldly-ignorant than she is. And so he begins, as they walk on, to tell her some of the wonderful

things which he will have to show her. When
suddenly, as he looks into her face, he sees it has
turned very pale.

He stops short. "Milicent, you are tired? This
is all too much for you! You should not have
walked out this morning."

"No — no." And then she says slowly: "Do
you suppose, if one should get one glimpse of paradise, and then the gates were shut, it would all be
much worse than it was before, outside?"

What man would not have drunk in the subtile
and unconscious flattery? He draws her hand
with eager ownership into his arm, and keeps it
there as he leads her on.

"What do we care about the outside, sweetheart? You and I will be inside, together."

"Ah, but if" — her voice is low and hesitat-
ing — "if there should be something that might
keep *me* outside?"

"We would stay outside together, and *that* would
be paradise. Why, Milicent, do you think there
could be any paradise for me, without you? Do
you not know there is nothing I would dread, but
being parted from you?"

Milicent stands still on the beach, and clasps
her two hands over his arm, in a sort of hurried in-
sistence.

"Say that again!" she cries, breathlessly.
"Again! — if you can."

Of course he says it again.

Perhaps, if the girl's eyes were not looking up
straight into his, he might remember there are

several other things he might have some dread of, besides that parting which seems an impossibility out of all reckoning. But as it is, he does not remember; still less, when Milicent lets her two hands fall, with a soft-drawn breath; and with the color coming back into her face, begins: —

"Then I may tell you " —

A footstep sounds behind them : it is Stephen coming to look for them. "The tide is turning," he says; "wind too in our favor; and the sooner we are off, the better."

Urquhart frowns. Why is the fellow always breaking in at the wrong time? — and just now, when Milicent has no doubt something to tell of "the old old story that keeps the world from growing old."

But Milicent has turned to meet Stephen; a smile, very like one of relief, dawning in her face.

It is near sunset when the Undine sweeps into Grand Passage, between the foam-lashed lighthouse island and the high red bluffs and cottage-sprinkled green slopes of Long Island : and the white street of Westport curves in front.

Stephen is steering; Urquhart, lying on a sail in the bow of the yacht, is asleep or very drowsy. Milicent is glad to see the old fish-houses, and says so.

"I always thought if I were once away, I should never care to come back. But now I am sure that, no matter where I go, I shall think of the old place with a sort of longing. Looking back may become in time as pleasant as looking forward."

"I am glad to hear you say so, Milly. I never liked to think you were willing to forget so much of your life as you said you were. It has not been altogether miserable? There have been some bright hours? I used to think, when you were a little one, you never heeded anything except a rainy day."

"Oh, they were wretched trials! and I was so dreadfully naughty every time a long storm came, that Aunt Ursula had a horror of them too. I never felt, until now, that I would be sorry to leave Aunt Ursula. She has never cared in the least for me; but that is from no fault of hers."

"It seems to me a fault not to care for you," says Stephen, glancing at the young, eager face, whose very earnestness makes it beautiful.

"But you never judge of me as others do. Besides," she adds with a laugh, "I do not think Aunt Ursula has ever seen me in her life."

"You mean she judges you hardly. I think it is a common fault with people as they grow older, and especially if they have passed through great trouble, to judge young people hardly. It always seems to me, Milly, Miss Ursula has gone through some great trial that has made her different from every one else in the world. Something you and I know nothing about."

"But that is not the reason Aunt Ursula dislikes me. My chief sin in her eyes is that I am like my mother."

"That is very unreasonable in Miss Ursula, I must say. How can you help your looks?" asks Stephen, smiling.

"I do not mean my face," she says, impatiently. "How much you men think of our appearance. Aunt Ursula disliked my mother, and in many ways she thinks I resemble her."

"I have heard that sisters-in-law are apt to have an aversion for each other; though I never understood the cause of it," remarks Stephen in excuse of Miss Ursula, of whom he is fond, despite her forbidding manner, and her evident coldness to Milicent. "Why did Miss Ursula dislike your mother, Milly?"

"I think Aunt Ursula's chief cause of displeasure was that my mother could not live through troubles as she did, but died and left them behind her."

There is such an unnatural ring of bitterness, one might say of cynicism, in Milicent's careless words, that Stephen is at once moved to defend Miss Ursula. "No doubt Miss Ursula thought if your mother had been braver, she would have outlived her troubles. It is difficult for strong hearts to sympathize with those who are weaker," he says, apologetically.

"She thought at least she could live without showing she was hurt," says Milicent, not at all resenting his warmth. "Aunt Ursula is of the same stuff martyrs are made of. She will never flinch, no matter how one tortures her; and, moreover, she has no patience with any one who has not just her amount of courage. Sometimes I wonder if I should die, as my poor mother did, if a great trouble came to me?"

"I do not think you would, Milly. You have more of Miss Ursula's spirit in you than you think. Perhaps that is just the reason she is hard on you at times: you hold out too bravely."

"I, like Aunt Ursula, indeed!" exclaims Milicent, derisively. "Why, the other night I cried myself to sleep, for no reason but because the world seemed so very big, and people so difficult to understand. Fancy Aunt Ursula crying herself to sleep!"

"I have no doubt she has, many a time, only she is not so honest in confessing it. Has the world grown smaller to-day?" asks Stephen, glancing over where Urquhart is making some sign of rousing himself.

"Yes, there are but three people in the world to-day," declares Milicent, merrily. "It was foolish in me to fancy I would like a crowd, — the world, I mean. I am afraid I never can. I hope I will find Aunt Ursula a little worried about us, so that I may have a chance to tell her I am glad to get home."

"Of course she has been anxious and unhappy about you, Milly."

"I hope she will say so, then."

"See what a crowd there is on the piers! I wonder if there is anything the matter?" says Urquhart, coming towards them.

"They have caught sight of the Undine. You don't suppose they will go on quietly drinking tea, when they know we are coming?"

"Vastly kind in them: though I don't think I

ever observed they took very much interest in us before."

"Why should they?" says Milicent. "As long as we were just like every one else around us, I can't see what possible interest they could find in us."

"Interest meaning curiosity," suggests Urquhart, coming to where they are sitting.

"Generally; but not with that little crowd on the piers," says Stephen. "They have been very anxious about us; and a fisherman is always glad when the sea is cheated of its prey."

"It being his habit to rob the sea, he does not like to pay it back," Urquhart supposes.

"He very often has to do it. There is nothing more pathetic than a fisherman's funeral, when the poor fellow is drowned, and the body found. Perhaps that is because it so seldom is found."

"I don't see Aunt Ursula, nor Thomas," says Milicent, scanning the crowd. "I wonder if any one has told them?"

They are at the pier now, and Urquhart and Stephen are occupied in bringing the Undine round handsomely.

A few minutes more, and they have all landed, and are receiving the heartfelt, though somewhat rough greetings of the little crowd. Certainly there are as many gathered together as on the Saturday of Urquhart's arrival with the fishing-boats. He recalls the scene of that day, with the odd impression of one's ignorance of what will happen to one in the course of but a very few weeks. A rather doubtful pleasure-trip, which was to have lasted as many days, has managed to shape the whole of his coming life. The rest of his days, though he might live long in the land, could never bear with such influence upon his happiness, he is very sure.

"We'd made up our minds the fish had got you. They are as greedy folk after us, as we are after them," says one of the fishermen, pressing forward to shake hands with him.

"We have fooled them this time," answers Urquhart, lightly. "Though I can't see much .difference between fish and worms, if one has to be devoured."

"Don't say it, sir, don't say it. It's bad luck to be uncivil to the finny folk where they can hear you."

"So, you're one of the lucky ones," remarks another fisherman, who has been attentively listening to Stephen's account of the squall. "A man who weathers a brown squall in these waters, in a craft like yon, is likely to die in his bed. And it's a heap more comfortable for the breath to go out of one little by little, than to have it choked out by a great, ugly wave. A quiet death-bed, with one's folks decently crying round, does a power of good, more than the parson's sermon. No matter how ill a man lives, he'll do his best to die respectably, if he has half a chance. But if one is drowned in the sea " —

"Then God himself preaches," interrupts old Angus. "And it's a solemn, awesome sermon, of

the same kind the thunder and lightning is made
of.   You 'll never think, while struggling with the
sea, what folks are saying or thinking about you.
It 's just wonderful for knocking the conceit out of
you ; for you are as good as nothing at all, when
the big waves are tossing you about, as if you were
no more account than a wisp of straw.   I was
picked up once for dead, on the shore over there,"
he adds, as if apologizing for knowing so much
more about drowning than the rest of them.

"Mrs. Featherstone," — asks Milicent of the village shop-keeper, who, with the broadest of smiles
on her round, rosy face, but the water standing in
her friendly blue eyes, has been the foremost with
her greetings, especially for Urquhart, — " have
you seen or heard anything of Aunt Ursula ? "

" Not I.   She is too handily in black to need
anything of me at short notice.   It has its drawbacks, though : for when afflictions come, folks are
apt to overlook you, if you wear the gown they 're
used to see you in," — and she smoothes down her
own black sleeve with a plump hand that trembles
a little.   " I thought may be Miss Ursula would
need a yard or so of black ribbon ; but she did n't."

" Not quite so soon as this !   Aunt Ursula cannot have given up all hope of us so soon ! " says
Milicent, hastily.

" I can't say there was much of what you call
hope about it.   It blew fit to leave the island bald ;
and such a sea as 'd bother a fish !   It was n't so
long : but none of the men put much faith in yon
pleasure-boat, — she 'd turn turtle in the squall,

they knew. But then, men always know so much, — more than the Almighty himself at times. Not that the women are far behind them. They make cocksure the prints are going to fade white before they are in the suds : unless they come out all right, and then they are ready to swear they knew they were fast colors. And that reminds me," — adds Mrs. Featherstone, dropping her voice confidentially, with what she would have called a lee wink, — " there 's that beautiful a-white muslin the Dominion fetched a-Saturday, by Miss Ursula's orders. I 'd hardly the heart to unpack my boxes, thinking upon the storm, — I was like a buoy that 's gone adrift, till I sighted that white muslin. And then I turned to, and clapped the scissors into it, and put on a puff here, and a flounce fore and aft, as it might be. Wheel there, steady ! says I to myself : we 'll make for the wedding-port, and that 'll be a lucky omen for the Undine. And it 's a mighty proud woman I am this day, that it 's the white that is wanted, not the black."

Milicent colors like a rose, and says hurriedly, —

" The men were wrong if they gave us up for lost. And as to the Undine, she behaved beautifully," she adds, with pride.

" You 're safe because you had Stephen along," declares one of the men standing near. " What ever made him a farmer, when he is a born sailor, I can't say ; only I always maintain it 's against nature, and so it 's all wrong."

" Mr. Urquhart was skipper," says Milicent stiffly, as she walks away. She would not confess that all the risk they had run was through Urquhart's headstrongness.

Apparently, Stephen and Urquhart have no chance to escape until they have given a minute account of their many vicissitudes, and listened to many remarkable comments upon them. The whole world might have been convulsed by some great throe, physical or political, and the little village would have been perfectly indifferent. But that a boat from its own harbor, and carrying some of its own people, should have been in imminent peril, is of vivid interest to the whole community.

Milicent has slipped away, unseen, from the group surrounding her two companions. It is very evident their return is a resurrection from the dead, to the people on the pier: and though she is anxious, perhaps a little curious, to see what effect the ill tidings had upon her own household, she does not wish for any spectators when she announces herself alive and well. Nor does she wish the news of her safety to reach her aunt before her. So she hastens on, with all the imprudent desire of youth to see things just as they are.

And Milicent is satisfied: for Miss Ursula, who seldom goes to the front of the house, has not seen the unwonted gathering of the village people on the pier, but is busy with her usual household avocations when Milicent comes into the kitchen.

Miss Ursula has her back to the door when the girl enters, — who, feeling very much as if she were the ghost of herself, and might startle the living, calls out softly : —

" Aunt Ursula "—

Miss Ursula turns, with a perplexed look in her eyes, as though she suspected herself of being nervous, or under a delusion.

But the bodily presence of Milicent standing in the doorway is of itself convincing.

A look of relief sweeps over Miss Ursula's face ; but it passes so quickly that Milicent is not sure it was not a delusion on her part.

Miss Ursula's sharp voice is none, as she asks :

" Where have you been, all this time ? "

" At the bottom of the sea, where I fancy you would rather I had stayed. Are you so very sorry to see me at home again, Aunt Ursula ? "

" Sorry ! Why should I be ? It is for you to judge whether your life is worth living or not."

" I have a little faith in its wholesomeness. At any rate, I prefer being alive, to undergoing the fish-devouring process our neighbors were fancying for us," says Milicent, carelessly, though inwardly deeply hurt by her aunt's cool reception.

" You believe so now ; nevertheless, the day will come when you will think a quick death preferable to a long life. But you never fished up a new hat from the bottom of the sea," continues Miss Ursula, with a glance at Milicent's head-gear.

" Oh, we have been shopping in St. John, and have had a rare good time of it," says the girl, lightly. " I cannot imagine why you never say one kind word for the great world, when it looks so pleasant."

" On the surface, perhaps. But you were scarcely

so imprudent as to go to St. John in the yacht! I
cannot see how Stephen could have consented to
anything so rash and indiscreet," adds Miss Ursula, with marked displeasure.

"He did, however, and was glad when a schooner
offered to take us in tow. I do not see why you
should care, since you were not anxious about us."

"Why should I be, if, as you say, you were enjoying yourself, and shopping for a new hat? If
you had been in any great danger, you might have
expected me to be anxious about you."

"I don't know that I would. It was Stephen
who expected it. I could have told him you wasted
nothing, not even so cheap a thing as pity," says
Milicent, bitterly.

She does not wait to hear Miss Ursula's reply,
but turns from the kitchen to go up-stairs to change
her dress; perhaps, too, to hide the bitter tears
flashing into her eyes. She had hastened home,
thinking to find some trace of sorrow or anxiety;
and instead, everything is going on as usual in the
great, dismal house.

It never occurs to Milicent, that, as she appeared
in the doorway, smiling and wearing a new hat, a
great fear died out of Miss Ursula's heart; and the
natural feeling of irritation after what one deems
a waste of pain is apt to make one sharp.

If Milicent had given only a hint of the great
danger just passed through, she would not have
been so cruelly hurt and mortified. Is it only
years, which separate these two? — the one thinking the other light and frivolous; and the other

very sure her aunt 'is always unjust and hard on her. Is it only the score of years between them? Or is it something they will not or cannot forget, and which belongs to the past?

As Milicent crosses the hall to the stairs, the open door shows her Urquhart coming to the house; he having followed her as soon as he had missed her. She goes out to him; and they are standing together at the gate, when Thomas comes up.

The Undine was riding at anchor, when Thomas's little fishing-boat sailed into the harbor. The crowd was dispersing; but there are always some stragglers ready to impart either good or evil news, so that Thomas had an opportunity to hear many versions of Milicent's adventure before he reached home.

He comes forward now, hastily, the lines which anxious hours have graven on his face not yet erased by the sudden good news.

"You are safe!" he exclaims, never heeding Urquhart's presence, and stooping to kiss the pretty, flower-like face, that blooms into a sudden scarlet under the unwonted caress. "We have had a fine scare about you, and I have been to the island to look for you. And lo and behold, you have been making a voyage to the world!"

Thomas does not offer to shake hands with Urquhart, who has shared Milicent's peril; but walks round to the back of the house, and disappears.

"I do not understand why you should refuse me your kisses, and yet give them freely to a fisherman," remarks Urquhart, with displeasure.

"I thought that was taken, not given," says Milicent, still deeply flushed, but trying to laugh it off. "You forget this is no common occasion, and I have been kissed by all the women in the village."

"But not by the men, that I perceived," remarks Urquhart, dryly.

Milicent half turns away; then she turns back, with a trembling pallor in her face where the color has died out: and her lips quivering. There is an air of hesitation about her. One might fancy she is trying to speak, and is afraid.

"You do not understand," — she begins, falteringly. "I remember him always — ever since I was so high," — marking the distance with her hand from the ground. "And — and " —

A voice is heard calling her just then: Miss Ursula's.

"I must go," she says, hastily. "Why will you never learn that you must not come here after sunset? That Aunt Ursula does not like it?"

"What do I care for Miss Ursula? Let her call."

"Presently she will come out and order you away: which you will not like in the least, for you will have to obey her. Discretion is much better than blind courage."

"The knowledge that this state of things will not last much longer, helps me to be discreet. Soon you will be all my own, with no Miss Ursula to interfere."

"And you will have the monopoly of fault-finding which Aunt Ursula enjoys. You will not deny

that you will profit by it. The few hours we were
in St. John proved your capabilities."

" But our position was so very peculiar, and you
were so vastly ignorant," begins Urquhart.

" Which is to say I am a sad dunce. No matter;
I shall learn so quickly, I will astonish my master,
and soon set up theories of my own. I don't mean
always to be in leading-strings. There, do not
grow really angry, for Aunt Ursula wants me, and
I cannot stop to explain myself."

It is Thomas who wants Milicent, though Miss
Ursula has called her. He is anxious to know
something of her adventure from her own lips.

But he is not to do so; for Urquhart has stopped
her.

" One moment, Milicent."

He is looking at two men who are coming over
the hill this way, together. Stephen, and —

Urquhart recognizes the new-comer at once.

To find more friendship than one is expecting
may chance to be irritating. Urquhart has been
looking for a letter from his former guardian, the
only person whom he considered it necessary, as a
mere act of courtesy or friendliness, to inform of
his speedy marriage. Mr. Raymond no doubt considered it an equal act of friendliness on his part
to remonstrate with his former ward against such
an unfortunate step as this marriage would most
certainly be. With his position and money, Urquhart ought to make a brilliant match; and that he
should throw himself away on a fisherman's daughter, — for such Mr. Raymond supposed Milicent,

— that gentleman was not inclined to contemplate
for an instant. He was too wise to write his re-
monstrance. Urquhart might read a letter or not,
as he pleased; but he would be obliged to listen :
and if his friend's eloquence or good common-sense
view of the position failed to convince the young
man, no doubt it would be possible to buy off the
girl's relations, so that they would interfere. For
Mr. Raymond had divined that poverty was a
marked feature of Milicent's surroundings.

He had arrived the day before, by the weekly
steamer from Yarmouth, which also brought, in
Mrs. Featherstone's stores, the white muslin dress
Miss Ursula had promised for the wedding. He
had shared, albeit silently, the anxiety of the village
for the missing Undine ; and being late on the pier,
and meeting Stephen there, he had been put under
his care, to be shown the house where Urquhart
was most likely to be found.

"I had no idea there were any gentry living in
these parts," Mr. Raymond had begun by remarking, as the two men crossed the hill, to Miss Ursula's. "I thought fishermen were too rough to
make pleasant, or even safe neighbors. But there,
over the fields, is a pretty place, evidently a farm-
house. By the way, Mr. Ferguson, what is Urquhart's fiancée's father ?"

"She has none."

"Indeed ! nor mother ?"

"No ; only an aunt."

Mr. Raymond does not say that is fortunate, —
though his tone of voice implies as much.

"Of course she is pretty: the girl, I mean, not the aunt."

"She is here at the gate," says Stephen, shortly: and it is now that Urquhart sees the two men coming, and stops Milicent.

He need not have done so. He could have gone forward alone, to meet Mr. Raymond; and Milicent's late arrival would have been excuse enough to postpone the introduction for a more convenient season. But Urquhart is too proud to make a sign as if he feared to introduce his friend to Milicent. He takes both the visit and the hour with perfect coolness; though how he wishes Milicent could appear in the dove-colored dress and cherry ribbons she wore one evening, to his great satisfaction! Yet fortunately she has the merit of being beautiful in any guise; and it is as well they should meet here, out-of-doors, rather than in that barn of a parlor.

But there is not the smallest use in Urquhart's hinting, when Milicent invites her visitors in, that it is pleasanter out-of-doors, and that the sea-view is perfect. Milicent will not understand him. It is not hospitality, to keep this friend of Urquhart's outside the house-door. She is not ashamed of her poverty, and she will not let her lover be.

There is one step too far in every course in life; and Milicent, instead of pausing to see her way, has recklessly gone forward.

When she opened the door and invited Mr. Raymond to enter, she expected to find the parlor empty. Instead, there is a bright fire of driftwood on the hearth, before which Miss Ursula is sitting with her work; near her, Thomas, lounging in a great rocking-chair, reading a newspaper, and smoking a cigar.

It is such a novel sight in the parlor, that no wonder Milicent pauses on the threshold for a moment, before she recovers from her astonishment, and makes way for the visitors to follow her into the room.

Of the four who enter, Urquhart is the most annoyed. How could he ever hope to explain to Mr. Raymond the primitive mode of life in this out-of-the-way fishing-village, where Milicent's aunt is on such terms with her hired fisherman that she not only permits him to share the parlor with her, but to fill it with tobacco smoke, — tobacco smoke from a cigar, forsooth, of unexceptionable aroma! Incongruous situations are always the most difficult to explain.

After the first shock of surprise, Milicent is not in the least disconcerted. "Aunt Ursula," she says, in her clear voice, "Mr. Urquhart has brought a friend to see us."

Miss Ursula is painfully embarrassed. She has scarcely lifted her eyes from her work, after the one glance she gave when they came into the room; and instead of receiving her guests, she makes a hasty apology or explanation to Milicent: something about the chimney in the kitchen smoking, and forcing her to make a fire in the parlor.

"So much the better," the girl says coolly. "This room is usually damp and uncomfortable."

No one but Stephen notices Miss Ursula's perturbation; for both Mr. Raymond and Urquhart are looking at Thomas, who rose to his feet when they entered, and is now slowly folding his paper, as if preparatory to leaving the room.

Urquhart has never seen Miss Ursula's fisherman without his hat; and, between its slouched brim and his heavy beard, there was scarcely anything of his features to be seen. That Thomas is a remarkably handsome man no one could deny; but it is not that which strikes Urquhart, so much as something very familiar in the fellow's face, which not only puzzles, but for some reason irritates him.

Mr. Raymond also is looking at the fisherman, with a perplexed expression of countenance: which quite suddenly lightens into one of recognition, and he starts forward, exclaiming, as he lays his hand familiarly on Thomas's shoulder : —

"Is it really you, Chaudron? You are the last person in the world I expected to see here."

"Is it not far enough out of the way? I might naturally be more surprised at seeing you in such an outlandish place as this," responds Thomas, with a short laugh.

"The impression is that you are abroad."

"So I was for a time. But I was not born under a lucky star. No doubt the impression also is that I am living like a prince; and lo, you find me a fisherman."

"One in disguise," says Mr. Raymond, smiling significantly.

"Not at all, but one actually. There is nothing to eat here but fish and potatoes; so I catch cod and herring to keep my family from starving."

"You are not alone, then?" asks Mr. Raymond, with evident curiosity.

Until this instant, some spell of lang syne has held his attention riveted on Thomas. There has been no slightest movement to distract it to the girl standing apart in the window; nor to the spare, elderly figure of the woman bent closely over the work in her lap, — so closely, that none could see the gray and rigid face, into which for one instant a startled look came, as of one suddenly confronted with the ghost of a dead past.

Now, as Mr. Raymond speaks, he half turns. But Thomas is answering him : —

"I am not alone. Of course you know my wife is dead. You may also remember I had a daughter. It is she who brought you here."

"That is false!" exclaims Urquhart, angrily. An intolerable annoyance seizes him at the mere idea that this rough-looking fisherman claims Milicent as his daughter. Urquhart has been watching with some interest Mr. Raymond's recognition of him; but never for a moment connecting him in any way with Milicent.

"I beg pardon for contradicting Mr. Urquhart," says Thomas, with mocking politeness; "but though a gentleman has occasionally been known to cheat, he is never known to lie. Perhaps if Milicent vouches for our relationship he will acknowledge that at least his assertion is a hasty one."

All four men turn to look at Milicent. She is standing at the window, her back to them, her brow pressed against the glass. Though they cannot see her face, her hands, which are clasped together in a strained, passionate way, give a strong hint of the mighty effort she is making to gain control over herself.

Stephen quietly moves near her, — near enough to touch her; but he does not, nor does he speak to her. Urquhart also makes a motion to go to her; but checks himself. He cannot bring himself to question her before so many witnesses; therefore he draws a little farther from her, and is silent.

"There has been a mistake somewhere," says Thomas, very quietly. "Or perhaps a complication would be a better rendering of our position. Milicent no doubt thought that her being the daughter of a fisherman would perhaps shock you; and that marrying her as such would have some effect upon your social standing. Of course that was her ignorance. Thomas the fisherman's daughter, perhaps only Mr. Raymond would have objected to, as your wife. But Mr. Chaudron's daughter holds a slightly different position."

"I never have heard the name, except as belonging to a banker who was both a forger and a swindler," says Urquhart slowly, looking at Mr. Chaudron as he speaks.

"So the newspapers said. They took great pleasure in the small spite of calling me names. However, this last swindle, which you are so fortunate, through the good offices of our friend Mr. Raymond, to discover, I must protest I had nothing to do with. I warned Milicent that her engagement was a rash and foolish one, and would end disastrously. But," he adds with a shrug, " it is in vain to argue with a girl in love. As to withholding my name, — even you who blame me for a too free use of it must see that, under the circumstances, this was only common prudence on my part."

Mr. Chaudron is standing with his back to the fire, his newspaper and long-extinguished cigar in one hand. His attitude is that of one who expects the interview to be a short one, though he in no way hurries his guests.

" If you had advised your daughter to tell me her parentage, you might have been sure I would have respected your incognito. A little honesty on your part would have done you no harm " — begins Urquhart.

" I am sure you are very good to say so," interrupts Mr. Chaudron, with irritating suavity. " But one may be a little particular about the use of one's name. My advice to my daughter was exactly the contrary to your wishes."

What answer Urquhart might have made it is not difficult to guess. Yet it is not Milicent's beseeching eyes (for she turns her face round when her father begins to speak) that silences him; neither is it Mr. Raymond, who has tried more than once to gain a hearing, but Miss Ursula.

She has risen from her obscure corner in the wide hearth, and now comes forward. " Gentlemen," she says, coldly and haughtily, " you must pardon my breach of hospitality, if I ask you to leave us to ourselves. We have long been unused to visitors, and would be alone."

The effect of Miss Ursula's words would have been exceedingly chilling and embarrassing, if Mr. Raymond had not turned towards her when she began to speak. " Are you here too, Ursula ! " he exclaims.

" Where else should I be ? " she asks, haughtily.

She stands with the western light from the uncurtained window slanting in upon her, broken only by the shadow of the girl, who, at the sound of her aunt's voice, turns aside again to resume her former isolated posture. That roseate glow tries to soften the hard and toilworn hands folded together before Miss Ursula; the straight folds of the black dress; the angular lines of the forbidding figure: and fails so utterly, that it does not attempt to reach up to the gray face, so still and set that it might be a mask.

Mr. Raymond, out of his comfortable ease, draws a hurried breath.

" I never dreamed of Chaudron's being here, of all places in the world," he begins, in haste to exculpate himself.

" The bow was drawn at a venture," answers Miss Ursula, bitterly. " It was intended only to wound a girl; but no doubt it was guided to its destiny. I never did believe in blind chance."

" I came here, I confess, to try to free my ward from what I feared would be a foolish marriage;

but I had not the slightest idea who the young lady really is. I ought not to have called your brother by his name; it was a mistake my surprise caused me to make. I meant no malice, — Ursula, you surely believe me," he breaks out suddenly.

"Is not Mr. Raymond's word always to be trusted?" replies Miss Ursula, in so quiet a tone that it is difficult to detect even the shadow of a sarcasm.

Yet Mr. Raymond flushes like a school-boy, and says in an aggrieved voice: —

"You are always keen in your thrusts, and never inclined to mercy. But now, even against your will, you will have to trust me as a friend."

"Having lost all I once deemed friends, I regard every one now as an enemy," answers Miss Ursula, coldly.

"That is a harsh creed," begins Mr. Raymond; but Miss Ursula interrupts him: —

"We are detaining Mr. Urquhart. He can hardly be interested in our meeting."

Urquhart is feeling his position awkward. He could not talk with Milicent, having so many witnesses; and he is too angry just now to trust himself to speak to her alone, even if she would agree to a private interview. Her manner does not tend to pour oil on the troubled waters of his temper; for she has again turned her back upon him, and seems absorbed in looking out of the window. He would give much, wrathful as he is, to see if there is pain, or only anger, in her face; but she is far too uncertain for him to use any rash means to make the discovery, even if his hurt pride would have permitted him to do so.

Urquhart's irritation is increased by the presence of Mr. Chaudron, who has made himself such an immense barrier between him and Milicent. Thomas the fisherman could have been quietly kept in the background, and need never have been heard of; but Mr. Chaudron is far too notorious to be hidden in a corner.

Miss Ursula's words have recalled Mr. Raymond to the fact that there are others in the room, and that Urquhart's position is unpleasantly awkward. "We had better go. There is nothing to be done at present," he suggests to Urquhart, in a low voice, as if the proposal were his own, not Miss Ursula's.

Not waiting for Urquhart's answer, he shakes hands with Mr. Chaudron, and would, if he had dared, have offered the same civility to Miss Ursula. But instead, he bows to her, and to Milicent, — a bit of courtesy the girl never sees, for her back is still towards them.

Urquhart leaves the room with Mr. Raymond, not noticing any one. He is too sore and wrathful to care for, or even think of, an ordinary act of politeness. Mr. Chaudron merely shrugs his shoulders at Urquhart's evident want of presence of mind; then signs to Miss Ursula, and the two leave the room together.

Still Milicent keeps her station by the window. She must have forgotten Stephen; for she starts violently when he comes closer to her, and speaks.

" Urquhart is taken by surprise, Milly. It will not be long before he comes back to tell you so," says Stephen, very gently.

" Are you sure he will ? " asks Milicent, turning on him two despairing eyes.

" Yes, I am very sure. It is not altogether unnatural that Urquhart should feel hurt and angry at first, especially as you turned your back upon him, and would say nothing in your defense. But after a while, when his anger dies out, he will be sorry."

" What could I say in my defense ? " interrupts Milicent, hopelessly. " It is perfectly true I deceived him. I have known for months now, that — that I have a father."

" It would have been better if you had told Urquhart; but of course it was a difficult thing for a daughter to do," says Stephen, sympathetically.

" I was not silent on my father's account. He would have let me speak to Mr. Urquhart. He would never permit me to confess everything to *you :* though he wanted me to marry you, and I told him I never would, unless you knew everything."

" Then it was not because you loved Urquhart, that you refused me, Milly ? " asks Stephen, eagerly.

" No, I did not care for him then. I wanted to get rid of my life here, that was all ; and I did not think it made much difference to him whether he knew or not, as we would go away, never to come back again. But my father did not keep me silent. Indeed, once he advised me to tell Mr. Urquhart everything; but that was because he believed he would go away, and — and not take me with him. I was afraid of other things; I was not afraid of that: at least, not until that glimpse I had of his world, of city ways. And then he said something that made me think I need not fear. Yesterday, is it only yesterday?" she cries out suddenly, wringing her hands together, and turning upon Stephen, her eyes widening with a look of terror of the long, long coming days and days.

Stephen's eyes could keep back his own pain.

"Milly, Urquhart will get over it. You must not be surprised that he was hurt by your not trusting him with your secret. All want of trust in those we care for is a slight put upon us. But Urquhart will get over it."

"Are you sure?" breaks in Milicent, willing to catch at any hope. "May he not go away without seeing me again?"

"No, no, Milly, you must not think so hardly of Urquhart. He loves you far too much to give you up so easily. He may blame you a little, and if he does, do not turn your back upon him as you did just now. You looked as if you did not care whether he were hurt or not, — the action, I mean; for no doubt your eyes spoke differently, — they often do, I find. Only let Urquhart see that you do care a little, and I am very sure all will be well."

"How could I speak, with that strange man

there, and — and every one looking at me? If he wanted to speak to me, he should have seen me alone, or at least have sent away his friend," says Milicent, losing her unwonted humility.

"He will, next time," promises Stephen. "And all will be right, Milly. You may be sure it will. What your father did cannot have any influence upon his love for you," argues foolish Stephen.

XII.

Mr. RAYMOND and Urquhart were both inclined to be silent while walking away from the old house on the hill. Each had received a heavy blow, though of a very different nature. With Mr. Raymond, it had sent him reeling back into the past: while with Urquhart, it had as certainly thrown him off from it.

For the one, Memory, with no great tax upon her, was fast shaping the past once more, — a kaleidoscope, with every bit and fragment taking definite shape: a shape he could not help seeing was distorted and unnatural. While Urquhart could find nothing to piece out even an action on his part, now that the present was so changed that the past was useless.

If Milicent had hidden from him only that she was Thomas the fisherman's daughter, Urquhart felt he could easily have forgiven her. He had so long intended to exile himself, at least for a time, on her account, that her humble parentage would not have changed a plan. Of course he would have preferred that she had been frank with him; and yet, if she had been silent only through fear of losing him, the flattery would have been sweet enough. She had been coy and uncertain during his whole wooing; and any evidence of a desire to hold him was pleasant. Besides, she was too artless and unaffected for one act of deception to change her nature; and he would not have distrusted her always, because once she had, through love of him, deceived him.

But with Mr. Chaudron's daughter, it is quite different.

The whole country had rung with the great banker's default and forgery; and though it had happened more than a dozen years before, yet his standing had been so high, and his fall so very low, that his name was still a slang term for an act of deep dishonesty. To connect himself with this man, even by the slender tie of son-in-law, would require an amount of moral courage, as well as the sacrifice of a large degree of family pride, which Milicent would not be at all likely to understand, much less appreciate.

Mr. Raymond's thoughts, being less involved by his feelings than are Urquhart's, are the first to shape themselves in words.

"Great heavens! Who would have expected to find Chaudron, of all men in the world, in such a place as this, and actually turned fisherman as a means of living! He must have lost immensely abroad. I cannot see why he did not take to something there, rather than run such a huge risk by returning."

"We are in Her Majesty's dominions," suggests Urquhart.

"Unfortunately for him, there is such a thing as the extradition treaty, and forgery comes under it."

Urquhart winces, but says nothing.

"And that I should have found Ursula here," Mr. Raymond goes on to say. "She has grown into an old woman; but not one I would care to offer a bribe to, in order to break off your unfortunate entanglement with her niece; as was my intention when I came here. I fancy you were too small a boy to remember how the town rang with her folly, — or heroism, as people chanced to call it, — when she gave up her handsome property to be made ducks and drakes of, in paying off her brother's — indebtedness, as she may have chosen to call it. She must regret it. She could not possibly help doing so," adds Mr. Raymond, with much asperity.

"Did she decamp with her brother?"

"No, she must have joined him abroad. At least she disappeared, no one knew where, until I find her here. Chaudron's wife had not half of Ursula's pluck. Certainly she did not follow her husband; and I never heard that he made the slightest effort to persuade her to do so. Of course she disappeared from society; and I heard she was very poor. But she did not live very long; and the child disappeared. It was an awkward bit of business for the whole of them."

"It could scarcely have been expected to turn out well," remarks Urquhart, sarcastically.

"I know some equally objectionable people who

are at this present moment flourishing like green bay-trees," replies Mr. Raymond, dryly. " I never could have any doubts as to the doctrine of future rewards and punishments. It is the only way of accounting for the seeming caprices of fate. Well, life is odd, very odd! I venture to bet a cool thousand, that if I asked any of Chaudron's friends, — or quondam friends, — when I go back to town, whom I met here, in this little fishing-village, not one of them would think of guessing Chaudron."

When Mr. Raymond begins to speak of his own theories and experiences, Urquhart's attention flags. It seems to him Milicent is again walking by his side, over the road where they had first walked together. It is as if he heard her voice pleading that she had nothing to do with her father's sin. That, like her mother, she loathed it: though, unlike her, she could not leave him, or die.

The few times Urquhart has ever seen Milicent with her father, he remembers she appeared either angry or frightened. Once only — to-day on their return from St. John, when Thomas kissed her — had Urquhart thought she had submitted to an unnecessary familiarity. Now he recalls that she had laughed at him for his fastidiousness. Why did she not tell him then that Thomas was her father? Was it only a false, foolish shame? Or was it a deliberate act of deceit? Poor Urquhart! All his thoughts and memories end in that overwhelming doubt.

" She is wonderfully like him." It is Mr. Raymond's voice which breaks Urquhart's reveries.

"She? Who is she like?" asks Urquhart, sharply.

"Chaudron's daughter. She is wonderfully like her father."

"What nonsense! Milicent's eyes are brown, while his are gray."

"It is their expression, not their color, I suppose. The girl puzzled me as soon as I saw her, she was so like somebody. It was the improbability of Chaudron's being here that misled me. Yet I wager if I showed her at the club, and said: 'Whose daughter is she?' nine out of ten would reply: 'The daughter of our Prince of Swindlers, Chaudron.' You need not resent my speaking of the likeness; for Chaudron was considered a handsome man, by men as well as women: and their tastes do not always agree, I assure you," says Mr. Raymond, didactically.

To this Urquhart makes no answer. He thinks his old friend tiresome, but he does not suspect him of probing his wound for the purpose of proving its painfulness.

They have walked a little way in silence along the quiet road-street, when Mr. Raymond says, with studied abruptness: "Of course this exposition will put an end to your engagement to the young lady."

"I do not see why it should," answers Urquhart, coldly.

"She can never hide her parentage. Chaudron is plainly written on her face; and not only that"—

"I never intended living in this country, so that would not influence me," interrupts Urquhart.

"You do not imagine you could keep your wife hidden? Such things will creep out: as witness to-day. My dear fellow, never try to conceal what is personally disagreeable. It is always best to mention such things yourself. It would be confoundedly awkward for some one to say: 'What a fine-looking fellow Chaudron was; and how much your wife is like him.' Such a remark might be made, you know. And it is difficult to be always on one's guard."

"There are not many men who would expect to insult me with impunity," replies Urquhart, coolly.

"It is deplorable when truths are insults," says Mr. Raymond. "And then, Urquhart, such a father-in-law as Chaudron is certain to prove troublesome. He must be very low down in the world; and men in his plight are not easily shaken off. I am sure the young lady herself did not expect you to keep faith, after you knew of her father: or she would not have been so anxious to conceal him from you."

"I doubt very much whether Milicent knew the whole truth," answers Urquhart. "She was a mere baby when the occurrence took place; and no one would be so cruel as to tell her the unvarnished facts."

"Yet it is evident she was holding something back from you. Rely upon it, she knew everything, and was anxious to keep you in ignorance. It is bad blood, dishonest from the fountain-head.

I am a firm believer in blood; and Chaudron's daughter could not possibly be worthy of trust," says Mr. Raymond, emphatically.

" You forget Milicent had an honest mother to inherit from; and Miss Ursula, though a Chaudron, you yourself have said was foolishly nice as to honesty."

" My poor fellow! I am vastly sorry for you," says Mr. Raymond, ignoring Urquhart's last remarks, perhaps discreetly. " She is pretty enough to turn an old man's head, let alone a young one's. Yet, as your father's friend, you must promise me not to see that unlucky girl again."

" I cannot promise that," replies Urquhart, hastily. " I must see Milicent. She shall have the chance to clear herself of all the dishonesty you so kindly impute to her ; and to prove to me she knew nothing worse of her father than that he is a poor fisherman."

" She will never tell you that, unless she tells you a falsehood. It is a very bad bit of business, very bad, indeed ; and the only thing is to get quit of it as soon as possible. I acknowledge it is not easy work ; and tugging at one's heart-strings does not make pleasant music. But we all go through it some time in our lives ; and then after a while we congratulate ourselves that we had the courage to make the break."

" What may be a matter of congratulation to one is not to another," remarks Urquhart, tritely.

" Not at first, I admit ; but it will be eventually. I speak what I know ; for I have gone through this thing myself, and can recall every wrench I suffered : and, thank heaven, I conquered."

Does Urquhart believe him ? Is it not the cry of every heart, — if there be any sorrow like unto my sorrow ? Can it be possible that this middle-aged, successful man, suitably married, and with children grown up around him, understands what a wrench from happiness he, as his father's friend, and brimful of worldly wisdom, is requiring of Urquhart ?

" Let me explain myself," says Mr. Raymond. " It is not always pleasant to go back into the past ; but experience may prove profitable. Now see if our cases are not similar. I was engaged to be married to Ursula Chaudron, and very much in love with her too, I can tell you : when her brother, who was looked upon as one of the most upright, honorable men in New York, was discovered to be a miserable villain. You cannot imagine the excitement his forgery made (for in those days they were uncommon occurrences), nor how many people were ruined by him. My engagement with Ursula was not announced, but I was willing to abide by it on two conditions, both of which she scorned. One was, that she should give up entirely her worthless brother, and hold no intercourse with him : the other, that she should not carry out her insane intention, which she had declared as soon as she heard of his villainy, of giving up her own fortune to his creditors. There were some stormy scenes ; Ursula was obdurate, so they ended in a complete rupture between us.

We have never met since, until to-day. She did not choose the firm, smooth road for herself; and I am shocked to see how much she shows the struggle. To think of her being an old-looking woman, so changed I did not know her, though I was in the room with her, until she spoke!"

Are Mr. Raymond's love reminiscences comforting to Urquhart? Is it possible for him to be consoled by the thought that a dozen years hence Milicent will be a prematurely old woman, showing signs of a hard, brave struggle he had stood aloof from? Would it give him any comfort to know that if life had gone hard with her it had been proportionately easy with him? Verily, some people are over-easily made happy. If they escape unscathed, is not everything well?

"Urquhart," says Mr. Raymond, finding his retrospection, tragic as he thought it, has brought out no response, "you can understand now why I ask you not to see Chaudron's daughter again. An interview will not do the slightest good, and will be painful to both. Let me entreat you to forego it."

"No," says Urquhart, with decision. "I am determined to see Milicent. Notwithstanding there is much that seems against her, I am convinced she can explain most of it." And then, observing that Mr. Raymond's shoulders lift themselves in a shrug of good-natured forbearance, he adds, irritably: "I owe it to both Milicent and myself, to see her. I do not care to be haunted all my days by the thought that I have made a premature old woman of her, because I had not the nerve to face what you are pleased to call a scene."

" As you will, my poor young friend," says Mr. Raymond, with undisguised pity for his weakness. "See your beautiful siren, if you will, and learn her frailty.   But do not for a moment give me the credit of Ursula's mutations.   Chaudron can very well bear the responsibility of both his sister's and his daughter's."

XIII.

UNTIL that night closed in hopelessly, Urquhart walked on the brow of the cliffs, carefully keeping himself in view of Milicent's windows. If he expected that the mere sight of him would bring the girl to him, he was disappointed; and certainly he was chagrined, when, after pacing back and forth until he was tired, he returned to his lodgings, and had to explain to Mr. Raymond that he had not had the interview he desired. Milicent's supposed avoidance of him had the unfortunate effect of confirming any doubt he may have had of her; and Mr. Raymond judiciously let fall a word or two now and then, to add to rather than diminish them.

Next day Urquhart wrote to Milicent, asking her to meet him on the cliffs, — only a few words of cold request, which he sent to Miss Ursula's house by a boy from the village.

This was half an hour ago; and now Milicent

is coming slowly down the path which Urquhart's
feet have helped to wear in the grassy slope from
the gate to the cliffs. He does not go to meet her
now, as usual; but stands waiting. and watching
her slow approach.

It is this waiting that chills Milicent. She was
glowing to the very finger-tips that let the gate
swing out of their trembling hold — glowing with
hope, glowing with shame. For she is deeply
ashamed of her deception, because of its cow-
ardice. That it would have sacrificed Urquhart,
she never guesses. Whether she were Mr. Chaudron's daughter, or Thomas the fisherman's, or
only Miss Ursula's niece, it could make no difference, since they love each other. All her fears
have arisen from her dread of her father's interference. During Mr. Raymond's unfortunate visit
Milicent had felt bitterly ashamed that Urquhart
should have made the discovery in the way he did.
The whole scene was terrible to her; and that Urquhart should be hurt and angry was the most
natural thing in the world. But Stephen had
given her comfort; Stephen who believed in the
love which "endureth all things" and is kind.
Stephen had told her to be meek and gentle, and
all would be well with her. And she had intended
to be both: only, while she walks down the path
and sees Urquhart stand quite unmoved, waiting
for her, she turns cold and still; for she thinks:
"If he loved me, he would come at least half way
to meet me. He is a judge who will vouchsafe
me his forgiveness."

" You will pardon me for giving you the trouble of coming to me," Urquhart says, when they stand face to face. " It is very necessary that I should speak to you ; and yet I could not seek you at the house."

" I thought you would send for me if you wished to speak to me," answers Milicent, her stiff formality being a copy of his own.

" Is it King Ahasuerus and the golden sceptre?" asks Urquhart, bitterly. " Are you waiting for permission to speak? Ah, Milicent, this unwonted meekness bodes me no good."

Milicent does not answer him, does not even look at him, as they turn and walk slowly down to the lower level of the rocks, for some fishermen are coming towards them.

This enforced silence is unfortunate, since it gives them both time to feel the bitterness of their position towards each other.

" Milicent," asks Urquhart, as soon as the men are out of hearing, " what am I to think? That you designedly deceived me ? "

" If I did, am I without excuse?" she asks.

" That I am unable to answer, unless you tell me what you wished to conceal. Was it the social position of your father? I mean his being a fisherman?"

" Would you have considered that a sufficient cause for our separation?" asks Milicent.

" Most assuredly not. I did not suppose you were of much better birth when I asked you to marry me ; though I confess I did not regret to learn from Miss Ursula that your family originally was a good one.”

“A good one!” repeats Milicent, with a hard, short laugh. “Perhaps you prefer Mr. Chaudron’s daughter to an honest fisherman’s?”

“It seems you did not care to give me any choice in the matter. Both you and Miss Ursula led me to believe you had no father.”

“Neither of us said so,” interrupts Milicent.

“Not in so many words, perhaps; but neither of you gave me a hint that there was such a personage in your family. The fact would have been of interest to me under ordinary circumstances; under such extraordinary ones, your silence was unpardonable.”

To this Milicent makes no answer; and Urquhart adds, with feigned urbanity, “It would be of much interest to me if you would deign to tell me how far it was your intention to deceive me.”

Milicent, instead of answering, suddenly takes her seat on a detached stone lying at the foot of an old sea-ruin, which, just beyond, looks sheer down over the withdrawing tide. She is pale enough to plead weariness; or, it may be, she does not care to prolong her walk so far as to be at a distance from home.

Urquhart does not take a seat, but stands leaning against the rough stone wall towering over against her. He has no doubt chosen the position for the view of Milicent’s face.

But evidently she has no desire to meet his gaze. She averts her head as much as possible; yet a faint pink tinge, which slowly mounts to her temples, proves her fully conscious of his scrutiny.

"Milicent, had you any idea who your father really is?" asks Urquhart suddenly, determined to learn the whole truth, even though he arrive at it painfully.

"I knew he was not a fisherman."

"But you knew nothing more than that bare fact? Pardon me for asking questions you show reluctance to answer. If you wish it, I will ask no more. But I warn you, it will be impossible for me not to draw my own inferences from your silence."

"I came here to answer any question you might please to ask," replies Milicent, still not turning to him. "You need draw no inferences. I knew perfectly well who my father is, also why he is hiding here, and why he has become a common fisherman. Shall I tell you," she continues, in a slow, monotonous voice, as if fearful that if she raised it a tone she would forget her task, — "my father forged his partner's name, and besides used for his own purposes money intrusted to him, thereby ruining hundreds of persons who had placed unbounded confidence in his probity."

"Great heavens, Milicent! Who could have had the cruelty to tell you this? You were far too young to have known anything of it at the time," exclaims Urquhart, shocked at her speaking truth undisguised by any of the soft epithets used for crimes in this polite age.

"Aunt Ursula told me ; so my authority is unquestionable. You need not doubt her, though. It was far more prudent for her to give me plain, unvarnished facts than only partial ones, as my conduct through life was to be governed by them."

"Blame her! I can only commend her prudence. Yet yours is even more praiseworthy," says Urquhart, bitterly. "Miss Ursula could trust you for an emergency; there were no circumstances, even the most sacred, that could tempt you to speak."

Milicent makes no answer. Perhaps she is thinking that, now that she has spoken, he is more shocked than sorry for her.

"Perhaps," says Urquhart, more gently, "your father would not permit you to tell me. It seemed an immense risk on his part, as I am a perfect stranger; and he could not be expected to trust me as you might."

"On the contrary," answers Milicent at once, but in the same forced monotone, "he one day advised me to tell you. He said you were a gentleman, and would not under the circumstances consider it honorable to inform on him."

"It is a pity you were not amenable to advice," says Urquhart, with ironical politeness. "If I had known something of the antecedents of your family I could at least have prevented that rather unpleasant scene yesterday, when Mr. Raymond discovered Mr. Chaudron. I must acknowledge, however, it is remarkable that your father was anxious I should know a secret he was guarding so jealously," adds Urquhart, not without suspicion.

“ The desire that you should break with me and leave here was much stronger than any fear of the risk. He was very sure you would not care to marry me if you knew his history,” explains Milicent. She has lost the hard, monotonous ring in her voice, and makes her unpleasant explanations eagerly, as if unburdening her conscience.

“ He was very good,” says Urquhart, ironically. It is rather hard on him to find such a man as this Chaudron objecting to his daughter’s marrying him, for any other reason than that of personal fear, or some latent feeling of honor. “ I should think your relatives might have made some excuse for breaking off a match they found disagreeable, without telling unpleasant facts. They have certainly not forgotten all their knowledge of the world.”

“ But I would not have allowed them to make an excuse which might have made me seem in fault, when I had nothing to do with it,” says Milicent with decision.

“ I might feel immensely flattered by your constancy, if I had any faith in your love for me.”

“ Do you mean to say you do not believe in that ? ” asks Milicent, turning round for the first time to face him.

“ I think I have very good ground to found a doubt upon. It appears to me that when a man tells a girl he loves her enough to wish to marry her, if she has a true feeling of love for him she will tell him of any just impediment to their engagement. Deception, then, certainly is not prompted by love.”

"Then you consider my father an impediment?" asks Milicent, quickly.

"I assuredly think I ought to have had the poor privilege of judging whether he is or not. And I infer that you thought the same, or you would not have been so discreetly silent. Unless you were really ignorant of how men look upon your father's conduct," Urquhart adds as a saving clause.

But Milicent will take no benefit of it.

"I knew it had separated my mother from my father, and had killed her. That told me far more of its guilt than the mere disfavor of strangers. I never had a doubt how you would look upon it."

"And I suppose you will tell me you were silent because you were in love with me," says Urquhart scornfully.

"Not at first. Certainly not the evening we were in the boat together, and you told me you wished to marry me. You tempted me sorely then. I was so wretched and miserably unhappy, and you opened to me a door of escape out of my troubles. If you had not said so much of the life we would live abroad, and had not promised that I should never come back here, I should have refused you at once."

"Do you mean to say I bribed you to engage yourself to me?" asks Urquhart, indignantly.

"I don't know that you really meant to bribe me; though I suppose you must have had some reason for dwelling on the subject so much."

"My only object was to make our marriage feasible," he begins.

"Aunt Ursula said you wished to live abroad because you were ashamed of me. That made but little difference to me then," interrupts Milicent.

"Why did it make but little difference to you? Most girls are sensitive as to their lover's opinions of them."

"Did I not say my great desire was to get away from here? And that was what you offered me."

"And I imagined I was so very fortunate in winning you! I was so sure you knew nothing of worldly advantages,—that you would marry me entirely for the love of me. I congratulated myself upon winning a fresh, unsophisticated heart, which it was my privilege to teach to love."

She answers nothing. She is looking not at him, but past him, far out over the sea, where the fog draws a veil of distance.

It is gray enough, blank enough. And yet it is the same sea that glowed and sparkled all about her, that first evening when he told her of that fairy-tale she was to live: the very waves then seemed to take the story up, and rippled past the boat's prow merrily. Now, she is listening to their long withdrawing moan along the ledges that more and more stretch out before her, black with the wet kelp. And now the moaning silence is broken by Urquhart's bitter voice:—

"What egregious fools we are, ever to trust you! I, who had run the gauntlet of all the matchmaking mammas and their well-trained daughters, and had managed to pass unscathed, was at last fooled by a pretty face, which I forsooth thought knew nothing of masks, much less dreamed of wearing one."

"I did not tell you then that I loved you. On the contrary, I only promised to learn from you," says Milicent, flushing scarlet under his bitter sarcasm.

"When a girl promises to marry, a man naturally infers she is in love with him, though he sometimes may think she is too shy to confess it. I acknowledge that was my mistake. If I had known you were Mr. Chaudron's daughter, I might have pressed for a stronger avowal of your feelings."

"At least our cases are parallel so far," says Milicent, quite calm under this taunt, though there is an evident effort on her part to be so. "You were not so very open with me, or you would have told me it was on my account you intended to exile yourself. That you were ashamed of me, and " —

"Not ashamed, Milicent; that I never was, in the sense you use it," interrupts Urquhart; "I was exceedingly proud of you."

"Of my appearance, perhaps: that is, when I was properly dressed. But as I am, you would never have cared to introduce me into your society. And I — I desired to get rid of a life I detested. We both had something we did not care to speak of."

"I must say I fail to see any parallel, simply because there is such an immense difference in the degree and kind of deception. I was deeply in

love with you, and, rather than part from you,
was willing to make a sacrifice which, if I had explained to you, you would not have understood.
Whereas, you, by your own confession, did not
care in the least for me, and only wished to marry
me to get rid of a life you detested. And the
thing which made it detestable to you, you were
bound in all honor to tell me."

"I grant all you say," says Milicent, wearily.
"I acknowledge that all I did was wicked and
cowardly. I ought to have said; 'My father is
dishonest, and in hiding.' I could not do it, that
is all."

The simple logic of those last words might have
been enough for Urquhart, if he could have seen
the dead-white face that is a comment on them.
But it is averted; and presently she says, in a
quite steady voice : —

"I never touched one penny of *that* money, —
and have lived hard and scantily all my life, but
honestly; and so ignorant am I of what you call
honor, I never guessed how wickedly I have behaved to you, until now that you tell me so. At
first my feelings were purely selfish. I don't believe I thought very much about them. I was unhappy, and impatient under my trials. Afterwards, when I had learned to love you, I saw fully
my mistake — or crime, as you may please to call
it. But I grew frightened at my father's secret.
My love for you made me all the more timid."

"Timidity is the last weakness I would expect
in you; and as to your love for me " —

"That at least you do not doubt," Milicent says quickly, turning towards him.

"It did not seem very much as if it were acted; and yet, when one loses confidence " —

"Not in that," she says, interrupting again. "I have deceived you in much — but not in that."

"But what a paltry love it was, when you could not trust me with your father's — secret."

"It was not lack of trust that kept me silent," explains Milicent. "I was afraid that words between you and my father might separate us. In fact, I feared that something very much like what happened yesterday would be a barrier between us."

"How long did you intend to observe this silence, may I ask?" says Urquhart, still feeling on unsafe ground.

"Only until after our marriage. My father could not have separated us then," she answers simply.

"And did you suppose it would strengthen my love for you, to hear you make such a confession when you had robbed me of all power of action?" asks Urquhart, in surprise.

"I never thought you would care to act on it. I considered anything would be preferred by you to the risk of losing me. You had said so more than once, and I foolishly believed you," says Milicent, with much of her old asperity. "I have not the slightest curiosity about *your* father. If he were hung, it would not make any difference to me," adds Milicent, with growing irritation. "I never thought of your family."

" You forget I was ready to give Miss Ursula full particulars on that head," says Urquhart, gravely.

" And if you had told her you had father and mother and a dozen brothers and sisters, it would not have made the slightest difference to me. I expected to marry you, not them."

" Not an uncommon mistake," says Urquhart, quietly; and then, suddenly bending down to look into her face, — " Tell me the truth, Milicent. Was there never a time when you had a desire to be frank and honest with me ? "

" Yes. I longed to speak that night we were driven out to sea, — the night of my birthday. I could not bear to think I might die, and some one else would tell you; or that we both might die, and you would in some way discover it. I fancy every one who has a painful secret must feel so at times; at least on one's death-bed."

She has lost her petulance, and says this softly, almost dreamily.

" Why did you not speak ? You must have felt sure I would not reproach you then."

" You forget Stephen was with us."

" Stephen would have held sacred what you say was as a death-bed confession."

" But I had promised Aunt Ursula not to tell Stephen; and then, of all times, I dared not break my promise."

" So you acknowledge you understand the sacredness of a promise ! " says Urquhart, with bitterness. " Why was it that Stephen was not to know what neither your father nor Miss Ursula objected to your telling me?" he adds, with ill-concealed curiosity.

"It would have been difficult for my father to have continued his disguise, if any one on the island knew his history; and Aunt Ursula would have been wretched about him: so many of the fishermen in the village dislike my father, and some of them are poor, and perhaps one might not mind making a little money on the misfortunes of others,—and they would gain something upon informing against him, would they not?" Milicent asks anxiously.

Urquhart nods yes.

"There were other reasons," she says, releasing him from her anxious gaze, and looking straight before her.

"What were they?" asks Urquhart, more eager to hear since she appears reluctant to speak.

"Both my father and Aunt Ursula wished me to marry Stephen," she begins; and then sits looking at a vessel in the offing.

"And feared, if he heard anything of your father's history, he would decline to do so? Their dread ought to have taught you how to act in regard to me," says Urquhart, reproachfully.

"Stephen would not have cared in the least; but I could not make them believe he would not," she answers quietly, not taking her eyes off the incoming vessel.

There is much in her voice, as well as in her manner, that causes Urquhart to ask sharply:—

"Why are you so sure Ferguson would not have cared? I know by his own confession that he was in love with you."

Then, bending towards her so that he can see her face the better, he adds, "Was there ever anything between you and Stephen?"

"Yes," she says slowly, returning his glance. "We were engaged to each other."

"For how long?" asks Urquhart, the old look of determination to know everything returning to his face: a suspicious look, as well as a stubborn one.

"When we were small children, we had an idea that some day we would grow up and be married," replies Milicent, with evident evasion.

"But after you were no longer children?" asks Urquhart, bluntly.

Finding Milicent disinclined to answer him, he shapes his question differently:—

"Was your engagement with Ferguson broken before or after I came here?"

"After, but not very long after."

"Of course you had a sufficient reason for breaking with him?"

"I had promised Aunt Ursula not to tell Stephen of my father," begins Milicent.

"And it was because of this promise that you would not marry him?"

Milicent's stiff silence is affirmation enough; and Urquhart continues with increasing bitterness, "You would have married me without considering it worth while to give me a hint of the mystery you lived in, though you were under no promise binding you to silence. Pray do not trouble yourself to make an excuse," he adds, seeing she is about to speak. " There is nothing you could urge that could in the smallest degree palliate your conduct to me. I could have forgiven your having kept from me your father's name, if fear for him had prompted your deceit. I might have thought the peculiarities of your life here had — well, had biased your ideas of right and wrong. But instead, I find you have the very nicest sense of honor where Ferguson is concerned; and that I am only so unfortunate that you cannot treat me openly. You must pardon me if, on my soul, I can draw but one conclusion; which is, that you had much better marry Ferguson than me."

" Did you send for me to give me this advice ? " she asks, icily.

" I sent for you, hoping you could make even a paltry excuse for your conduct. I was willing to take one so threadbare that it could scarce serve as a covering to your error " —

" And you failed to find one ? " — interrupting him.

" I failed to find even the shadow of one. Your desire to get away from here seems to have been so great you never chose to consider whether I might object to being made a fool of. In commonest honesty " —

" If dishonesty is a taint in the blood, you ought not to be too hard on me," interpolates Milicent, with a mocking assumption of humility.

" You sin with a full knowledge of your guilt, only you choose your victims. Ferguson you would not be persuaded to deceive : while you had not the slightest compunction where I was concerned."

" Yet there was a difference between you and " —

" I never imagined for a moment that there was not a difference between us," interrupts Urquhart ; " only I flattered myself that if you had to make a choice between us, I would not be the one you would sacrifice. But it appears that I have been egregiously in the wrong."

" There was a difference, if you will let me explain it," Milicent begins again, in a hard, forced voice. " Stephen, living here and knowing my father, and not knowing of the relationship between us, disliked him ; and I never could have kept the peace between them, for every sign of displeasure to me on my father's part Stephen would have resented. I had foolishly promised Aunt Ursula not to tell Stephen ; and I could not possibly have lived on, day after day, deceiving him."

" I can very plainly see the difficulties in your life as Ferguson's wife," Urquhart replies, sarcastically. " My stupidity is in not discovering how marrying me would not have been at least quite as awkward."

" Abroad, no one would ever know I have a father " —

" Do you imagine that your father's reputation has not traveled ? That Mr. Chaudron is not as well known and remembered as Thomas, Miss Ursula's fisherman, is known in the village? Are you aware of the very strong likeness you bear to your father? That three months' skulking from place to place would, short of a miracle, be as much as I could reasonably expect to hide your parentage; and Mr. Chaudron's daughter would be far better known than my wife, I not having the distinction " —

" Stop ! " she cries out vehemently, and raising both hands as if to ward off a blow. " I see it all now. I was terribly blind."

One instant's gasping pause, in which her color flickers from white to red, and red to white again. But when Urquhart, startled, would have spoken, she stops him.

" I do not wonder you are shocked at the magnitude of my offense. I only thought to deceive you as to my father, whom I presumed the world had long forgotten, and would never dream I had anything to do with. I did not know his name was written on my face, and you would blush to own me. I never thought I would be a reproach to you. A little rusticity and awkwardness was the worst I feared : and never even that, until I went for that little while to St. John. I cannot expect you to pardon me," Milicent goes on to say, her eyes all ablaze with some feeling not akin to contrition. " And I do not wonder that you have said to me all you have."

Urquhart is aghast. His jealousy of Stephen has goaded him into speaking words he would gladly have Milicent forget. She was so quiet under much of his merited reproaches that he is utterly dumfounded by her sudden indignation under his unmerited one.

“ I did not mean to reproach you for being like your father,” he begins, with an uncomfortable assurance of his absurd position.

“No, that would be rather unjust,” interrupts Milicent, so quietly that one would never suspect her ebullition of wrath just a minute before. “ One difficulty has been our seeing everything by so different a light, — I by the light of a penny candle, and you by the sun’s full glare. No wonder I overlooked all the corners you saw so plainly.”

“ And now you are looking at the shadows,” says Urquhart, quickly. “You should not recall my inadvertent words. I was angry — jealous, if you will. I have always been jealous of Stephen.”

“ Jealous of Stephen ! ” repeats Milicent, with unfeigned surprise in her voice. “ I cannot see how you could fancy that I could appreciate such a man as Stephen. None but a woman as unselfish and as good as he is himself could do so.”

“ It is infinitely pleasant to hear the girl one is engaged to so very appreciative of one’s friend,” says Urquhart, politely.

“ But we are no longer engaged,” protests Milicent, with ill-suppressed vehemence. “ Have you not told me you have no desire to marry Mr. Chaudron’s daughter ? Unfortunately, I cannot deny my father.”

“ I am very sure I said nothing of the kind. I

was naturally angry to find you had deceived **me,**
and perhaps I did not weigh my words sufficiently.
But of course, if you would like to make a choice
again, and Ferguson is willing " —

" Why do you mention Stephen's name, or anything but the fact that we have met to say good-
by?" interrupts Milicent, hotly. " I will not say
I am sorry you came here : but I will ask you to
leave at once."

" Thank you. At last you deign to be frank
with me."

" I am not so stupid that I cannot learn the
lesson you set me," says Milicent, with a slight
lifting of her shoulders. " I shall certainly never
try to deceive you again."

" If you had learned the lesson sooner, we should
both have been spared this scene," remarks Urquhart.

" If it were what you please to call my deceit,
that separated us, I should but reap of the seeds
of my own sowing," says Milicent, more quietly.
" But it is my being my father's daughter that has
divided us. I cannot tell what it is, in what you
call ' the world,' that makes such cowards of otherwise brave men ; but I see it would require great
courage in you to say, ' My wife is Mr. Chaudron
the famous forger's daughter.' For myself I would
rather live on here alone " —

" Alone, Milicent ? "

" I could scarcely ask you to come here to live.
Thomas the fisherman would be no more to your
liking than Mr. Chaudron is."

"Milicent, be careful!" says Urquhart, sharply, as if she were in some sudden peril.

"I shall run no risk," she answers calmly. "It is needless to lose patience, and Aunt Ursula is constantly warning me I am too hot-tempered. Why should we tax each other's politeness? There is nothing left to us but to shake hands and say good-by."

"Could we not even dispense with the formality of the hand-shaking?" asks Urquhart, ironically.

"Certainly." Milicent places her hands out of all danger, by clasping them behind her. "Good-by, Mr. Urquhart, and may you and the Undine have a safe voyage."

Nettled, indeed stinging with anger as if Milicent had given him a blow in the face, Urquhart lifts his hat politely, and walks away. This daughter of Mr. Chaudron's should not treat him so. One would fancy he was in fault, not she. She was glad of a quarrel, — glad of the smallest chance to break with him. Stephen —

He puts away the thought before it has more than suggested itself to him. Just now he cannot harbor it.

Urquhart strides on, over the rocks. Once he turns to look back, and sees that Milicent has not moved. Her girlish figure stands out sharply defined against the pale autumn sky, — such a forlorn, lonely little one, sitting there amidst all that dreary waste of rock and water. Could he leave her so? Leave her to battle alone against such a cruel fortune as hers must be? Has she not said she deceived him because of her love for him? Because she feared just what has come to them, their separation? After all, would it not be easier to forgive her than to walk away, as he is doing now — to leave her? Would not anything be better than this parting in utter bitterness and anger? It is small comfort to think it is Milicent's own fault, not his, that has sundered them.

Still Urquhart walks on, not back. He cannot in his heart forgive Milicent, and her sharp words cannot be forgotten in a moment. As he said, he is by no means sure of her love for him; and he could not overlook that she has been far more loyal and tender to Stephen than to him. He glances back no more, to see what has become of Milicent.

It is impossible to hear a footfall, for the thunder of the waves: but presently he hears some one calling his name.

He stops, and looks back.

Milicent is coming towards him. After all she has said, she could not let him go! Poor little Milicent! this is her love for him. He wronged her cruelly when he said — not only to her, but also to himself — that she does not love him.

He stands still, waiting for her. In his eyes, she had never looked fairer, not even when she wore the dove-colored silk, than she does as she comes to him, her paleness all gone, her eyes bright with eagerness. She has taken off her hat, and the sea-wind has played roughly with her hair, which she has to push out of her eyes with her two hands, as she stands quite near him.

Urquhart could have caught her in his arms and kissed her; but knowing her coyness, he takes the wiser part of standing to wait for her.

"We must not part in anger," says Milicent, never looking up into his face when she comes to him. "As we shall never see each other again, we should not have only bitter words to remember. It is much easier to ask forgiveness than to go through life uncertain whether it has ever been granted us."

"Will you forget the hard things we have said to each other?" asks Urquhart, eagerly.

He wishes he had been less harsh; that if they must part, there should have been no anger, only sorrow.

"Yes. I shall forget them."

Urquhart looks at her wistfully. He does not know how to take the sting of utter coldness out of this parting. Could they shake hands as friends would, and go their several ways, never hoping to meet again in life? It was easier to part in anger than in cool friendliness. But Milicent comes to his help.

"Do you remember," she says, "the evening you told me you loved me, I was angry with you because you kissed me, and you said the next time I should ask you myself? Will you kiss me for good-by?"

Urquhart's answer is to take her in his arms.

He knows perfectly well that she not only means it for their farewell, but also for a sign and seal of mutual forgiveness. But as he rains down kisses on her mouth, her brow, her eyes, while she lies for one little moment passive in his arms, there is no farewell in his heart.

He could no more have left her there and then than he could have turned his back on heaven, if he had had a glimpse of its joys. What to him were the sneers of a few worldlings, in comparison with Milicent's love? Even Mr. Chaudron might become bearable as father-in-law, if Milicent were the bond between them.

"Milicent," says Urquhart, softly, "I cannot live without you. Let it be as it was between us."

She has freed herself from his embrace, and moves a pace or two from him. "No," she answers, firmly. "That was our farewell; we cannot go back now."

"Why can't we? Who is to say us nay?"

"It never would have done," Milicent goes on, never heeding his questions. "Even if there had been nothing else, I never could have borne the knowledge that your friends pitied you for being caught by what you considered a pretty face."

"I am not going to listen to such nonsense as that," interrupts Urquhart, hastily. "I care very little for the sympathy of those you call my friends."

"But you care for mine," says Milicent. "I should feel sorry for you, if your friends thought lightly of you. Sorry for you and much more for myself. Every time you were quiet or sad, I should think some one you liked had slighted you on my account. If you found fault, or suggested a change

in my dress or manner, I should torment myself
with fear that you were ashamed or weary of me.
I could never be meek and gentle except fitfully,
for it is not my nature; and I should tax myself
with being wicked and ungrateful, every time I was
cross and unreasonable. I should fail so utterly in
my new life that you could not help feeling tram-
meled and burdened with me."

"Do you imagine your love will grow colder by
being with me?" asks Urquhart, half tenderly, half
beseechingly. "Do you think I intend you shall
not love me more than you ever have loved me before?"

"It would never increase in that big world of
yours. The little time I spent in St. John proved
that to me. I cannot tell you how it irked and
chafed me; and you seemed changed and unnatural,
scarcely kind to me. I would have tried to make
myself like the women I saw; and no doubt I should
have succeeded in a measure then. But it would
be impossible now: for there is far more for me to
overcome than a few gaucheries. I should much
oftener recall the fact that I am my father's daughter, than your wife. Here, I can live without shame
at least."

"How can you talk of a future without me, Milicent?" asks Urquhart, reproachfully.

"Because it will be better for you to be free from
me. Yet you will not altogether forget your summer here?"

"I want you, not a memory," says Urquhart, sullenly.

“Not if I would do you a harm?　You will not ask me to do that,” she says gently.　“People must not say of your wife, that she was even less honest than her father.　That he only took money: but that I tricked you into marrying me.”

Urquhart would have replied indignantly, but Milicent stops him.　“It would be all true, you know.　Let me be honest, now that I see how dishonest I was.　And won’t you say good-by?” she pleads, in a weary, broken voice.　“I cannot tell why, but I am so very, very tired.”

Unconsciously, to Urquhart at least, they have in their slow walk reached the little path down which Milicent came alone from her own gate to meet him.　It is here that she intended to part; and here she stops, and holds out her hand.

But Urquhart is not inclined to say good-by now or at any other time.　He has no idea of abiding by this too hasty decision of Milicent’s; even though a little while before he expected only so much grace at her hands.

He has changed his views of many things in the last ten minutes; and so he would as flatly have refused to shake hands as he had before, and would have gone on arguing his points, if he had not chanced to look into her face.

It is a pale, weary face, with a strange, strained expression about the mouth, which tells that the poor child cannot bear very much more just now.

He must wait a little ; giving her time to think, and grow calmer.

“I will not say good-by.　I must see you

again. You look sadly tired, and I am cruel not to have seen it before. You must go home and rest, my darling. It shall be good-by until to-morrow; and then "—

Milicent smiles, in as near an approach to her old saucy way as she is able to do, and then holds out her hand, which Urquhart clasps, and lightly kisses, not as a sign of farewell, but as an earnest of the next day's meeting.

Then he watches her pass through the gate, and over the path that leads her home; and it is not until he has lost sight of her altogether that he goes back to his lodgings and tells Mr. Raymond, much to that gentleman's disgust, that he had better return in the Dominion's next trip, without him : as his, Urquhart's, stay in the fishing-village is necessarily indefinite.

XIV.

"A faint sea without wind or sun,
A life-like flameless vapor dun,
A valley like an unsealed grave
That no man cares to weep upon."

MR. RAYMOND could not be persuaded to leave without making one more effort for Urquhart's emancipation. What was to be that master-stroke which was to free his friend he gave no hint; but certainly he had great faith in it. Urquhart's interview, according to his own showing, had terminated most unfortunately, Mr. Raymond thought. He naturally dreaded another: his great desire was to prevent it, if possible. So he chose the cowardly mode of writing a letter to Milicent, in which he told her in plainer words than he would have had the courage to speak, how Urquhart's friends and Urquhart's world would regard his marriage with her.

It was not a very pleasant letter for Mr. Raymond to write to Ursula Chaudron's niece; yet he was closely following the golden rule, for he did for Urquhart very much what, in like circumstances, he had done for himself. He never guessed that Milicent had taken her final leave of Urquhart. That it was an unnecessary wound, he never suspected; for Milicent was silent under it; and Mr. Raymond for the rest of his life is under the hallucination that this last effort of his has been a great success, a bit of well-performed duty on his part to Urquhart, of which he is willing to enjoy the fruits, without hinting how they were produced.

But the letter has driven Milicent out of doors. The sparks are flickering out of that harmless-looking bit of cindery ashes on her hearth, as the flash dies out of her eyes; but somehow the fumes of the burnt paper seem to fill the room, and she does not breathe freely until she has shut the house door on them.

There is no fear that any one will see her: the fog gathers so closely about her, as she clambers down, the nearest way, upon the cliffs. The fog-horn has been moaning on the Fundy side of the island the whole morning, showing that the fog was lurking in that bay; and by the time the sun is well overhead, it is no longer sun, but moon, floating silverly in the warm haze.

Milicent has gone far out; far out of sight of any one who might be skirting the cliffs. She is in a strange, still world all her own, with everything shut out in the silver-gray of the mist blending with the silver-gray encircling sweep of waters. Everything, that is, but the wild rock-world in which she sits and listens to the shrill cry of a fog-hidden sea-bird; the tinkle of a sheep-bell on the cliff's green brow; the lapse of almost sleeping eddies round the rocks.

She is staring far down into the clear water of a pool; down on the manifold tints the dark rocks have taken on, with their long tangle of rock-weed, — the golden-brown, the vivid green, the long, broad ribbons of the kelp, that float in and out, upon the least stir of the water, with brown-fingered dulse clinging about them. Now and then, one of the long ribbons turns over in the eddy, like some strange sea-thing, and catches one glint from the sun that just now opens a round, dim, yellow-white window, peering into that strange underworld, which has its mystery and its fascination for us all. Here wave, far under the deep water, brown-green tossing tips, which might be the close-pressing tops of some weird sunken forest. And there a pool lies sullen and still, until some breaker leaps up, curving itself for the plunge over a low, white-barnacled rock : until the rock seems slowly to up-heave itself, and to move forward, a huge gray-green sea-monster.

Milicent watches it all ; and, for the first time in her life, the sea looks to her a terrible thing, full of all hidden cruelties. It is going to isolate her here forever ; and fate, like that stealthy wave, has crept about her, until, as it roots up her garden of delight, she finds out for the first time how many hopes were budding there.

Yes ; but what right has she to their blossoming ?

Ought she not to have known, that evening when she drifted with Urquhart upon yonder golden sea — now blotted out — that she had no right ? But her shame was so new to her then : it seemed something apart from her ; something she could leave behind her on this wave-washed rock, while her gay lover sailed away with her into that new world he promised her.

Miss Ursula would never have trusted her brother's perilous secret to a child; and the girl had grown up with a shrinking dislike of her aunt's fisherman, which now and again, though rarely, some familiarity, or touch of authority on his part increased. Then, suddenly, chance as it were tore away the mask; and Miss Ursula had to tell her the whole story. Was it one that, like a magic word, could make the tender blossoms of love and faith spring up from such bitter seeds as had been carelessly sown in the girl's heart?

She is not thinking all this; she is but feeling it, and feeling it only dimly and blankly, as the fog drifts round her like a windy veil. She hears the fog-horn's long three moans across the island, and the longer repetition of the echo on the rock-bound coast; and then suddenly there is the brisk rocking sound of oars upon the water. Her world is no longer blank to Milicent.

She sits there, quivering in a breathless expectancy, half hope, half dread. What if it were Urquhart's boat? What if he were to come this way, and find her here?

She will not make a sound, not a movement, to call him to her. But if he comes —

He does not come.

That long, long waiting — which is in truth so brief a space — is over: not a footstep breaks upon the coming and retreating of the waves about the rocks, and the long-drawn approach of the tide-rip in the distance. Now a sheep-bell tinkles out, as it were overhead; and then there is no more. The boatman, whosoever he may be, has gone by on the other side.

The girl throws her arms against the rock beside her, and buries her head on them. She is not weeping. She is only hiding her face, as the man fallen wounded by the wayside might have hidden his, in his despair, when the priest and the Levite passed him by upon the other side. Wounded, almost unto death,—and no one coming near her!

After a while she grows impatient of her pain. She will not lie prostrate under it: there is no Good Samaritan coming to her by the wayside. She will stagger to her feet, and keep the road, and hide her wounds as best she may.

But now that she is literally, as well as metaphorically, on her feet, she finds it impossible to turn homeward, and to face at once the old life there. Somehow the sea soothes her with its strange, mysterious voice: she longs to get nearer to it still.

She flings herself down from rock to rock, lightly, and not as if her heart lay so heavy within her. Her foot falls without a sound that can be heard for the waves' gurgle in and out among the pools. The tide is far out still, only just beginning to turn; and she knows the cliffs directly under Greenhead are accessible.

But Milicent is in no rambling mood; she goes no farther now than to the ledge which juts out, facing the outer one. She sits in a roomy elbow-chair at its entrance, and turns her face towards the sea, and means to wait until it steals round her, and but just leaves her a narrow stairway in the rocks to climb back by the way she came.

As she sits there, and gazes blankly out into the fog which is so like her life, so dull and gray and dim, she thinks how well for her it would be if the tide were to creep up and up, hemming her in, past flight, — sweeping her out into the wide sea of eternity. One gurgling struggle, perhaps —

Nay, she knows she would never do it; she has started up, as the first tiny wavelet creeps sighing to her footstool. Not many moments now, and the full tide, that here sweeps in so rapidly, will be covering the great rock-pile about her, broken columns and pinnacles and beaches and all, beneath those inaccessible cliffs.

As she starts from her seat, half frightened, as if her wicked thought had taken shape and menaced her, the memory of the last time she was here with Urquhart keeps her lingering; and presently draws her to pass round the near cliff into the next cove.

Once more she will see them all; once more — and then, she thinks, never again.

As she passes through the sort of gateway leading behind one of the buttresses, she starts back. She is not alone. A man in the dress of a fisherman is lying prone, face downward, on the shingle, his head hidden on his arms.

At first, the girl's heart stands still within her. Is he dead, — drowned, — cast up by the sea here, — that he lies so motionless?

But her second glance shows her his clothing is not wet: his slouched hat is pulled down to shade his eyes. He is asleep, perhaps?

At her second glance, her pale face grows yet paler; she goes a step nearer, and says: —

" Father " —

Her voice is low, hardly above the hoarse murmur of the incoming wave. Perhaps he does not hear it; for he does not stir.

A little nearer. " Father ! "

He lifts his head then, with a start.

" Milly ! "

She is quite near him now, but he looks up at her with a far-away look in his eyes. " Milly ! "

He never calls her " Milly."

He has raised himself upon his elbow, and is looking up at her so strangely. The girl has never seen that soft look in his eyes before.

" The tide is coming in so fast. It is hemming us in. You must come away, at once ! "

He has not moved, save when he raised himself to look at her. A gray dimness like a cloud has risen in his eyes and shadows his face. Milicent grows frightened. When again she speaks to him, and still he gives no sign, she goes to him, and puts her hand upon his shoulder.

" Come ! "

It is her left hand, which chances to be nearest to him as she stands with her back turned on the sea. He puts his up, and draws the small hand down, and looks at it, stroking it gently as it lies in his toil-hardened palm; lingering over it, as if he were groping half blindly for a ring on the third finger. All Milicent's blood rushes to her face; then ebbs again as suddenly, for he is saying : —

" Milly's hand would have had my ring upon it. I must have been dreaming, child. I took you for your mother, as I saw you standing there in the mist between heaven and earth."

He has never before spoken to her of her mother.

Milicent stands voiceless, breathless; but perhaps her eyes press him, for he says hoarsely : —

" I thought it was all over, child, and that Milly, your mother, — that she had come to tell me she forgave me, for the little one's sake."

" All over, father ? " There is something in his face, in his voice, that terrifies the girl. " Come," she cries, with a glance over her shoulder at the hurrying water.

He flings her hand almost roughly from him, as he rises to his feet. " Yes, I *am* coming. But you do not know, you foolish girl, what you have done. You cannot get free now from the past, its blots, its stains. A few short moments more, and the sea would have washed away — would have washed away " —

But Milicent is clinging to him in a very frenzy of terror.

" Father ! father ! "

Is it possible that what she idly dreamed of for a moment, as the end of all these doubts and dreads, he had deliberately set himself to bring about? Death, that would put his grim finis to the ill-told story —

Chaudron understands her cry. He puts out his hand to lift her to a higher rock — the water is creeping up to their feet now, laying its white, treacherous hands about them. "I was half mad, I think," is what he answers her. "It would have been well for you if you had not come, my girl. Chaudron safe out of the way, his daughter would be no worse than many a nameless girl besides. And Milly might have forgiven me, for the child's sake."

He has half forgotten that he is speaking his thought aloud. Face to face with death and with despair as he was a moment since, it is not all at once that he can feel the healing virtue that goes out of those small hands clasped tightly round his arm.

And Milicent —

As they together climb up the wet rocks, into that gray and foggy life of theirs, the silent tears come dripping down over her white cheeks.

A hand has touched, but gently, and not smiting it, that heart of hers which lay cold and hard as a rock within her; and the waters have gushed out, not bitterly, but as a healing flood.

With the heavy tread of the climbing waves upon the rocks no lighter footfall can be heard.

Thus, if some one passes her by, not very far upon the other side, — only with that dense wall of fog between, — Milicent does not know.

XV.

THE passer-by is Urquhart, who has just come away from the house, where Miss Ursula coolly told him Milicent was out. He has come away angry and disappointed, very sure that Miss Ursula and her brother are keeping Milicent from seeing him. He does not believe she is out; and yet, in the slight hope it gives him of meeting her, he wanders through the fog in every direction he thinks it in the least possible for her to have taken.

The fog baffles him at first; then the sun disperses it. Then later, after long and aimless wandering, he finds himself in the road near Stephen's cottage.

Urquhart opens the gate, intending to take the shorter path across the field to the village. He has not seen Stephen since the day Mr. Raymond came to Miss Ursula's house to be introduced to Milicent. That day seems very long ago. If all the rest of Urquhart's life is to lag like these four days, his allotted threescore years and ten will be interminable.

The frost has stripped the vines against the cottage, which stands out a white blot in the gathering twilight. It is a hint to Urquhart that he has no time to dally. For though the sea lies before him unchanged, as if for it the cold had no death-touch, yet he knows from the fishermen's well-spun yarns, that not very many weeks off the sail to St. John, even, would be not only uncomfortable, but hazardous, — and in the fogs and storms the Dominion could not be trusted to steam out of her way to seek the difficult harbor of the little village. And yet Mr. Chaudron and Miss Ursula are both using their influence, if not their power, to delay Milicent's seeing him.

Suddenly it occurs to Urquhart that Stephen is the very best person to bring about an interview with Milicent, the very one he could send a message by. No doubt it is the sight of Stephen crossing over the field that suggests to Urquhart the idea of using him as a medium of communication with Milicent. But it is not until after tea, — Stephen's mention of which substantial meal reminds Urquhart that he has eaten nothing since early breakfast, — when the two men are smoking before the bright wood fire, that Urquhart broaches the subject.

"Have you seen Milicent lately?" he asks, stooping over the hearth, to knock the ashes off his cigar.

"Not since we were at the house together," says Stephen in reply.

"Then you do not know what is going on there;" indicating the direction of Miss Ursula's house by a motion with his cigar. "They are preventing the poor child from seeing me, and I hoped you could tell me something of her."

"I do not understand how they could prevent Milly from seeing you " — begins Stephen.

"Nevertheless, it is a fact. I have tried in various ways to get access to her. I wrote, and got no answer. I even went to the house, but was not permitted to see her. If you don't call that coercion, I don't know the meaning of the word."

"Do you mean to say you have not seen Milly since the day we were at Miss Ursula's together?" asks Stephen, sharply.

"I have seen her but once. Then she came to the cliffs, by my request, and " —

"Perhaps, then, it is your own fault that you have not had a second interview."

"Not at all: for though we had a little squally weather at first, Milicent calmed down, and was reasonable, and — well, you know what she can be after a quarrel."

"Then of course things are as they were between you," says Stephen, not sparing himself.

"Not altogether," admits Urquhart. "Milicent understood, much better than you seem to do, that our marriage will at least bring me some annoyance, as well as herself. Not that I believe she thought of herself: women so seldom do when they are in love."

"The more reason their lovers should think first of their happiness," — rather curtly.

"Exactly," returns Urquhart, in the same tone.

"But unfortunately Milicent looked so very pale and weary that I did not dare to keep her longer; so we parted with the understanding that we were to meet next day. So you see, Ferguson, in any case, I must see her. You must acknowledge it is better for Milicent to marry me; and I am willing to put up with a good deal, rather than lose her. If she *is* Mr. Chaudron's daughter, she is by far the most lovable and bewitching woman I ever met."

"Perhaps, as you think so much of blood, the Chaudron stock is happier in its females. Miss Ursula is certainly a most uncommon person."

"Most uncommonly uncomfortable. I hope Milicent will avoid growing like her aunt, as well as like her father. Yet that Miss Ursula once loved is not easily forgotten," — his thoughts reverting to Mr. Raymond. "I ought to be off," he adds. "Poor Raymond, who is putting himself to all kinds of inconvenience for my sake, must be wondering what has become of me."

Nevertheless, he makes no movement to go; but comes forward, staring moodily into the dancing firelight. He has not yet made his request of Stephen.

"I am quite sure," Urquhart says again presently, "the poor child has very confused ideas of the wrong she was doing me in deceiving me." Then, apologetically, "One must make allowances for her bringing up, and her surroundings, as well as for her strong feelings."

"Those are a great many allowances to make," Stephen remarks, dryly.

" I never did think women ought to be judged by our standards. They are far more impetuous in their feelings than we ; and their happiness is so much in the hands of other people, no wonder they grow restive."

" Weaker vessels, in other words."

" Because finer in their texture. I, for one, would not have them stronger and tougher," says Urquhart, lightly.

"I should not call Milly weak," says Stephen, gravely, as if resentful of Urquhart's good-humored laugh. " She has twice the strength of purpose that I have."

"It was you who used the word. What surprises me is to find that Miss Ursula, with that peculiar spite common to middle-aged single women, has told Milicent the whole story of her precious father's villainy. And she must have had to explain the full force of his crimes, to make her niece understand them ; for they could never come under her observation in such a community as this. She must have known Thomas the fisherman was her father ; yet neither you nor I, who saw them so often together, ever suspected the relationship."

" A heavy secret for so young a heart to carry."

" But which she managed to do," replies Urquhart, the more coldly because of Stephen's low, pitying tone. " The fact is, it would have been far better for both of us if Milicent had been less strong. The oddest part of all to me is that in all these years you have had no suspicion of this Thomas."

" There has been nothing more to arouse suspicion in the past years than in the last few months, where your opportunities have been equal if not superior to mine. And if there had been, I should not have tried to discover what both Milly and Miss Ursula desired to keep secret."

" All right and highly honorable in you, under ordinary circumstances. But a man's intention to marry a girl makes a world of difference. Milicent has told me you were engaged," he adds in parenthesis, not choosing to notice that Stephen winces under Milicent's frankness to her last lover. " Then I think it not only natural, but your duty, to know all you could of her."

" Of *her*, yes, I grant you that. Milly was right to tell you of me, for instance. But as to her family, that's another matter; for what her father is or was does n't touch her."

" Does n't it, though ? I only wish her father's act did n't touch her. Do you suppose Mr. Chaudron's daughter is not branded, only in a lesser way, as Cain was ? No hand will be raised against her for any other purpose than to point her out. But she will feel keenly the sneers that will be flung at her."

" Are there no right-judging, charitable people in your world ? "

" Very few, I fancy. When I marry Milicent, all my acquaintances will consider me a fool; my friends will tell me so; and my few relations will treat me as one," says Urquhart, concisely.

" I am very glad my list of acquaintances is so

small that I do not dread their criticism ; my friends too far away to express their opinion of me ; and that I have no kinsfolk."

" All of which advantages I did not appreciate a week or so ago," replies Urquhart, coolly; and then adds, relighting his cigar, and speaking more confidentially than before : " Of course it is a thing a man hates to talk about: but there is no use in disguising the fact that there is a deal that is disagreeable before me. When Raymond croaks, and points out unpleasantnesses, it is human nature to pretend to be blind. Nevertheless, I see much more clearly than is at all agreeable to me."

" Then I would not look," says Stephen, with more shortness than is natural to him.

" There is one thing that I have determined upon," continues Urquhart, in his desire to give his own opinion of the situation, rather than to take the opinion of others, " and that is, not to make a mystery of Milicent's parentage. Raymond thinks her wonderfully like her father, — which I must say I fail to see. I could not bring a wife back with me, and people not be curious to know who she was. I do not say it from vanity : it is the question one always hears, when a man marries. So I am determined to give at once the fact that my wife is Mr. Chaudron's daughter."

Urquhart says this with the pleasing sensation of unburdening himself of a well-matured course of action ; while Stephen is listening to what he considers the most natural thing in the world, — that a man should acknowledge who his wife was.

"It will be much harder on Milicent than on me, I am afraid," Urquhart goes on to explain. "She is not one to overlook small impertinences, but will blaze up grandly at a mere trifle. It will be the women: they being non-combatants, you cannot make them responsible for their words, or insolent actions. If I could only take the poor child abroad, as she expects me to do, she would have much more peace and comfort."

"Why cannot you?"

"Because of my will-be father-in-law. For his own reasons, he will ignore what you call the States; but one could never be sure of not meeting him in Europe, Asia, or Africa."

"If you did, I do not see that any harm could come of the meeting."

"Some unpleasantness. If Milicent wishes to help her father in a pecuniary way, I shall never object; but I do not intend that there shall be any other intercourse between them."

"Perhaps Milly will object."

"Object! when you remember what her father is, the sacrifice cannot be immense; and I fancy she would be willing to make some sacrifice for me," says Urquhart, coldly.

Stephen is not inclined to argue the question, so he changes the subject somewhat abruptly by asking, "Why did you suppose Milly coerced?"

"When we parted, I told her I would certainly see her again; and though she understood me perfectly, she has not been able even to answer any of the notes I have sent her. A further proof: to-day, when I went to the house, Miss Ursula told me she was out — which is not at all likely."

"I do not see why Miss Ursula should say so " —

" Nor do I, unless upon the ground that she did not wish Milicent to meet me. Miss Ursula does not come of such upright, honorable blood that one shrinks from doubting her."

" Be careful, Urquhart ! " exclaims Stephen, sharply. " If you permit yourself such speeches, you may chance upon them before Milly, and wound her cruelly. Besides, you cannot blame others for saying what you say yourself."

" I admit that is the worst feature in the case : for what we resent as a wrong, our righteous indignation makes more bearable. However, I had no intention to discuss this question ; but, instead, to ask a service of you."

" Of me ! " Stephen shrinks back slightly, as if dreading a blow. " You do not wish me to be best man, I hope ? "

" I am hardly the brute you take me for," says Urquhart, quickly. " I must see Milicent ; and I cannot get word to her. Miss Ursula is not afraid of you, and I want you to take a message to Milicent. Nothing written ; only a few words. When will you go ? "

" To-morrow, I suppose. It is too late to-night," Stephen adds more cheerfully, as if glad of the respite.

" Will you remind Milicent that winter is near at hand, and that we have very little time to lose ?

And, Stephen, pray be particular to impress upon her that our not seeing each other has not been my fault. That I even braved the dragon in her den, and went boldly to the house."

" I can't understand, if Milly still intends to marry you, why there should be any difficulty about your seeing her," says Stephen, with that persistency of unbelief which is so irritating.

" That is because you absolve Miss Ursula of all interference. There is not the slightest difficulty between Milicent and myself. There was, as I said, at first; and we even went to the absurd extreme of saying good-by. But we made it up between us."

Urquhart has risen to go, and is standing with his back to the fire. He does not explain to Stephen the process of " making it up ; " but it seems to him that the child, with her pale, upturned face, is once more in his arms.

Many a time afterwards in his life he holds her thus again ; but the sweet face is never a shade older, nor less pale.

XVI.

LAST night, when Urquhart left him, Stephen sat a long while over his fire, — thinking, thinking. Urquhart's love was so much more selfish than his own, that it was difficult for Stephen to believe it deep and lasting. And if it was not? If Milicent believed it was not, would it be well to urge her to test it once more?

But when the fire had died entirely out, and the new day began to dawn, chilly and bleak, and he went up-stairs to try to get an hour or two of sleep, he had determined to go to Miss Ursula's, and give Milicent Urquhart's message. For a great dread had come to him, that perhaps the poor child thought Urquhart had deserted her, and that she was left alone to bear the bitter fruits of her father's sin. If the rest of her life were a long regret, for which he, Stephen, no matter with what good intention, was responsible —

No, that he will not bear; and so the early morning finds him walking over to Miss Ursula's.

There is nothing unusual about the house. Miss Ursula, always an early riser, is busy getting breakfast ready; and she tells him, as she has dozens of times in his life, that Milicent has not come downstairs yet, but that if he will wait in the parlor, she will tell her he is there. There seems nothing like harshness nor coercion on Miss Ursula's part towards Milicent; and as Stephen sits in the great bare room, his doubts of Urquhart's inferences strengthen.

Milicent is not long in coming to him.

Stephen is greatly shocked to see the change so few days have made in her appearance. It is more than a hint of the struggle she has gone through.

"Are you ill, Milly?" asks Stephen, coming forward and taking the hand she holds out to him.

"Yes," she answers, with hesitation. "That is, I suppose I am. I don't sleep, and I am more restless than I need be. Yesterday I could no longer be in the house, and walked out on the cliffs. But it did not help me in the least," she adds, with a weary little sigh.

"Then you were really out when Urquhart called."

"Yes. Did he think we had put on grand, worldly ways, and told falsehoods if we did not wish to see him?" asks Milicent, unconsciously to herself showing an interest as soon as Urquhart's name is mentioned.

"He thought perhaps Miss Ursula did not wish him to see you. He never doubted your truth, Milly," Stephen hastens to assure her.

"Why should Aunt Ursula have cared? But I would not have seen him, if I had been at home."

" He is very anxious to speak to you " — begins Stephen.

" Did he send you to tell me so ? "

" Yes. You do not mind my coming ? " asks Stephen, deprecatingly.

" Oh, no. I am glad you came, no matter for what purpose. I thought he had seen it is best to go away," she adds, in a voice far from steady.

" You did not think it would be so easy for Urquhart to go away ; for you know, Milly, that is the same as giving you up."

" But he knew I had said good-by to him. He could not have thought I meant it for anything but that," says Milicent sharply, a flush mounting into her cheeks, and then suffusing her whole face.

" Meant what, Milly ? " asks Stephen, bewildered, and then regretting his question.

" Nothing," she answers, with a face as pale as a moment ago it was crimson. " Only, Stephen, he must go. Cannot you warn him if he lingers he will be weather-bound ? You must frighten him with the winter storms, which you know are often terrible. I could not bear to have him here in the winter ; you must not let him stay," she adds sharply and impatiently, as if the very thought were unendurable.

" He knows all about the storms, and the peril of lingering, Milly. He wants you to marry him at once, and go away with him."

" But you do not tell me to go ? That is not your advice ? " she asks quickly.

"I can but think of your happiness first, Milly.
And so I beseech you to be careful how you decide: it is not only for now, but for always. If
you regret it, dear, no matter which way, there is
no turning to the right hand nor to the left."

Stephen speaks gently, but firmly and with em-
phasis, as if he would have his words make all the
impression they are capable of.

"I know," she says slowly. "If I went with
him, and he tired of me, what then?"

Milicent has slipped down into a chair by the
table, near which she was standing; and resting
her elbows upon it, she shades her eyes with her
hands: though indeed she is really watching Stephen's face, as she propounds her difficult question.

"You have no cause to distrust Urquhart, Milly."

"I do not distrust him: at least not in the way
you mean. I know he will be sorry to give me up;
and if he married me, he would be kind, and try
to make me happy. Do you not think, Stephen,"
she goes on to say, no longer shading her eyes
from him, but making a frame for her face with
her two hands, "that if one feels perfectly sure
that by doing a certain act, one would wrong another, it is God Himself who has given the fore-
knowledge, to keep one from the act? And is it
not selfish, as well as wicked, to do what you like,
or some one urges you to do, when you are confident that in the end it will bring trouble?"

Milicent asks these questions eagerly; so eagerly,
that it is plainly to be seen she has long ago given
herself the task of answering them.

"Of course one ought not to be selfish," Stephen replies, gently and gravely. "But, Milly, unselfish people very often unwittingly sacrifice others unnecessarily and cruelly. It is not only wicked people, who do wrong; but often those who are anxious to do their best."

"But he told me just how it would be. How people would sneer at him and think slightingly of him, on my account. And," she adds, her eyes contracting as if in pain, "I have no right to his love, for I never gained it fairly. If from the first he had known who my father is, he would have taken care not to fall in love with me. Even when there seemed nothing against me but my poverty and my not being exactly what he called a lady, his friend came all this distance to remonstrate against his folly; and I think this Mr. Raymond is a little glad to find an acquaintance in my father, to add more to break what he and his kind consider an unfortunate affair. Ah, Stephen, you and I know nothing of the world, — his world. We know where the sun rises and sets, and the wind blows from. We understand the fishing seasons, and when our village is pinched or comfortable. But neither you nor I quite understand why the daughter of my father would bring shame to the man who loves her; and why good, honest gentlemen who live in the world frown upon her. And yet it is all an indubitable fact."

Stephen stands looking uneasily at Milicent, who speaks with flushed face, and a ring of bitterness and wrong in her voice. But both color and bitterness die out before she ends.

He finds it impossible to answer her at once; for he recalls much that Urquhart said about the sacrifice he would make in marrying Milicent, — a sacrifice, at least, in the eyes of his friends.

Milicent detects his hesitation, and adds quickly:

"You must not judge hardly of him, because, indeed, you do not comprehend him. I too thought him cruel at first; and that he was making more of even my own wrong-doing, than there was any necessity for. Of course, when he was angry he naturally said more than he intended to. But," — this with a quivering little smile that seems on the verge of tears, — "there are true words spoken in anger, as well as in jest. I am convinced, now, that it would have been unbearable to me to marry and then to discover that a heavy sacrifice had been made for me. Indeed," — with a flash of her own willful self, — "I would have died of it. It is better to part at once."

"But you have not entirely decided!" exclaims Stephen, somewhat startled to find she has come to a definite decision.

"Yes. I am quite determined. Do not think I have been hasty. It was not so easy to see at first what was best for both of us, because he wished it different. But his friend wrote to me. Don't mention it, Stephen. It was not an unkind letter; only it showed me I could do him little or no good, and very much harm."

"Milly, no one but Urquhart has a right to show you that. I would not permit any one to meddle with me in that manner; and I am certain Urquhart would not."

"I told you he knew nothing of the letter, and he must not," says Milicent, a little impatiently. "And after all, Mr. Raymond's words were not very different from his own, when he was angry with me. I have no wish that his friends should say he did a foolish thing when he married me."

"They will not, when they know you," answers Stephen promptly.

"He is not so sure as you are, and Mr. Raymond thinks differently. Stephen, it is not like you to persuade me to turn away from a good resolution."

"I wish you to be very sure it is a good one, before you act upon it, Milly."

"I am very sure. There is a stronger Hand than mine steering the boat. Let us trust to a safe guidance."

Stephen turns away, and walks to one of the many windows. He must find another argument; and there comes no suggestion from the sullen sea, and no less sullen sky above it.

In a little while he returns to the table, at which the girl is still sitting.

"I must take Urquhart some message, Milly. He trusts so much in seeing you again. Will you not speak to him, even for a few minutes?"

She shakes her head; and there is a pause of utter silence between them.

Then her words come, very slowly:

"Tell him that it is far better for us both not to meet again. That I thought he understood our parting on the cliffs was to be our final one, or —

or I would never have been so bold. And Stephen,"
— more quickly — " take care that he does not go
away thinking me so very lonely and unhappy as I
must be: it will do him harm to feel too sorry for
me. And for myself, it will do me no good, and I
do not wish it."

She buries her face in her arms folded upon the
table. Stephen stoops, and gently kisses the warm
brown hair: kisses it as he has many a time when
he wished to comfort her in some burst of childish
sorrow.

Milicent looks up at once.

" Thank Heaven, you are not going away too,
Stephen. You will not forget your promise to help
me in my need?"

" You may always be sure of my help," Stephen
says quietly.

He recalls the day he made Milicent the promise. He wonders, had he then withheld his sanc-
tion to her engagement with Urquhart, if it would
not have been better for her? She has since confessed that she did not then care very much for her
new lover ; only she was weary and impatient of her
life with Miss Ursula, — the life Stephen had been
so blind to, in the great, windy house. Now that
he has the key to her unhappiness, he wonders
why he needed it to unlock what he had never
thought a mystery.

Milicent seems to have nothing more to say; and
again her head sinks down upon the table. Stephen
stands and watches her a moment or two; then goes
softly out of the room, closing the door after him.

He does not go towards the village, where he is sure Urquhart is waiting for him. He walks in quite a contrary direction. He must gain his wonted calmness, before he gives Milicent's message.

XVII.

" The sea of ill, for which the universe,
With all its piled space, can find no shore—
.   .   .   the billowy griefs come up to drown."

STEPHEN is some time in gaining his composure; it is fully an hour later, before he goes to the village in quest of Urquhart, who, evidently on the watch, meets him not very far from his lodgings.

"You have seen Milicent?" Urquhart asks at once, heedless of any other greeting.

"Yes. She was really out yesterday. It was no subterfuge of Miss Ursula's."

"Where will she see me? I hope she has not named the house; it would be worse than awkward to meet Mr. Chaudron. I should have told you to suggest the beach, or somewhere else out of doors," says Urquhart, impatient at his own want of thought.

"It does not make the smallest difference"—begins Stephen, dryly.

"Not to you. But then you are not about to marry the fellow's daughter, so you have only to be coolly civil. I shall find it deucedly awkward to meet my future father-in-law."

"Milly thinks it best that all should be over between you," says Stephen, not finding it as embarrassing to speak as he had feared, or as if Urquhart

had taken a different view of his position. And
Stephen, as gently as he can, gives Milicent's message.

"What nonsense!" exclaims Urquhart, sharply.
He is bitterly disappointed, and has misgivings as
to the loyalty of his messenger. "Has Milicent
no idea that I am suffering, as well as she? If I
could only get at her, I could soon persuade her
that it is best, for both of us, not to part. I did
think, for Milicent's sake, you would have helped
me a little," he adds, reproachfully.

"I did all I possibly could, — for her sake, as
you say," replies Stephen, quietly.

"She has gotten into her head that it would be
better for me to lose her than to have her. It can't
be that you repeated to her any of the nonsense I
said last night," exclaims Urquhart, stopping short
in his walk, and looking suspiciously at Stephen.

"I repeated nothing. But I doubt whether you
were as judicious; for she said some of your own
words to her made her see that it would be better
for you not to marry her. She did not seem to
blame you in the least."

"It is hard to have the words we say in anger
brought up against us," Urquhart says, bitterly;
then adds, tenderly: "If I could only see the poor
child, and could judge for myself how much she is
suffering. I shall be forever tormented with fears
if I do not see her. Poor little Milicent! How
shall I ever be sure she is not breaking her heart!
How is she looking, Stephen?"

"She is very pale, and says she does not sleep

well. That was her reason for going out yesterday. But her walk was not of much service."

"That I should have had such bad luck as not
to meet her, though I walked in every direction!
No wonder I believed that old witch, Miss Ursula,
had misled me. But see her I must. I will write
to her. Perhaps I can manage to say more to persuade her, even on a bit of paper, than by another
man's lips, eloquent though they be," adds Urquhart, sarcastically.

To this Stephen cares to make no answer; and
Urquhart strides off to his lodgings, to write the
note that is to have more influence than Stephen
has over Milicent. A note which, if he can only
get duly delivered, he has no fears of finding fruit-
less. It is such a small thing he asks for, — only
that she would see him again. Another farewell, or
a promise never to part from him. He is not afraid
of her decision, if he can but speak with her.

Urquhart's note is diplomatic, in so far as that
it dwells on his own feelings rather than on Milicent's, thereby hoping to touch her pity. It is his
last request. Not such a great one; only to see
him for the briefest moment. If she sends him
away then, he will not say a word, but silently do
her bidding.

He walks over to the house with his messenger,
to be sure of no delay, and stands at the gate,
watching his progress to the house. Indeed, he
even waits until the boy returns, and reports the
note given into the hands of Miss Ursula, who
promised to deliver it at once.

So there could be nothing more for Urquhart to do, but to return to his lodgings, and feed his expectation on the peppery diet of impatience and disappointment, as every sound of an approaching footstep promises a note from Milicent, which never comes. The only relief he has is in smoking, and talking to Mr. Raymond, who proves a good listener, only now and then dropping some covert remark upon the wisdom of society in keeping such men as Chaudron in the background, with a reminiscence of the excitement the great banker's fall made when it was discovered. But Urquhart is restive under all such attacks; which makes his friend think him as sensitive as he wishes him to be. Indeed, Mr. Raymond has good hopes of his quondam ward, if he can only get him away at once.

Mr. Raymond is watching the whole proceeding with curiosity, as well as with anxiety. He is fearful that this daughter of Chaudron's may not be able to hold out. She is trying to do well; and if Urquhart would only let her alone, she might succeed; but it is n't in her sex to be so very strong of purpose. Possibly he forgets that Milicent is Miss Ursula's niece. Perhaps — for time does dull the past, almost to obliteration, with some minds — he thinks of himself as more of an actor in those few painful scenes in his life than he actually was; and draws comparisons as to the strength of his own will, and the shilly-shally weakness of poor Urquhart's.

And so the hours go by. The morrow's sun is

glinting on Grand Passage ; two or three laggards
of fishing-boats are skimming towards the Fundy
entrance of the harbor ; and Mr. Raymond, who
stands watching them from between the tall geraniums in Mrs. Featherstone's bow-window, is secretly regretting that this favorable wind to St.
John should be a sheer waste, so far as the Undine
is concerned. Why should this girl keep his poor
friend so long on the tenter-hooks of indecision ?

His poor friend is walking restlessly about the
small parlor, where the breakfast-table still stands
in the middle of the floor, bearing witness to his
preoccupation, as well as to Mr. Raymond's calm,
untroubled appetite. The door opens unheeded
by either: until, instead of Mrs. Featherstone,
entering to remove the cloth, the shock-head of
the landlady's youngest child is thrust in, with
the announcement that " somebody's coming to
speak to them."

Urquhart starts forward eagerly : Milicent has
come to him. He forgets the awkwardness of
such a visit with Mr. Raymond as witness. He
has only the delicious feeling that he is to see her
again, and that he has conquered.

Mr. Raymond, who has made no such flight of
the imagination as to suppose that Milicent is
here, is surprised, when, as soon almost as she is
announced, Miss Ursula stands in the doorway.
Her entrance might have been awkward to a guest
who looked for a welcome ; but Miss Ursula has
no such desire, and coldly refuses the chair which
Urquhart tardily bethinks himself of offering.

" I shall not detain you a moment," she says, turning to Mr. Raymond rather than to Urquhart, who nevertheless asks hastily : —

" Is it about Milicent ? "

" Not directly. Though of course it will affect her."

She almost turns her back on Urquhart after giving him this small bit of satisfaction, and takes a step or two towards Mr. Raymond.

" Is it with me you wish to speak? " he asks, with ill-concealed agitation. " Do you wish to see me privately ? "

" Certainly not. A witness is rather to be desired, since I have come to ask a favor."

" Times have changed," Mr. Raymond says. " I remember hearing you say once, Ursula Chaudron would never stoop to ask anything of me. Rash vows are brittle things."

It is an ungenerous reminder, which perhaps escapes him unwittingly ; or her reference to a witness may have provoked it.

But Miss Ursula does not appear to care in the least. That straight, angular figure, with the nun-like black falling in stiff folds about her, would never hint to a stranger of a past less cold and rigid and precise, of luxurious surroundings, the brilliant setting to the picture of a young Ursula Chaudron. And yet it is that picture at which Mr. Raymond is looking, with a bewildering light in his eyes, though he stands in the window with his back to the sunshine which streams in on her. There is no apparition out of the past, it seems, to her, in the fine and somewhat portly presence opposite; the voice in which she answers is calm and unfluttered, not that of a ghost-seer: —

"All vows are worth the keeping whole that are worth the making," she says. "I at least keep mine to the letter. The favor I spoke of is not for me, but for another."

Urquhart at once supposes she means Milicent, and eagerly draws a little near her; while Mr. Raymond, who has recovered his nerve, says, blandly: "I would much prefer that the favor, if indeed it is one, had been for yourself. Though I will gladly be of service to any one in whom you are interested."

"You have most unexpectedly discovered — our home, I was going to call it — our hiding-place," Miss Ursula goes on to say, not heeding his politeness. "Of course it can no longer be one to us; and what I request is for my brother's safety. It is not so very much," she adds, smiling sarcastically at Mr. Raymond's eagerness. "I only wish you not to mention, for the next two weeks, whom you have met here. Two weeks of silence are not very much to ask of a man. There is a superstition that to a woman it would be onerous."

"Do you think I have turned into an old gossip?" Mr. Raymond is smiling, though angry at heart. "Why do you not ask Urquhart there the same remarkable favor?"

"He will be silent on his own account. A love-affair with Mr. Chaudron's daughter is enough to keep him dumb."

" We will both be dumb, if you so desire. You need not leave here on our account," replies Mr. Raymond, decidedly curtly.

" Of our movements you are not perhaps a very good judge," answers Miss Ursula, coldly. " Your visit here has excited the curiosity of the village people, and curiosity is a sharp wedge for forcing a secret. Prudence is a wise protector, and certainly points to our leaving."

" Where will you go, Ursula? " asks Mr. Raymond, with a strange blending of interest and curiosity.

" To Europe," she answers, without hesitation. " One is more easily lost in a crowd than in a desert."

" And when? "

" To-morrow, if possible."

" It will be much safer for — for Louis. Ursula, if I can help you, — advance you any money, for instance, — I will gladly do so. These sudden moves are often difficult to compass," he adds, without explaining that the convenient money was to have been used to buy off Milicent.

" Thank you," says Miss Ursula, with studied politeness. " I have long learned always to have a sum of money ready by me in case of an emergency. All I wanted was your word pledged for a two weeks' grace."

" For a year, or forever."

" Two weeks are all-sufficient. I have no desire to hamper your conscience."

" But a great desire to wound me by an innuendo," answers Mr. Raymond, sharply. "Your brother is as safe with me as with you."

"I was not thinking of my brother, but of Mrs. Raymond, who might feel aggrieved if she did not know some time or other that you have seen us. Will you tell her, in a fortnight's time, that you saw Ursula Chaudron, and that she has grown into quite an old woman?"

"But in many things unchanged," he says, with a meaning smile.

"In more than you think. Time is a great dispeller of illusions. I must thank you for giving me what I came to ask for. I am too young a beggar to have learned the trick of calling down blessings from Heaven for a dole."

Miss Ursula has turned to leave the room, when Urquhart stops her. "Does Milicent intend to go to Europe with you?" he asks.

"Certainly. What else could she do?"

"Several other things, I should think," answers Urquhart, bitterly. "At least she might have hinted her plans, instead of keeping me here, waiting her pleasure."

"I thought there was nothing between you now? I heard her tell her father so," returns Miss Ursula, in surprise.

"She might have answered my letter, at any rate," Urquhart says, deeply hurt.

"Ah, so she did; but she came very near being unfortunate in her messenger. She is nearer right in parting with you than you think," adds Miss Ursula, almost gently. "She is not fitted for your life; and, believe an old woman's experience, you will get over this disappointment."

Urquhart smiles as he takes the note she hands him. "You will pardon me if I prefer not to make the trial you advise. And you will also pardon Milicent if she does not go abroad with you."

For has he not Milicent's consent to see him, in his hand? It would be hard indeed, if he could not persuade her to make a different arrangement.

Miss Ursula does not answer him: she seems in haste to go.

Mr. Raymond follows her to the front-door of the cottage. He would willingly detain her for a longer parting. It is scarcely possible that they will ever meet again; and he feels inclined to linger over the farewell.

But Miss Ursula is in haste, and walks away with swift, firm steps. "Poor Ursula!" Mr. Raymond says, pityingly, as he stands watching her. "If she could only walk over people as she does over the road, she would be satisfied."

Urquhart has time to read Milicent's note while Mr. Raymond is politely seeing Miss Ursula out of the house.

It is a poor little note; so very short, that he reads it over two or three times in the few minutes of Mr. Raymond's absence.

Two or three times; not because it is hard to understand, but because he had expected a conclusion so different.

He is dull in taking in the fact that she refuses

to see him. It would do neither of them any good, she says, as their parting is inevitable. It would be only a grief to her to see him again; and he had better go away at once.

"I did not intend to persecute her," Urquhart tells himself, bitterly. "If she wishes me to go, I will."

There is no sign of weakness in that poor little note, in his eyes. It never hints to him that Milicent is afraid to see him. There are some soldiers, it is said, who do not know when they are whipped; and there are others, who cannot tell when they are conquerors.

Urquhart has turned his back to the door, and is looking out of the window, when Mr. Raymond comes in. "We had better sail by dawn to-morrow, if this wind holds out," Urquhart says, without turning round.

Stephen is on the pier when the Undine is ready to sail.

"Tell her you saw me off," says Urquhart, as they shake hands at parting. "It was a sweeter, fairer dream, than I ever imagined; but scarcely paid for such a rough awaking. After all, Milicent is to have her wish, and live abroad; but she will scarcely have the life there, which I intended she should have."

"Live abroad! what do you mean?" asks Stephen, sharply.

"Have n't you heard? Miss Ursula told me, yesterday, that they are going to hide themselves in Europe. Chaudron has a fright on him. It is by no means uncommon under his circumstances. I understood they will leave at once."

Stephen makes no answer. He stands stunned under this bit of news, given with such good authority for its truth as Miss Ursula. Urquhart, glancing at him, is conscious of a satisfaction almost amounting to a pleasure. If he must lose Milicent, Stephen will have no hold on her as her friend. It is not a very noble feeling on Urquhart's part; but very few of us, when we are beggared, like to see another enjoying even a moiety of our past wealth.

As for Mr. Raymond, he is beaming with satisfaction, as he comes forward to shake hands with Stephen. Mr. Raymond may well congratulate himself upon freeing Urquhart from his unfortunate entanglement. Once safe in the world after his many weeks of exile, there need be, his sometime guardian is very sure, no fears for the future. Even if, in years to come, Urquhart should meet Milicent, he would see her in the disenchanting, tawdry glare of a make-shift foreign life.

It is a light which shows everything in very different proportions from those revealed by the sunshine here, which darts over wave and rock, to twinkle on the window-pane of the bleak old house upon the hill. Though Mr. Raymond, on Urquhart's account, does not regret his discovery of Mr. Chaudron there, he turns sharply away from this reminder. Some old wounds, ill-cured, have made themselves felt, and have proved more troublesome and painful than he imagined they could possibly be. It is to be hoped he will be a more skillful surgeon for Urquhart than he has been for himself.

The sun is shining, but "the sullen rear" is threatening ; a low, dull bank behind it.

"We'll have a storm before another sunrise," an old sailor declares.

"Ay ay, it's piping up."

But the wind is fair for the Undine to reach her haven first. Stephen helps to cast off the ropes that hold her to this rock, where, for all her bonny looks, her master has suffered shipwreck. A knot of men, with a proper proportion of small boys, are lingering on the pier to see her off. A handsome vessel will always receive her full quota of admiration, not coming a whit behind a blooded horse, or a beautiful woman, in the sight of a connoisseur. The Undine courtesies and dips gracefully and coquettishly ; until, the wind puffing her sails, she turns her back upon her small crowd of admirers, and shows her heels in the most approved style.

But just as she is slipping past the pier, Urquhart from the stern calls to Stephen.

"There is something I had forgotten," he says ; and Stephen leans over to catch the undertone : —

"The box of dresses, — you know what I mean. I left them at my lodgings. Distribute them among the village girls. They will like them, perhaps, better than Milicent seemed to."

From her window Milicent is watching the sun rising. As she leans with arms folded on the sill, she can hear the heavy thud of the waves against the cliffs, and the sweep of the tide-rip toward Grand Passage, as the tide begins to turn, in yonder long white line, outside. Far in the distance, a sea-gull, in its flickering pause against the sky, looks like a star that lags behind to twinkle after dawn. The low pile of heavy gray clouds in the horizon has shorn the sun of his rays, and he comes up looking like a pale, round moon. Then he brightens, and shows Milicent on the nearest pier quite a crowd of the fisher-people. Doubtless some of the fishing-boats are going out; so the storm is not as imminent as Milicent had thought, when she first glanced at the sky from her window.

As she stands there listlessly, watching, she gives a sudden cry. The poor child had not seen the Undine, until now that she has slipped past the pier, and is sailing swiftly away before the wind.

After all, Milicent discovers that Urquhart said truly, when he told her there were some sorrows in life much worse than death.

Milicent makes no other sound, after that one sharp cry of astonishment. She stands quietly at the window, watching the yacht sailing away under a pressure of canvas which the fishermen are discussing; or reprobating, if one might judge from their gestures. And now the water seems to have swallowed her, leaving no trace of the pretty pleasure-boat.

It is what Milicent asked Urquhart to do, — to

go away. She has thought it would be less painful to them both, when they knew there was no
hope of a meeting. And now that that hope is
really gone, all others have slipped away with it.

She turns from the window with a moan, as if in
pain. The inevitable is seldom a source of strength
to young hearts.

Urquhart has gone, and seemingly has left no
trace behind him. He has gone, "as a ship that
passeth over the waves of the water, which, when
it is gone by, the trace thereof cannot be found,
neither the pathway of the keel in the waves; or as
when a bird hath flown through the air, there is no
token of her way to be found, but the light air being beaten with the stroke of her wings, and parted
with a violent noise and motion of them, is passed
through, and therein afterwards no sign where she
went is to be found." So the memory of him also
vanishes from the village.

When Stephen some days afterwards recalled
Urquhart's last request, there was one thing he did
not find in the box : the only one he could have recognized. The dove-colored silk, with its cherry
ribbons, which Milicent had worn for one evening,
was missing. Whether Urquhart had destroyed
the dress, or whether he had taken it away with
him, Stephen could not guess. If the latter, how
it must keep Milicent's poor little story before him.
It would be like the nail with which the woodman
fastens some quivering, transfixed victim in his
sight.

XVIII.

"Come in, Stephen."

It is Miss Ursula's voice that bids him enter: though it is Mr. Chaudron, who, as Stephen pauses at the parlor door, gives him the ready greeting : —

"Come in, Stephen. We are in a dilemma, and perhaps you can advise us. I am not generally in favor of a multitude of counselors; but just now we want a suggestion."

Miss Ursula had taken up her knitting when she heard Stephen's knock. She gives Mr. Chaudron a startled glance, as he asks for Stephen's advice, and her needles work nervously. She is losing the self-control she has exerted for years.

"Our difficulty is this," Mr. Chaudron goes on to explain. "Raymond knows my whereabouts, so it is wiser in me to decamp. Not that I think for a moment he will formally inform on me ; but he is a tremendous talker, very fond of giving his personal experiences ; *à propos* of something or other, his meeting with me will slip out. Besides, Ursula would never feel comfortable, since so many know her fisherman is really her brother."

"Then what Urquhart told me is true, and you are all going to Europe." Stephen comes to this conclusion the instant he knows there is a dilemma to discuss.

"You see I was right, and that already they have spoken of our plans!" cries Miss Ursula to her brother, with that inflection of voice which says so plainly — "I told you so." "Not that we are at all troubled by your knowing," she adds, turning to Stephen, "but it proves they are imprudent."

"Urquhart only wished to explain to me why he left so suddenly," Stephen apologizes.

"He may chance to have another explanation to make," says Miss Ursula, dryly.

"Well, it can do no harm, as we have no idea of trusting either of them. Our difficulty is not my leaving: that is decided upon. But unfortunately there is not money enough in our purse to take both Ursula and Milicent," Mr. Chaudron adds, turning to Stephen.

"If you will let me advance you what you need, I can do so," says Stephen; but slowly and reluctantly. It is not the money he regrets; but it seems always the poor fellow's luck to be able to further the plans and wishes of others at the expense of his own. It is not so easy, cheerfully to open a path to take Milicent away from him forever.

No doubt Miss Ursula thinks he does not wish to part with his money; for she says at once: "I could not think of accepting" —

“ Oh, the money is nothing,” interposes Stephen, hastily. “ It is whether it will be wise in you to leave here.”

“ The practicability is the question, not the wisdom,” replies Miss Ursula, shortly.

“ And unfortunately the question has two sides to it; for I cannot think how you and Milicent can live on here alone ” —

“ Let Miss Ursula and Milly come to the cottage. That would overcome all obstacles,” exclaims Stephen, with eager hospitality.

But Miss Ursula will not have the difficulty so easily done away with as the two men are inclined to wish, and curtly refuses. “ Poor Ursula! ” says Mr. Chaudron, laying his hand half tenderly on her shoulder. “ Is it so very hard to give up a good-for-nothing brother ? ”

Miss Ursula makes no answer; but her needles work rapidly. “ Who will knit your socks, Louis? or look after your comfort ? ” she says presently, looking up at him.

“ You do not expect me to wear yarn socks in Paris ! ” says Chaudron, laughing. “ You forget my rôle of fisherman is played out.”

“ If it were not for Milicent, you would not be forced to leave me. Could you not send her to her mother’s relations ? ”

“ Do you judge from the past that they want her ? ” asks Mr. Chaudron, bitterly. “ No, I will keep her from their cold charity, if I have to starve the child in doing so.”

“ It is hard that she should separate us ” —

begins Miss Ursula. But it is useless to argue against the inevitable. The hard, set lines about Miss Ursula's mouth deepen, and she drops her eyes and goes on with her knitting as if she were in haste to finish it before her brother leaves.

Stephen is inexpressibly sorry for her. "Miss Ursula," he says, "you must not be separated. I have n't the money in the house, but I will write to St. John for it. Surely such an old friend as I can be permitted to advance a little money."

She shakes her head sadly. "There must be no delay. Louis must leave to-day, and so he must go alone."

"No, he shall not go alone. We must not permit that, Aunt Ursula."

It is Milicent's clear voice that makes all three turn toward the doorway.

How long she has been there, how much she has overheard, no one can tell from the startled young face. The little flush of resolve in it makes its wanness only the more apparent, as she glances across the great, bare room lit up rather by the bit of drift-wood fire on the hearth than by the dull day staring through the uncurtained windows.

She glances in, just as she did on that evening of her coming home — how long ago? — only Urquhart is not with her now, and Stephen turns from his leaning posture against the mantel-shelf, to look at her. The rest of the picture is the same: the gray, straight figure in the chimney-corner, with the knitting on her lap, and Mr. Chaudron, leaning forward in his arm-chair.

It is he who breaks the silence; answering for Miss Ursula, as if there had been no pause, —

"I don't see how it can be helped. I cannot bear to cross Ursula; and yet I cannot leave you alone."

"Of course you must not cross Aunt Ursula, — Aunt Ursula who has done so much for you, while I am but a burden. If only one of us can go with you, it must be my aunt. Unless," she adds, trembling, "it is my duty to go."

"I can dispense with duty," answers Mr. Chaudron, with a short laugh. "The truth is, Milicent, that pretty face of yours would be sadly in my way, for it would be continually attracting attention. No; as Ursula can't leave you, I must go alone."

"But Aunt Ursula must leave me. Not here, not in this house" —

It is involuntary, the meaning glance which Chaudron turns upon Stephen, who, with his eyes fixed on Milicent, cannot see it. But the girl does. An intolerable blush overspreads her face, and she turns angrily on her father.

"The old thorns will grow out of the old stem." That root of bitterness between these two had struck too deeply down, through years of growth, to be all plucked up in one such moment as theirs under the cliff, in the grasp of the threatening waters. That moment might well seem unreal to the girl in the face of the man's customary mood of careless cynicism. But, that once swept aside like a mask, she could not long forget the bleak face of despair that had looked out at her from under it. Her wrath dies out as quickly as it flashed ; she answers quietly, —

" You would never guess my plan unless I told you. It is to live with Mrs. Featherstone. She can't manage to keep her accounts straight, and often brings them to me to add up for her. She will willingly give me the little room behind the shop, if I will help her with her figures, and in the shop. And for the rest, I can sew for the women, or net fishing-nets for the men."

Miss Ursula has dropped her knitting, to watch her brother.

He is walking up and down the room, his hands clasped behind his back, his head bowed on his breast.

Milicent also is watching him. Stephen has gone behind Miss Ursula's chair. " Milly shall never want as long as I live," he whispers.

Presently Mr. Chaudron stops before Miss Ursula. He has determined that she shall decide. He owes her far too much to set even his daughter before her. One debt at least he will honestly acknowledge ; and if this poor pay of following him satisfies his sister, she shall have it.

" Ursula," he says gently, " you shall decide. Will you go with me or stay ? "

He has made his question as simple as possible, so that his words shall not bias her judgment.

" Let me go with you, Louis. I am getting old, and have nothing in life but you. Milicent is young yet, and may have much in the future."

" One must be satisfied to live day by day,"

Milicent answers, sharply. "What is the future to either of us?"

"Then it is decided," interposes Mr. Chaudron, abruptly. "Ursula and I go together; and Milicent is to sell sugar and tobacco to the fishermen. Milicent is right about the uncertainty of the future. That Louis Chaudron's daughter should peddle out small groceries to fishermen seemed scarcely possible a dozen years ago. Well, at least you'll get an honest livelihood"—with bitterness.

"It will not be long, Louis. We can send for her in a little time. Once in the world again, you must find some employment which will better our fortunes."

"So we will," returns Mr. Chaudron, hopefully. "Keep a look-out for a check, Milicent. Stephen will see you started to us. But, Ursula, we must get off as soon as possible, if we would catch the next steamer from Halifax. Will a couple of hours be enough for you?"

"There is a storm coming up," suggests Stephen. "You had better wait until it is over."

"No time to lose. Ursula and I have weathered many a storm together, and are not afraid. Is it not so, Ursula?"

"No, I am not afraid. It is harder to sit still and fear for others than to run great risks."

"Than even the risk of shipwreck? Stephen looks as if he thought us foolhardy," says Mr. Chaudron, laughing.

"If that is to be your fate, I would rather share it than live to hear it," answers Miss Ursula, briefly.

"It won't be as bad, as that. I have always been lucky in escaping death. People who have very little to live for generally are. We will start before the storm comes, and reach Halifax before it."

The two men go out together: Mr. Chaudron to get his fishing-smack ready for the short voyage; and Stephen to see Mrs. Featherstone.

Stephen is glad Miss Ursula needs her niece's help, so that she has to let him go alone to arrange matters with Mrs. Featherstone. For he has determined that if Mrs. Featherstone wishes to make a good bargain for herself, he will permit her to do so, and will go surety, with her promise to be discreetly silent.

Miss Ursula and Milicent have their hands full. The scanty furniture Milicent may dispose of afterwards; but there is the cooking of provisions for the voyage, and then the packing.

As Milicent is kneeling over an old trunk, Miss Ursula stoops and kisses her. It is such an uncommon action on her part, that Milicent in her surprise does not return the embrace. "God will reward you, Milicent. I never will be able to. A kind, brave act is a debt to Him."

"Then there is some little good in me?" Milicent says, half crying. "I was afraid I should only feel bitter and unkind to every one, now that I have no one to take care of me. If I had not been sure that only you could have been of use to my father, I am not so certain that I would have said I would stay here."

They have not much time for talking. Mr. Chaudron sends a boy to tell them to come ; and Stephen follows quickly, to hasten them. The sky is darkening with clouds ; the sea reflects the dull shades dismally. The fishermen are standing together in groups, predicting a blow ; their fore-warnings have infected the man hired by Mr. Chaudron for the run to Halifax ; he grows faint-hearted, and refuses to leave. Miss Ursula waxes sharp and impatient, but Mr. Chaudron seems unruffled. " It is a pity you are not going, Milicent. You would be useful in steering," he says, lightly.

" It is too late now," interposes Miss Ursula in haste, as if afraid at the last minute Milicent would go in her place.

But there is a young sailor who is willing to join them for a free passage to Halifax, and Mr. Chaudron gladly closes with his offer.

" Now we must be quick."

Miss Ursula is swifter than her brother's hint. She has kissed Milicent hastily, and Stephen helps her on board. " We will write from Halifax," she promises.

Milicent stands on the edge of the pier watching Miss Ursula, who is busied in placing her baskets and packages so that they shall not be wet by sea or threatening rain. Already she seems to have forgotten the fishing-village and its inhabitants, and is altogether absorbed in her arrangements for the voyage ; never even heeding the wind, which is blowing her black dress about her, and which is damp and chill enough to be shivered under.

Milicent hurriedly takes off her plaid shawl, her only possession of value. "Put it around Aunt Ursula," she says, as her father kisses her good-by. "The wind is much too cold for her."

"We will send you another from Paris," Mr. Chaudron promises, hastily.

There is no time for separate leave-takings; he has only a moment to speak to Stephen, while he keeps the girl's hands still in his. "I leave her in your charge," he says. "I know she is safe."

A moment more and the sails are set, and the little sloop darts off. "It's a foolhardy voyage," Milicent hears old Angus grumble, as she brushes past him. "A body might think they were running away from a bigger storm than the sea will give them."

Mr. Chaudron, in the boat, is waving a farewell. His hand falls, but his eyes are still on Milicent. There deepens a yearning pain in them, as once when he stood and watched the light figure flitting from rock to rock beyond Green Cove, with the young stranger of the Undine at her side. He had turned sharply away then, as if there were something in the bright picture defined against the rosy sky which he could not bear. The picture is none too bright now. The lonely, wind-swept figure standing forward on the pier against a background of gray, weather-beaten fish-houses; at her feet, the gray sea, chafing sullenly on the black rocks and the gaunt piles that lean about in the water, stained a dull, yellow-brown by the sea-weed. Behind lies the white village; the green ridge rises beyond the gray, bleak, empty old house upon the knoll, to where the smoke from Stephen's homestead lays a white touch on the low, brooding skies. But Mr. Chaudron's haggard eyes fall short of that. Only there comes some gleam of light across their gloom, when he sees Stephen quietly draw nearer to the girl upon the pier.

Miss Ursula never once turns to look back.

It is the second boat Milicent has watched sailing away to-day.

The first went laden with her future; this one with her past.

Has it altogether vanished, yonder in the distance? — or is it her tears that have blotted it out?

"Shall we go, Milly?" It is Stephen's voice behind her. "You forget you have no shawl, and the wind is keen."

She turns to him at once. Then there is some one to think of her, to care for her?

They pass through the village together, stopping at Mrs. Featherstone's to look at the box of a room Stephen has secured for Milicent. He sends for one of his carts to move her possessions; and then they go back to the old house, where their voices sound loud and startling in the silent rooms. Stephen seems to fear to leave Milicent by herself, and follows her closely, making excuses to keep her in sight. And she makes no effort to get rid of him; indeed, she would have broken down utterly, if it had not been for that sense of companionship.

It is sunset, the hour for tea in the village, when the two come out of the house together, and Milicent locks the door on her old life.

The rain begins to fall, and the wind is moaning as if impatient of being restrained.

When Stephen returns to Mrs. Featherstone's, later in the evening, he finds Milicent weighing sugar for a customer, under Mrs. Featherstone's supervision.

Milicent brightens when she sees Stephen come in ; and asks how she can serve him, so exactly like Mrs. Featherstone, that she might have cheated him into the belief that she is amused with the novelty of her position, had she not looked so worn and weary.

"You come in good time," says Milicent, lightly, as this last customer goes out. "For here is Mrs. Featherstone flatly accusing figures of lying and stealing."

"It 's Wilkins's account," explains Mrs. Featherstone, looking up from her books at the other end of the little counter.

"Any fool could tell," she goes on, "that the cod, which are as thick in the sea as the pebbles on the shore, could never balance the weight of the groceries and dress-goods his folks manage to use. I don't say they could n't be more saving; but I do say when things square to a penny I have my doubts as to the figures. Even a penny over, on one side or the other, makes a better looking account, to my thinking. But that Wilkins! he 'll never have enough till his mouth's full o' mouls, as my Scots grandam used to say."

"I am sure you have the right on your side. I can soon prove it by your figures," says Milicent, soothingly.

"Oh, as to the figures, they slip out of one's head like herrings out of a rent net. But come into the parlor, the two of you. There won't any more customers be in to-night : and I 'll bring you a cup of tea ; — Miss Milicent there took next to nothing at tea-time."

She has come out from behind the counter now, and stands before them, her plump hands on her hips, her comely, friendly face wearing an expression of concern.

"Next to nothing," she repeats, shaking her head over it. "But we 'll get her over that. She 'll soon be working on to a level keel again. There 's nothing like feeding up. Why, look at me! and I knew the day when I did n't weigh a quintal of hake. No more than missy there " — nodding at Milicent.

The girl laughs, just the ghost of her old merry laugh ; and Mrs. Featherstone bustles away to bring the tea in here, as Stephen proposes, — he having divined that Milicent is afraid of the parlor, this first night. The parlor, where she has never set foot, since the day Stephen led her through it to see Urquhart in the room behind.

Poor little Dickon! Milicent's eyes follow the mother wonderingly. Can she have forgotten, so soon ?

She does not know a mother's heart is fashioned somewise in the image of its Maker's: one day is as a thousand years in its sight, and a thousand years as one day.

There is one little cup which is hidden away, to be used nevermore; but her best tea-things Mrs. Featherstone brings out in honor of her guests. Milicent, seated on the broad sill of the shop-window, with Stephen leaning against the near end of the counter, sips her tea out of a cup on which the Queen, in the purple, and the Prince Consort, look down from the throne upon the Princess Royal in pea-green frock and pantalettes, trundling her hoop with the small Prince of Wales. As for the gingerbread, the hostess declares the plate must speedily be cleared, that Milicent may see the jolly shepherd in the centre, with the posy: —

> " When I had one sheep,
>   Your heart I could not keep:
> So now that I 've a flock,
>   At you I mock."

The lamp upon the counter does not shed too broad a glare on Milicent; whom Stephen watches with a great longing in his heart to have her at his own fireside, even though there were a cloud on her young face which he could not chase away. After a while, when Mrs. Featherstone, who has been dozing off comfortably for some time, rouses herself, and begins to close the shop, Stephen goes away. The storm is rising now with vio-lence; and Milicent reproaches herself for not having sent him home some time before.

With wet eyes, Milicent glances round her nest of a room under the eaves, when Mrs. Feather-stone sets down her lamp on the small white dress-ing-table, and leaves her alone, with a cheery good-night. The kind soul has evidently been bent on doing honor to the desolate girl's coming. The home-made carpet is brightened by the newest mats, done in such roses and fuchsias as one could hardly believe had blossomed out of strips of colored rags, hooked through a coffee-bag, and clipped into the semblance of a Persian rug. The gayest prints are on the sloping walls; and the Queen herself, in royal robes, looks down a wel-come from what seems to be the post of honor — the square white chimney-shaft, which runs up al-most through the middle of the room, like the mainmast in a cabin. The wooden paneling of the walls also suggests a ship's cabin; and the creaking and straining of the vines under her window in the wind puts Milicent drearily in mind of the rough night at sea.

But it is not until Milicent has fallen asleep, worn out with the excitement and fatigues of the day, that the full force of the storm comes. The small house rocks in the gale; and the sea seems wildly endeavoring to break its bounds, making a dreadful tumult in its useless efforts. Milicent lies listening; praying, as only those on the coast can, for the imperiled sailors. It is not for Ur-quhart she prays: she is sure he has reached St. John long ago. But whether her father and Miss Ursula have outsped the storm is doubtful.

Towards morning, she falls asleep, and dreams she is with Urquhart in the Undine again, and they are drifting out to sea before the wind. It is the night of her birthday; Urquhart's arms are around her, and she has no fears.

In the morning, she finds that the wind has died out. Only, to remind one of the storm, the sea rises and falls in the great throb of the ground-swell; and all the village street is heaped with kelp and dulse, which the villagers are gathering together for their fields.

Such poor spoils, the ravening sea has not cared to keep back; but for the more precious things, the lives, the faithful hearts —

The days grow into weeks, and Milicent begins to get used to the changes in her life. She makes no complaint; and the toil which was once so intolerable to her proves now a help. Even the weeks are gliding by; and yet there is no letter from Halifax, neither does the new shawl arrive from Paris. Milicent's anxiety and fear have grown so great that there is no room in her heart for even a longing to hear something of Urquhart. Secretly Stephen hires a boat and sends it to Halifax to make inquiries; but it can find no tidings of Mr. Chaudron's little fishing-sloop there, nor at any of the smaller ports it stops at, on its way.

The fishermen of the village say it was a tempting of Providence, to start when such a storm was gathering; and they knew very well how it would all end. But the sea keeps her secret for the Judgment Day. Whether the brother and sister, who let no earthly trouble separate them, had clung together even in the mighty throes of death; or whether the water had divided them asunder for a little time, until they "had crossed the waves of this troublesome world," and stood side by side in the one safe haven, — no one could tell.

XVIII.

A LONELY, wind-swept figure, standing on the green crest of the tiny lighthouse island, shading her eyes with the hand that holds the bunch of bluebells and buttercups, and dandelions as small as buttercups, just gathered from the springy turf under her feet.

Shading her eyes from the level rays of the setting sun. It is going down in flames; and the harbor glows blood-red, as though Moses' rod were lifted over it. But there are heavy, ominous banks below, on the horizon; a ragged black cloud is driving up, with fringes fluttering in the wind; the tide-rip turns with a hoarse threat, along the whole line of its yeasty surges from St. Mary's Bay. And Milicent is standing, half afraid, upon this sea-lashed rock, of which she and a helpless invalid within yonder lighthouse cottage are the only inhabitants just now. There is no sign of the keeper's boat returning homeward; the girl is watching vainly for it.

Over there, from Long Island, it ought to be putting out. Milicent's glance wanders past the low, deep cove of Freeport, to the high red bluff with its green slopes besprent with cottages; and

then across the harbor, to Westport, and to the
old gray house upon its stony hill.

Sea-gulls are drifting over it, like white waves
set free from the ocean-bed. But there are waves
enough left: great sheets of foam, that scale the
ledges, and are flung from them high into the air,
in drifts through which the sun strikes, tinting
them, and giving to the swirling green upon the
rocks its complementary shade of lilac.

Milicent is watching; gazing across so far that
she does not quite at once see, near at hand, a
skiff, with sides painted in black and white squares
like a checker-board, shoot in on the rising tide of
the tumultuous passage between this islet and the
Bryer Island point of rocks.

When she does see : —

"Stephen!" she cries, under her breath: "Stephen!"

There is something of terror in her voice; but
more of eager gladness. That passage might be
perilous to any one but Stephen: Stephen who, as
his strong frame bends to the stroke of the oars,
and the westering sun is on his fair hair and his
resolute face, looks, Milicent fancies, like one of
those old-time sea-kings for whom the waves held
no threat.

The sun which lights him up lights up the girl's
slight figure as well.

Thrice has the summer come, since Milicent
locked the door of the old house behind her, on
that stormy evening, to reënter it no more. Thrice:
bringing changes gradually, as time is sure to do,

even though we may fail to mark them as they come.

At last is laid aside the black dress which Milicent's first fishing-net bought her, and which Stephen disliked, — though he said nothing, — for it made more evident the extreme pallor of the young, sad face, with the dark circles under the eyes, which told of long fits of weeping. That black dress was to Stephen not merely the badge of mourning for her dead; he was sure Urquhart had his share in the tears Milicent shed in the little room above Mrs. Featherstone's shop: tears which Stephen's long patience and unselfish love have staunched, and which Urquhart at least has now no power to call forth again. There are no traces of them, in the clear eyes watching Stephen's progress now.

He has lifted his head just once, to look at her; and then his whole attention is strained to reach her, over the stormy passage rushing like the rapids of a mighty cataract.

Just across it is the point of rocks upon the Bryer Island side, where Urquhart pushed his boat and landed Milicent, the day he went to the rescue of the drowning boy and nearly lost his own life in the attempt.

Many of us have felt, at least once in our lives, when we have returned to an old haunt where we lived through some great personal tragedy, or even a mere happiness, and have found those who were equally interested passing tranquil days, unruffled by a memory which stirs us to the very depths, —

we have felt angry and hurt by their indifference. We forget they have long lived in the remembrance; and the scenes which come before us so painfully vividly have been daily before them, and have been blurred by many a touch of passing time since then. There are many scenes which Milicent can conjure up, on the cliffs or in the harbor, that have happened in these two years since Urquhart's wooing and farewell, and have quite blotted out both. Urquhart, whenever he sees in memory the little fishing-village, the cliffs, the bay, the harbor, lives over the past again; but Milicent looks, and sees Stephen now.

He has beached his boat, and comes over the rocks and the green crest, to where she stands and waits, an expectant smile in her brown eyes.

"Stephen, you have not come to take me back? Did not Mrs. Featherstone tell you I was to stay with poor Ellen until her brother gets home from Freeport? He went to see the doctor for her."

Stephen takes her hands, and draws her back a little from the spot where she is standing — the smooth brink of a gash in the turfy crest, a black chasm where the waves that enter unseen flash up with a wild, hoarse moan, then are dragged back, out of sight.

"No, I have n't come to take you back, Milly," he says, when he has her in safety. "On the contrary, — what do you say to turning lighthouse keeper?"

She looks up at him, a pretty, puzzled gleam in her eyes.

"Because, though the tide has helped me in through the strait (my boat was in Green Cove, and Mrs. Featherstone told me you came over here this morning), to cross from Long Island would be impossible, in the teeth of wind and tide, and the storm that is fast coming up. I doubt Dixon's being able even to attempt the passage ; indeed, I propose to let the lighthouse send him an early message that he is not wanted. What do you say? Shall we two tend the light? When he sees its first flash, he will understand the lighthouse has a keeper, and his sister is not alone in the storm."

Milicent looks up at her old friend, with a smile.

"You would serve very well for a lighthouse yourself, Stephen. Whatever we think on sun-shiny days that we might do, in stormy nights you send out such rays of help and hope, that we could never make the harbor without you."

With a glow in his face, Stephen listens to the pretty plagiarist ; as unconscious as she, that a modern poet has said much the same thing. But after all, do not true thoughts dwell in many hearts, before they find their way to the one pair of inspired lips that gives them fitting utterance?

When Stephen comes down to the cosy family-room, after sending his kindly message from the lighthouse tower to the absent keeper, the table is set for the nondescript tea. To the inevitable finnan haddies and dish of potatoes steaming with mealy promise, Milicent has added a plate of Mrs. Featherstone's famous lemon patties ; and, fringed round with bluebells and buttercups, there is a glass bowl of small crimson wild-strawberries in the midst, of so powerful a fragrance that the room is full of it.

There is a tiny driftwood fire, for good cheer; Milicent throws on another stick, which catches and blazes up at once. She stands on the hearth, dreamily watching the bright flame. She is still wrapped in the soft folds of her Shetland shawl, and she looks wonderfully pretty, as she stands there, smiting her hands gently together, to free them from the fibres of the wood. She is thinking pleasant thoughts; for there is a smile on her mouth, and the wild-rose flush in her cheeks comes and goes too fitfully to be the effect of the blazing fire.

There is no need of a lamp here, for the long northern twilight ought to last a couple of hours more; and Stephen, as he mounts the few steps from the outer room, and pauses in the open doorway, takes in the whole picture at a glance.

It is a homely scene enough; but the girl lends spirit and life to it. The other occupant of the room sits at the window looking seaward; the gray, fading light resting on a gray and fading face, where pain has set its seal of patience. It is a face not yet past youth; but pain and patience know no youth; and the mouth has that plaintive wistfulness which, just as surely as the stooping shoulders, tells of spinal curvature. The busy hands for once lie idle in her lap; but it is they (her stalwart brother the keeper would tell you, with hearty pride in them), it is they which have made the pretty rugs that lie about the room; they which have knitted that wonderful, tall bunch of worsted flowers under the glass case; they which sometimes, opening the parlor organ in the corner, let loose simple melodies that go floating all about the twilight harbor.

There is no such peaceful sound this evening: the crash of the great waves flinging themselves madly about, among the rocks, grows loud and louder as the hours go by.

Once, when Stephen has gone anxiously into the little tower where the lights are burning steadily, he hears in the lull a faint sound behind him, and turns, to see Milicent at the head of the stair.

"I could not help coming, Stephen," she says, apologetically. "Ellen is used to it all, and she has fallen asleep in her chair: but I could not help thinking — suppose those waves" —

She catches her breath: up to this moment, the foremost of them, pressing on, could only reach to lay white, angry hands about the foot of the cottage and the tiny lighthouse tower. But this one, gathering strength, and urged more fiercely on, leaps up, and sends a shower of spray against the windows, in the midst of Milicent's words.

Swift as thought, she is at Stephen's side; catching by his arm, holding by him as he sits in the elbow-chair, under the lamps, which glow on their stand above, — a circle of great student-burners reflected far out through the Passage, to St. Mary's Bay. Milicent's eyes, glowing as much with excitement as with fear, flash out with them; while the mighty billows hurl themselves against the glass, and go hissing past, overhead, in great glittering handfuls of prismatic diamonds now, and now in showers of wind-driven sparks.

It is too beautiful to be all terrible.

Milicent says as much, presently, in one of those treacherous pauses before the coming onslaught, when her clear voice can make itself heard above the more distant muffled thunder on the ledges.

"What a night! Stephen, are you sure there is no danger, as Ellen declares? But she can't know anything about it; I'm sure this is a much worse storm — O Stephen!" stopping short, and then beginning again: "Did not that shake your very heart? I am sure it did mine; and all the place swayed."

"It is founded upon a rock, Milly," he says, smiling up at her.

She has to wait for another crash and long withdrawing boom; and then she responds softly to his hidden thought: —

"'Upon a Rock.'"

Presently he shows her his watch.

"The tide is beginning to turn; we won't have many more such onslaughts as this last. Sit down, Milly; you are just a thought pale, and this hand is not so steady as it ought to be," he says, as he lifts it from his arm, and puts her in the chair from which he has risen.

She takes it, and turns her back upon the seaward-looking panes, idly drawing towards her the newspaper he thrust aside when she came to him.

He makes a hasty movement, as if to take it from her. But she does not see, and has gone on:—

"What were you reading, Stephen, when I came in? You looked so grave over it that the storm frightened me."

"An American paper," he answers, hurriedly, "which Dixon probably got from some trader in the village. It is not very late, and "—

He stops: his hand, extended for it, falls to his side. He is too late. For she sees already.

It is a "Herald": Urquhart's name in the list of American arrivals in Paris.

Milicent has a strange look in her eyes, as if she saw a ghost,— not a ghastly corpse, but a vision.

Then she lifts her eyes straight to Stephen.

"And you thought it would startle me?" she says. "And so it has. I had a vision of the sunset bay, and of the fairy-tale I listened to there, of sailing away and away into shining foreign bays. — It would never have done," she cries, breaking off. "Such a voyage is for light summer breezes; but there must come storms — like this "—

She turns to him with a half smile; and Stephen stretches out his hands to her.

"Milly, if we might slip back into our old moorings "—

The smile dies out of her eyes; there comes a startled look into them.

"Safe in harbor, Stephen? Is that what you are thinking of, for me? No: when I left the good holding-ground "—

If she means his heart, he has drawn her masterfully back to it.

"Milly, I loved you when you were little Milly, my one playmate and friend, and I have never found any reason why I should not love you. It is not in the nature of some women to be forgotten."

"Not in the nature of some men to forget."

But they have both forgotten — as the storm is now withdrawing, and they make their way back to the lighthouse parlor and Ellen — they have both forgotten Urquhart, and the paper that has fluttered to the floor, with his name on it.

Neither of them gives one thought to him; but it is a question whether Urquhart has never a thought of Milicent, as he wanders idly, and certainly a little wearily, to and fro along the Paris thoroughfares. He assuredly has never dreamed of her as still in the little fishing-village. Living abroad with her father a life far worse for her than that which she had detested in the old house, he has often pictured to himself. While, for all the friendship of his world, — of which, though fond of and kind to him, he has yet a little dread, — it is in vain he strives altogether to blot from his memory that Fundy summer-tide, when he, if not the Undine, suffered shipwreck in port.

Not that he may not find another woman to love; but it will not be another Milicent.

And, after all, that huge bugbear with which Mr. Raymond had managed to frighten first Urquhart and then Milicent would never have existed.

They could have married, with no objectionable father-in-law to start up at inopportune moments to annoy Urquhart; and Milicent's parentage would have been forgotten, after the story of her father's violent death had been worn threadbare through excessive handling. If Urquhart could only have foreseen this future, — but prevision is not a human attribute.

"And the cottage, Milly?" Stephen is saying, staying her hand on the latch of the door downstairs. "It has waited so long for its mistress."

"But poor Mrs. Featherstone?" says Milicent, breathlessly, and opens the door.

She has been lingering so long in the pleasant border land, the Debateable Ground between Friendship and Love, that she is in no haste, now, to cross the line.

Only, when the two are standing together before the flickering fire, the invalid's regular breathing from her easy-chair by the window filling the pauses of the retreating waves, Milicent glances up at her lover, with a shy little laugh in her eyes.

"I 'll tell you what I will do. I will teach one of Strainer's girls to keep accounts. Besides," she adds, "I don't think Strainer's new wife treats Victoria well. I found her the other day sitting by herself and crying. She would not tell me why, but I could guess. So, when she knows the ropes, as good Mrs. Featherstone would say, — the cottage" —

"Shall have its mistress!"